Praise for 'Alice

'I was hooked before the prol... what happens to Alice. With beli... memories of my own teenage year ... ...ked by the descriptive passages and a real insi... into 'behind the scenes' in theatreland, I couldn't put it down!'
Kathy Taylor – *Television Personality*

'This terrific story is inhabited by fabulously wicked people who are easy to loathe. Counterbalance this with an endearing heroine and friends we'd all love to have as our own and you understand why this novel works so well. And the ending…, oh, the ending!'
Anne Woodward – *Author*

'The era is re-created with authenticity; the characters wholly believable… I see productions as the polished outcome of this intriguing, often unpleasant world where characters reflect individuals from all of society. And, the ending… astonishingly cleverly crafted!'
Alison Chambers – *Amazon review 30th April 2017*

Praise for the Liberty Sands Trilogy

'I assumed it would be lightweight, formulaic chick-lit, an enjoyable read but little else. I was wrong. It is well written with a pace that grips the reader and believable characters that I cared about.'
Linda's Book Bag

'**Entertaining & Heart-Felt Emotions** – Julia Roberts writes believable story-lines for characters that come across as real and imperfect. Holly's story is captivating and emotional.'
David Reviews — *Top 500 Reviewer on Amazon.co.uk*

Julia Roberts' passion for writing began when, at the age of ten, after winning second prize in a short story-writing competition, she announced that she wanted to write a book. After a small gap of forty-seven years, and a career in the entertainment industry, Julia finally fulfilled her dream in 2013 when her first book, a memoir entitled *One Hundred Lengths of the Pool*, was published by Preface Publishing. Two weeks later she had the idea for her first novel, *Life's a Beach and Then…*, book one in the Liberty Sands Trilogy, which was released in May 2015.

Julia still works full-time as a Presenter for the TV channel QVC, where she has recently celebrated her twenty-third anniversary.

She now lives in Ascot with her partner of thirty-nine years and occasionally one or other of her adult children and their respective cats.

You can find out more about Julia and her upcoming books on her Facebook page www.facebook.com/JuliaRobertsTV and her website www.juliarobertsauthor.com

You can also follow her on Twitter @JuliaRobertsTV and on Instagram @juliagroberts

By Julia Roberts

Life's a Beach and Then…
(Liberty Sands trilogy, book one)

If He Really Loved Me…
(Liberty Sands trilogy, book two)

It's Never Too Late to Say…
(Liberty Sands trilogy, book three)

One Hundred Lengths of the Pool

Time for a Short Story

The Shadow of Her Smile
(free short story on www.juliarobertsauthor.com)

Alice
in
Theatreland

Julia Roberts

A **ripped** book

I can't go back to yesterday
because I was a different person then.

Lewis Carroll
Alice in Wonderland

Prologue – September 1976

Alice closed her eyes, battling the feelings of nausea that washed over her in waves. The stench of vomit with its acidic undertone always had this effect on her. How long will I be able to hold my breath before I start to feel faint? she wondered, breathing in through her mouth as deeply as she dared to minimise the pungent aroma. An image of Mr Wilkins, her swimming coach, filled her mind as her lungs expanded with air. The repetitive practising of underwater lengths had given her an edge over the other competitors in the regional finals that he was so proud she had won. A tear squeezed out of the corner of her eye. He wouldn't be so proud of me now, she thought.

Alice was fearful of taking her next breath but she knew she had to. Her stomach contracted, and bile started rising in her throat. The retching resumed, adding only tiny amounts of clear fluid to the pool of her own puke in which she was lying. Bits of it were already drying on her face and stuck in her hair, but Alice was beyond caring. The effort of vomiting doubled the excruciating pain in her lower abdomen. Her hand moved down across her belly towards the top of her thigh and connected with something warm and sticky. She knew without looking that it was blood.

I don't want to die, she thought, drifting back towards unconsciousness, but perhaps that's the best thing for everyone after what I've done.

'Alice, are you in there?'

She recognised the voice but couldn't place it.

'Alice! I need to pee. I'm busting. Open the door.'

'Help me,' Alice murmured to the only person who could save her, before darkness enveloped her once again.

CHAPTER 1

Five Months Earlier

'Alice, are you ready? Your dad's already in the car, and he told me to tell you that the train won't wait, even for a "soon to be West End star",' Sheila Abbott called from the foot of the stairs.

'Coming, Mum,' Alice replied, releasing her younger sister, Mary, from their tight embrace. 'I'd better go before Dad gets his knickers in a twist! We're going to be at the station way too early, but Dad wouldn't hear of me wasting money on a taxi. Promise me you'll try not to get into too many arguments with them.'

'I'll try,' Mary said, surreptitiously brushing a tear from her eye. 'The problem is, you're a hard act to follow. Nothing I do ever seems good enough. I wish you weren't quite so perfect.'

'You know that's not true. We're just different. You've always enjoyed going out to the youth club with your friends, and I've always preferred going to dancing class, which is why I don't have many friends to go out with round here.'

'You have me.'

'I know, and you're my best friend in the world. Listen, they only give you a hard time because they care about you and, if everything works out with this job and I get my own place to live, you can come and stay with me in London for a while once you've finished your exams.'

'You are so lucky, Alice. For as long as I can remember you've always known you wanted to go on the stage and have your name up in lights, whereas I haven't got a clue what I want to do with my life.'

'It didn't go down that well with the careers officer at school,' Alice said, remembering the patronizing expression on Mr Tomkins face. 'If I recall, he wanted to know what I was going to do to earn a living. Obviously he hasn't heard of the Young Generation and Pan's People, who probably earn more in a month than he does in a year.'

'He is a bit of an old fossil,' Mary laughed. 'He keeps suggesting I should get a good solid job with the bank… boring or what?'

Alice was pleased to hear her sister laugh. This was different from the summer shows, which were for a set period with a date for returning home. It must be difficult for her with me heading out into the big wide world and leaving her behind, she thought. If I do well in London, we may never share this bedroom again. She looked around her at the familiar faded floral wallpaper, partially covered with posters of their favourite popstars, and swallowed the lump of emotion that was forming in her throat. The girls had been having one last listen to their favourite song, Johnny Bristol's, 'Hang On In There

Baby', which held a different significance for Alice and her 'baby' sister.

'Pass my cassette player will you. I've left a space for it but I'm still going to need your help if I'm to get my case closed.'

The girls wriggled around on the soft lid of the battered old brown suitcase until the hard sides met and obscured the brightly coloured contents. Alice pressed the T-shaped fastener on her side, and Mary followed suit.

'Are you nervous?'

'What about? The audition, or going to live in London?'

'Both.'

'Not so much the audition. I've had to do those before for my summer seasons and pantomimes, although not in London of course. All the girls will probably be from proper stage schools like Bush Davis and Arts Educational, and there's little old me from Miss Nora's.'

'I bet you'll be the best dancer there.'

'We'll see. It might be a bit of an eye-opener for me. Maybe I'll find out just how good, or bad, I am and come home with my tail between my legs.'

A car horn sounded.

'I've got to go, sis. I'll miss you,' she said, dragging the suitcase to the top of the stairs and bumping it down tread by tread.

'At least I'll have my own room with no one nagging me to keep my side tidy.'

'I'm not sure what Mum will have to say about that.'

'Say about what?'

'Nothing, Mum,' Alice said, wrapping her arms around her mother for a hug, hoping that she wouldn't be able to feel the thumping of her heart against her ribcage seemingly in a bid to escape the confines of her chest. Her mother placed a hand on each side of her face and peered deep into her eyes as though examining her soul.

'Are you sure this is what you want, Alice? It's not too late to change your mind. No one will think any less of you.'

'It's what I've always wanted, Mum, you know that. I'm just a bit nervous is all.'

'Of course you are. I'd be surprised if you weren't. Do you remember what the Cheshire Cat said in your favourite book? "Every adventure requires a first step". This is your first step, darling, the first of many.'

'Thanks, Mum. Don't come out to the car,' she said, anxious to avoid a tearful farewell. 'Dad and I can take it from here.'

'You make sure and ring me when you get there. Have you got coins for the phone box?'

Alice shook her purse. 'Plenty. Stop worrying. It's only London, not New York,' adding under her breath, 'at least not yet.'

Ted Abbott made no effort to get out of the car to help his elder daughter with her heavy suitcase. The way he saw it, she was going to have to manage it on her own once the train pulled into St Pancras station, so she might as well get some practice in now. He had suggested she take a smaller case, with fewer clothes and shoes, until she knew for sure that she would be staying in London, but Alice had stuck to her guns. She had somewhere to live for the next eight weeks, until her friend, Linda, returned from touring with the Royal Ballet Company, by which time she would hopefully have a job and a place of her own to live.

Suitcase safely stored in the back of her dad's Mini Traveller, Alice closed the wood-trimmed doors and climbed into the front seat, her dancing bag and her shoulder bag on her lap.

'Have you got your ticket?'

'Yes, Dad.'

'And the sandwiches your mum made you?'

'Yes,' she said, patting the white paper bag sticking out of the top of her shoulder bag which contained four cheese and pickle sandwiches, neatly wrapped in greaseproof paper.

'Good. That'll keep you going on the train. Your mum's sandwiches are a darn sight fresher than British Rail, and you can't be paying those extortionate prices either. And here's 50p for a drink – hopefully that should cover it.'

'Thanks, Dad,' Alice said, accepting the coin and slipping it into her purse. She didn't need it, and she knew her dad couldn't really afford it since losing his job at the colliery, but he was a proud man and to refuse would hurt his feelings.

'Right, we'd best be off then. Like I said to your mother, the train won't wait.'

They arrived in the station car park less than fifteen minutes later, just as Alice knew they would, with still an hour to go before the scheduled departure of the train that was going to lead Alice to the promise of a new life. This time, Ted carried his daughter's case and purchased a platform ticket so that he could see her on to the train safely.

'So what time did you say your audition is?'

'Eleven thirty.'

'Right. You'll have time to leave your case at the lost property office, so you're not lugging it around on the underground with you. Remember to put the ticket they give you in a safe place, or they might not let you have it back.'

'Stop worrying, Dad. I've got all my instructions written down. We went over everything last night.'

'Sorry, love. Am I making you nervous?'

'Just a bit, but nerves are a good thing for a performer. Apparently, adrenalin brings the best out in people.'

'Is that so?' Ted said, wrinkling his forehead, clearly unsure what adrenalin was. 'Well, you just show them Londoners how it's done.'

'I will, Dad. I'm going to make you proud of me, I promise.'

CHAPTER 2

The sun streaming in through the lead-light windows of the dining room caused Richard to raise his newspaper higher to prevent him squinting as he read. Most of the time, he flicked through stories with little interest, but at least it meant he didn't have to try and make polite conversation with his wife, Anita, who was sitting at the other end of the dark oak table. The jingling sound of her charm bracelet each time she reached for her cup of tea or another slice of toast was jangling his nerves. Who gets up in the morning and puts their full make-up and jewellery on before breakfast? he thought, lowering his paper slightly. Anita was staring at him.

'What?' he asked, barely able to keep the irritation out of his voice.

'You're not even aware that you do it, are you?'

'Do what?'

'Tut,' she said. 'Every time I move my hand, you tut.'

'It's that bloody bracelet. It's so annoying. Do you have to wear it all the time?'

'You know why I wear it, Richard. It makes me feel closer to Mum,' she said, fingering the gold charms and battling to hold back the tears that were welling in her eyes, threatening to spill over and cause her perfectly applied make-up to run.

Oh great, here come the waterworks, Richard thought, lifting his paper back up so that he didn't have to witness the salty tears, coloured black from mascara, streaking down his wife's face.

Anita had struggled to come to terms with the death of her mother following a stroke three years ago. The effect it was having on their relationship was carefully hidden when they were out in public together, but at home the strain was becoming unbearable. Richard had considered filing for divorce when Anita began making excuses to not have sex with him. Surely, it's unreasonable behaviour to deny your husband his conjugal rights, he thought. Mind you, knowing my luck, I'd get some pro women's lib judge who wouldn't look too sympathetically on me, given the circumstances, and the last thing I need is bad publicity.

There was also the money to consider. It was always difficult to get financial backing for staging a West End show. It was so much easier to keep it in the family, and Anita's inheritance was bank-rolling his latest project. Talk about being caught between a rock and a hard place, he thought, sighing loudly.

'Can I get you another coffee?' Anita asked, apparently recovered from her emotional wobble.

Richard glanced at his watch. It was 8.30 and Max, his driver, wasn't due until nine with the car taking him to the theatre. He didn't want another coffee, but at least she was making an effort. He smiled, the warmth not quite reaching his eyes.

'Go on then, but just one sugar. I need to try and lose a few pounds.' And I'm not the only one, he thought uncharitably, watching his wife's once slender body waddle from the room. After the initial period of mourning when she had refused to eat and had become almost skeletal, she had gone in completely the other direction and taken solace in the biscuit tin at every available opportunity. He was surprised there wasn't a country-wide shortage of Gypsy Creams the amount his wife munched her way through each week.

'Daddy! Thank goodness you're still here.'

Richard motioned for Miriam, his fifteen-year-old daughter, to come and give him a hug. She had inherited her father's chocolate brown eyes and dark hair, although his was now significantly grey at the temples.

'Shouldn't you be on your way to school by now?' he asked, kissing her forehead.

'I hate walking,' she said, a sulky expression settling on her face, 'especially when it's raining. It makes my hair go crazy. What's the point of sleeping with it wrapped around my head to keep it straight if the moment I step outside I look like a frizz ball? Can Max take a detour and drop me at school? Please, Daddy?'

Richard had never been able to deny his daughter anything, and Max would do whatever he asked him to. Twelve years ago, Max had killed a woman in a hit-and-run accident while under the influence of drink, and Richard had provided not only his alibi but also had the car repaired before the police came sniffing around. Since then, Max was unswervingly loyal to his employer. Whatever Richard did, or asked Max to do on his behalf, was never questioned.

'All right, princess, but not a word to your mum, she'll tell me off for spoiling you. Max is always early, so fetch your school bag and wait for me in the car and she'll be none the wiser.'

Miriam smiled, happy in the knowledge that she still had the ability to wrap her father around her little finger.

'You're the best daddy in the world,' she said, bounding out of the room and almost knocking the coffee out of her mother's hand.

'What's all that about? What have you agreed to buy her now?'

'Nothing. She just appreciates me more than you do.'

For a moment, it looked as though Anita was going to rise to his provocative remark but instead she shrugged slightly and said, 'Are you in for dinner tonight?'

'Probably. Audition days are always long and tedious. I'll most likely fall asleep in front of the television.'

Out of the corner of his eye, he noticed the black Mercedes pull up across his driveway. Moments later, Miriam called goodbye from the hallway, slamming the front door behind her. Could she make it any more obvious? he thought.

'Thanks for the extra coffee,' he said, to distract his wife from looking out of the window. 'I wonder how many more I'll have had by the end of the day to stay awake?'

'Who are you auditioning today?'

'The girl dancers. The advert in *The Stage* clearly stated that only Full Equity members should attend, but you just know there will be dozens of kids who've travelled to London from the provinces in the hope that the blue card rule doesn't apply to them. What a waste of their time and money. Still, not my problem.'

'How many are you looking for?'

'Twelve, although Larry's probably already got his chorus line in his head from girls he's worked with before, unless someone is really outstanding, of course.'

'It doesn't seem very fair on all those hopefuls if Larry has already made his mind up.'

'Life isn't fair, Anita. I would have thought you would have realised that by now. Right, I'm off. I should be back around seven,' he said, placing his barely touched cup of coffee back on its saucer. 'Have a good day.'

CHAPTER 3

Gina's head was pounding. If only I'd been brave enough to ask Franco for last night off, she thought, reaching for the glass of water on her bedside table, swallowing two Panadol and sinking back on to the fluffy feather pillows to wait for the tablets to take effect. He didn't take kindly to the girls letting him down, and she had to admit she was more than a little frightened of him since Pam, one of her closest friends, had come into work with a badly camouflaged black eye the night after she had been absent without permission for her birthday celebrations.

The plan had been to arrive at the Ostrich Club around 10.30 p.m., encourage a few of the customers to buy her the extortionately priced drinks and leave around midnight, feigning a headache. Unfortunately for Gina, a group of around a dozen businessmen rolled into the club just before she was about to make her excuses, flashing wads of twenty-pound notes. They were already very drunk, and that meant easy pickings. Franco had welcomed them effusively and instantly sent his most experienced girls over to their tables to attend to their requirements. Five minutes later the Moët & Chandon was arriving in ice buckets, and corks were popping like machine-gun fire. There was no way she could leave, fake headache or not. Business had been a little slow lately, but tonight Franco had pound signs in his eyes, and he would do everything he could to milk the drunken idiots dry. The first few bottles of Moët were always the real thing, but once the boss was comfortable that the punters wouldn't be able to tell the difference between the real thing and a cheap imitation, the empty bottles were refilled with something not so palatable and much less expensive.

It had been past three when she had finally got away from the Ostrich, but at least she hadn't had to endure too much in the way of fumbling and fondling. Most of the attempts at bottom pinching and grabbing at pert young breasts had fallen short of their mark, such was the level of inebriation. From Franco's point of view, it had been a great night, which was reflected by the extra ten pounds he had given each of the girls as a bonus on top of their wages.

From Gina's point of view, it was a disaster. She needed to look her best today to compete with girls half her age at the auditions for Larry's new musical. She and Larry went back a long way. They had done their first West End show together in 1964 and had even had a little fling until he had realised he preferred boys to girls. They had remained firm friends throughout the past twelve years, but while Larry's career, once he had moved into choreography, had taken off, Gina's had begun a slow downward spiral that was more a reflection of her age than her ability. Stage schools provided a constant supply of quality young dancers, and it was becoming increasingly difficult for thirty-two-year-old Gina to compete. Larry had all but promised her this job, but yesterday he had dropped by her flat to deliver the bombshell that the show's producer would be sitting in on the auditions and he was renowned for favouring younger girls.

'You're gonna have to be at the top of your game, sweetie,' Larry warned. 'Most of the big stage schools have put girls up, and then there will be all the kids who have seen the ad in *The Stage*. It's going to be tricky insisting that I have you if you can't pick up the steps. Fortunately, you are my best friend in the world, and I've come up with a plan. Go and change into some practice gear and I'll move the furniture.'

Two hours later, sweat-drenched and exhausted, Gina flopped on to her leather Chesterfield sofa after Larry had taught her the routines he was planning to unleash on the hundreds of hopefuls the following day, effectively giving her a head start. Performing had never been a problem; eyes, tits and teeth was Gina's mantra.

'Jeez, Larry. I'm shattered. You're definitely going to sort the wheat from the chaff with that little lot.'

'That's the idea. I think this show is going to be huge,' he said, flamboyantly extending his arms as wide as he could reach, 'and when it transfers to Broadway, I want everyone to be talking about my choreography and my brilliant chorus line. Maybe I could even get you a role as my assistant, if you think you're getting too old to be a dancer.'

'Do you think I'm getting too old?'

'Don't be ridiculous, darling. You are one of the best

dancers I've ever worked with, and you've got a better body now than when we first met. I don't know what you do to stay in such great shape but keep it up, it's clearly working.'

Gina doubted that Larry would approve if he ever discovered her secret.

'I'll get you a drink, and then we'll go over the routines one more time. Pepsi?' he asked, padding softly across the polished parquet living room floor in his suede-soled jazz shoes and pushing open the door to the kitchen.

'Just water, thanks,' Gina replied, slipping her sweatshirt over her shoulders and pulling her knitted jazz trousers back on to keep her muscles warm. The towelling strip she was wearing across her forehead as a headband, to prevent the sweat from dripping into her eyes, had worked loose with all the exertion, so she undid the knot at the back of her head, re-folded it to have dryer fabric next to her skin and was re-tying it when Larry walked back in with their drinks.

'Here you go,' he said, handing her a glass of water before pulling the ring on a can of Pepsi, releasing an expanding mound of light brown froth. 'You are so lucky living here. I still can't believe a long-lost relative left you this in their will. It must be worth a fortune.'

Gina sipped her water and shot him a sideways glance. Since she moved into the Barnes riverside apartment two years ago, Larry had often commented along similar lines. She was convinced he didn't believe her story and was giving her the opportunity to tell him the truth, but that was never going to happen. Lying to her best friend was not something she was proud of, but it could ruin their friendship if he found out how she came to be living in the luxury two-bedroom apartment.

The Panadol had started working on the thumping headache brought on by a combination of last night's fake bubbly and a lack of sleep. Gina glanced at her travel clock. It was quarter past nine. Larry had expressly told her not to be late for the audition, knowing that time-keeping wasn't her best asset. Time to get up and get my slap on, she thought, and I'm probably going to have to take a cab if I'm going to make it on time. There goes last night's bonus.

CHAPTER 4

A lice heard the queue before she saw it. She had arrived at the front entrance of the Duchess of York's Theatre a little after 11 a.m. and initially thought she was one of the first before she spotted the sign taped to the glass of one of the entrance doors. It said, *Auditions This Way*, and had an arrow underneath pointing around the side of the majestic old building. Approaching the end of the street, the sound of excited chatter increased in volume with every step she took and, on rounding the corner, she almost bumped into the girls at the back of a very long queue which snaked round the next corner. The butterflies that had been flitting around in Alice's stomach since she had climbed on the bus at St. Pancras station were now doing somersaults. What am I even doing here? she thought, as groups of girls, who obviously knew each other, were lending each other lip gloss along with words of encouragement.

Alice wasn't wearing any make-up. She had thought that this would be like her previous auditions where girls were selected on their dancing ability rather than their looks, but glancing down the line it was clear that the minimum she would need was blusher, mascara and lipstick. She put her dance bag down on the pavement and reached into her shoulder bag for her make-up.

'I wouldn't do that if I were you,' said the pretty brunette she had almost bumped in to.

'Sorry?'

'I wouldn't put your bag on the pavement. If you take your eye off it for even a minute it's likely to get pinched.'

'Oh. Right. Thanks.'

'I take it you're not from London.'

'No. I've just come down from Nottingham this morning.'

'You mean up. London's the capital, so you come up to London from everywhere else in England, even if you've travelled south. I like Nottingham. My friend was in pantomime at the Theatre Royal last Christmas and we had a few really good nights out.'

'Really? I must know her. I was in the panto too. Is she here today?' Alice asked, hoping for a familiar face among the hundreds of girls.

'No. She's moved on from doing chorus work. She played the princess.'

Alice flushed and reached down to pick up her dance bag to avoid eye contact. Erica Lindsay, who had played Princess Balroubador, was one of the bitchiest girls she had ever met. She only had a dozen lines in the whole show and a singing duet with Aladdin but anyone would have thought she was the headliner the way she behaved. She was particularly spiteful about the girl dancers, constantly complaining to the company manager that they were making too much noise in their dressing room, which was next door to hers. Alice had vowed at the time that if she ever made it big she would never behave in such an arrogant manner.

'Move up,' said a voice from behind her.

'It's okay, you go ahead, I'm just picking my bag up,' Alice said, relieved to put some distance between herself and the pretty brunette, thus avoiding an awkward conversation about Erica.

It took fifteen minutes to reach the stage door, by which time Alice had managed to apply a little make-up. It had been tricky holding both her bags while spitting onto the Miner's mascara block and applying black to her fair lashes, but the end result was worth it. Her china-blue eyes were now defined and the coral pink lipstick made her full lips even more voluptuous. In front of her, the girl who she had allowed to queue jump seemed to be having a heated discussion with the stage-door keeper.

'But I have done my forty weeks. I applied for my full Equity card last week, it just hasn't arrived yet.'

'Sorry, love. The ad in *The Stage* clearly stated that you would be required to show your blue card. You should have gone up to Harley Street and got some kind proof before coming to the audition.'

'I didn't have time,' the girl wailed. 'My train down from Manchester was late.'

Up from Manchester, Alice thought. She was a quick learner, which was just as well in the world of the professional dancer.

'The management said no exceptions to the full Equity rule. If you can't show your blue card, you can't come in. I'll have to ask you to step aside, there's still a lot of girls to check, and the auditions are due to start in ten minutes.'

The girl was crying. Alice wanted to speak up for her, but the advertisement had been clear. There was so much competition for every job, the rules had to be stuck to. She showed her blue plastic wallet to the stage door keeper and in exchange received a piece of card with the number 257 on it.

'Follow the paper arrows taped to the walls and join the back of the queue,' he instructed. 'Next.'

It didn't take long to reach the back of the queue which was filling the narrow Victorian corridor that led to the wings at the side of the stage. Alice couldn't help wondering if the paying public were aware of how different the conditions were backstage compared with the splendour and opulence of front of house. Although the girls were now talking in hushed voices, the concrete floors and painted bricks intensified every sound, making it very noisy until somewhere at the front someone said, 'Shhhhhh, pass it back.'

Moments later, from the general direction of the auditorium a voice, amplified by a microphone, said, 'Thank you for coming today, ladies, and thanks for your patience in the queue. I'm Richard Sherwood, the show's producer, and this is Larry, my choreographer, who will be putting you through your paces. Because of the huge turnout, we have to be strict about enforcing the height requirement. Please can the first twenty of you come on to the stage and remove your shoes.'

A collective gasp filtered back along the line of girls queueing in the corridor. It wasn't unusual for an advert to stipulate a minimum height, but it was generally thought of as only a guideline. By wearing a slightly higher or lower heel you could add or remove an inch or two. If everyone had to take their shoes off, there was no room to hide.

'Surely they are not going to send people away without letting them dance?' Alice whispered to an auburn-haired girl behind her in the queue.

'Looks like it. You shouldn't have a problem though. What are you, five foot six?'

'Five foot seven.'

'Me too. Just don't stand up too straight or you'll tower above the minimum height.'

'Thanks for the tip.'

'No problem. I heard you mention that you've travelled from Nottingham to be here. It's an expensive day out if you're not even permitted to dance.'

The throng of girls shuffled ever closer to the stage, and as they did so, girls in floods of tears and others muttering furiously under their breath pushed past on their way back out to the street.

Finally, it was Alice's turn to be scrutinised. She undid the green leather ankle strap on her platform-sole wedge sandals and dropped four inches as her feet made contact with the wooden planks of the stage.

After a few moments, a voice from several rows back in the stalls said, 'Numbers 242, 249, 250, 256 and 259, please step forward.'

Alice's heart sank. She had not even made it past the first hurdle.

'Thank you for coming, but I'm afraid you don't meet the height requirement. The rest of you: leave the stage to your right and follow the signs to the changing area. You'll be assigned a new number when you come back.

And please keep the chat to a minimum.'

Relieved that she was through the first two screening processes, Alice knew that now the serious business began. Pulling on her purple footless tights, matching leotard and pink leg warmers, she surreptitiously checked the room, eyeing up the competition. Erica Lindsay's friend had not made it through the height check and Alice felt a pang of guilt. If she hadn't warned me about putting my bag down on the pavement I might not have any practice gear to change in to, she thought, slipping her feet into her well-worn jazz shoes and tying her long mane of hair into a ponytail.

'Haven't you got any heels?' hissed the girl with auburn hair who had previously been number 258.

'Yes, but I thought—'

'Put them on. You're auditioning for a West End show, not a holiday camp summer season. You'd better stick with me, or you'll be chucked out with the next lot. I'm Gina, by the way.'

'I'm Alice. Thanks for yet another tip. It seems I've got a lot to learn.'

'You certainly have, but just concentrate on learning the steps for the time being. Larry's a stickler for getting the feet right, but that said, don't forget to perform. Come on, let's make your journey down from Nottingham worthwhile.'

'Up.'

'You what?'

'Oh, nothing.'

CHAPTER 5

Peter lay in bed staring up at the ceiling. He could hardly believe he had finally had the balls to dump his model girlfriend, Lisa. He smiled at the use of the word 'model'. The only model thing about her had been her profession. She was lazy, moany and lately had got into a nasty habit of hitting him when she didn't get her way. Peter had been raised to never lay a hand on a woman in anger but at times, over the six months of their turbulent relationship, he had been sorely tempted, only prevented by the fear that she might break because she was so thin. It seemed that everything she did lately was to see how far she could push him. Well, last night, she had gone too far.

The evening had started off well with a quiet dinner for two at their favourite restaurant in Knightsbridge. It was difficult for a pop star and a top model to have any privacy on a night out but Mario's was used to accommodating A-listers in secluded booths with dim lighting. As usual, Lisa had picked at her food which was one of the ways she maintained her almost skeletal figure.

When they had first met at a charity ball in Manchester,

she was a perfect size 12, shown off to great effect by a gold maxi dress that plunged to the navel at the front and almost as deep at the back, but that was only part of the attraction. She was funny and self-deprecating, and Peter could sense that they shared the same insecurity that people only liked them because of what they were, rather than who they were. They had laughed together about the supposedly glamorous worlds they inhabited, sharing stories of freezing cold 5 a.m. starts and evenings spent alone in front of their respective televisions.

After the first photograph of her and Peter leaving a London nightclub together made it on to the front page of one of the tabloids, Lisa's agent, Kathy, had called her into the office. Her modelling work had mostly been for catalogues, specialising in lingerie and swimwear, but they were aware of the secret desire she harboured to become the next big supermodel. Not only could it be Lisa's big break, but it would also put the agency on the map, not to mention the commission they would rake in. 'Now that you're dating a pop star,' Kathy had said, 'the phones are ringing off the hook with assignments. It could be your chance to break into catwalk if you're prepared to drop a couple of dress sizes.' It was the chance of a lifetime for Lisa. Plenty of sex with very little food proved to be the perfect diet, but as the pounds melted away, so did her bubbly personality and the rows had started, mostly about Peter's adamant refusal to let her move into his mews house or even give her a key to the front door.

After the restaurant, Lisa had insisted on going clubbing, ignoring Peter's protestations. 'You're so boring,' she had said, 'you're more like a sixty-four-year-

ALICE IN THEATRELAND

old than a twenty-four-year-old.' As usual, he had caved in, not wanting an argument in public, and when they got to Lucinda's he made a beeline for the bar to order champagne while she hit the dance floor to work off the calories from the six bites of salmon and the three lettuce leaves she had consumed. He stood watching her cavorting around in a mini skirt that was so short he could see the occasional flash of bright pink knickers.

'You're Peter Flint, aren't you?'

He dragged his eyes away from his girlfriend to be confronted by two girls, who looked far too young to have passed the club's over-18 policy. They were standing on the other side of the thick velvet rope that cordoned off the VIP section.

'Guilty as charged,' he said, smiling.

'Can we have an autograph?'

'Of course; if you wait a few minutes, I'm sure my girlfriend Lisa will sign your paper napkins too.'

He had turned back to the dance floor to point her out to the two fans, but there was no sign of her.

'Or maybe not. She seems to have disappeared.'

'Was she the one in the blue mini dress?'

'Yes.'

'She went with a man towards the fire escape door.'

'She's probably gone outside to cool down after all that leaping around. I suppose I'd better go and see if she's all right.'

Leaving the bottle of champagne in the ice bucket by the table he had reserved, Peter went to the bar to ask for a glass of water. It wouldn't be the first time Lisa had felt faint from lack of food. Twiggy has a lot to answer for, he thought, pushing down on the bar to release the fire

35

escape door which led out to a narrow alley. No one was there, and he was about to go back into the club when a movement caught his eye in a doorway further down the alley. Probably just a cat, he thought, straining to see in the dim light. A car passing the end of the passageway briefly illuminated the doorway with its headlights, revealing a flash of blue fabric.

'Lisa?' Peter had said, moving forward across the cobbles, 'is that you? Are you throwing up?' That was another of Lisa's tricks to keep her weight down.

There was a scuffling sound and in a flash of light from another pair of headlamps, Peter was treated to the sight of a man with his trousers around his knees and his dick hanging out, over whose shoulder was a shocked-looking Lisa.

'You're disgusting!'

'Christ man, I'm sorry. I didn't know she was here with her boyfriend.'

'She's not. Goodbye, Lisa,' Peter had said, turning on his heel, depositing the glass of water on the metal railing of the fire escape and heading towards the street whose traffic had been so illuminating.

Peter turned on his side, checked his bedside clock and, despite it being almost midday, rolled back over pulling the covers up over his shoulders. He'd been trying to find the right moment to end their relationship so, in a way, she had done him a favour. Not a very pleasant thing to witness, he thought, but imagine if she'd pulled a stunt like that after I open in my West End debut. The press would have had a field day.

CHAPTER 6

By the time Larry called for an hour's lunch break, it was 2.30 p.m., and the number of dancers had dwindled from many hundreds to just twenty-four. Alice had stuck to Gina's side like glue and had been amazed at how quickly her new friend had picked up the steps and the confidence with which she had performed them.

After one step sequence, as they moved to the side of the stage to let the next group of six dancers try to secure themselves a place in Larry's final chorus line, Gina had whispered, 'You're a bloody good dancer, but you need to get your head up and smile, or you'll be out in the next round.'

Once again it had been good advice. Technically, there was very little to choose between the remaining dancers, but the ones who were less expansive in their presentation were gradually being sifted out. Looking around the group that had made it to the lunch break, Alice hoped she wasn't going to be among the twelve disappointed girls. It would almost be worse to have got this far only to fail at the final hurdle.

'Do you want to go for a bite of lunch? I know a salad

bar on the next street if you fancy it?' Gina said.

Alice hesitated. 'My mum packed me some cheese and pickle sandwiches. I'm happy to share if you like.'

'Put your jacket and outdoor shoes on and bring them with you,' Gina said. 'Let's get a breath of fresh air.'

Alice could sense several pairs of eyes on her as she fastened the buckle on her sandals and she could have sworn she heard a couple of the girls sniggering.

'Come on,' Gina urged, 'we haven't got long.'

After spending hours in the gloom of the theatre, the bright afternoon sunshine dazzled the girls as they spilled on to the pavement, but Gina didn't hang around to allow their eyes to adjust. She took hold of Alice's elbow and steered her in the direction of a cobbled passageway.

'I know this area like the back of my hand. Let's take a short cut through to Floral Street.'

'Was it my imagination, or were some of the other girls laughing at me back there?'

'It's a bitchy business being a professional dancer. You'll need to grow a thick skin if you're going to make it.'

'What do you mean?' Alice asked, following Gina into a small café called Joe's.

'Ciao, bella. I don't see you for a long time.'

'Hi, Giuseppe,' Gina replied to the man behind the counter. 'It must be all of a month.'

'It seems longer. You bring the sunshine through my door. You have the same as usual? And your friend?'

'Yes, for both of us please and pronto. We're in the middle of an audition,' she said, heading to one of the small wooden tables at the back of the café.

The girls had barely taken their jackets off and sat down before Giuseppe was at their table carrying a tray with two plates of egg salad and two glasses of water.

'I bring cappuccinos in one minute.'

Alice stayed quiet until Giuseppe moved away.

'I thought we were going to share my sandwiches?'

'Don't you like egg salad?'

'Yes, but…'

'Don't worry, it's my treat. Joe only charges me half price so it will be like paying in full for once. A salad will be lighter on your stomach. We've still got a lot of dancing to do,' Gina said, forking grated carrot into her mouth and studiously avoiding eye contact.

'Oh, I get it now. That's why those girls were laughing. They heard me mention sandwiches and they think I shouldn't be eating them because I'm fat.'

'You're not fat, just… "curvier" than most West End dancers. You'll soon drop a few pounds when we start rehearsals, particularly if you cut bread and potatoes out of your diet.'

Alice was mortified. Despite being so kind and helpful, it was clear from her comment that Gina also thought Alice needed to lose weight. She could feel the prickle of a blush rise up her neck and on to her face. Having felt starving hungry moments before, after a morning of serious exertion, she had now completely lost her appetite.

'Is there any point me going back for the afternoon session? With so many skinny dancers to choose from, why would the choreographer go for me?'

'Don't be like that. When I was starting out, I was on the curvier side too and couldn't understand why I kept getting rejected at auditions until I met my friend Joanna, who took me under her wing. The truth hurts sometimes but I'm eternally grateful for her honesty. Losing a few pounds takes a bit of willpower but being able to dance like you can is special. It's a God-given talent and, trust me, Larry has noticed it.'

'That's the second time you've referred to the choreographer by his first name. Do you know him?'

'Let's just say we've worked together a lot over the years. I pointed you out to him in the early stages of the audition, and he gave me a thumbs up. If it was purely down to him, you and I would already have the job, but Richard, the producer of this show, is very hands on, and in more ways than one if the rumours are to be believed.'

Alice wasn't so naïve that she didn't understand what Gina was getting at. In show business, the dancers were looked on as easy pickings and not only by the management. It was often the star of the show making lewd advances. It could make for a difficult situation but fortunately was one Alice had no personal experience of.

'And here we are ladies. Giuseppe's special cappuccinos. Enjoy.'

Once again waiting until he was out of earshot, Alice said, 'What is it?'

'It's a frothy coffee like they drink in Italy. It looks and tastes like a treat but Joe does it with espresso and then froths up skimmed milk so it's not too calorific. He even holds off on the chocolate sprinkles on the top for me so I can enjoy it without any guilty feelings.'

Alice sipped it.

'That's really good. I'll remember that I can have this as a treat when I start my diet.'

'That's the spirit. I said you would need a thick skin to survive in theatreland and I wasn't joking. Eat up, we need to be getting back, and when we do, we'll show those bitches a thing or two. If you think the choreography has been tough up to now, Larry is about to unleash a masterpiece. Don't panic: with your ability you'll be fine, but some of them will be laughing on the other side of their skinny faces. At least all you and I need to worry about now is impressing the producer.'

CHAPTER 7

Lunch for Richard and Larry had been of the liquid variety in the Four Keys public house across the road from the front entrance of the Duchess of York's Theatre. Larry, who rarely drank alcohol and needed to keep his wits about him for the afternoon session, had stuck to soft drinks but Richard had fortified his Coca Cola with a double scotch each time he had visited the bar. Larry could smell it on his breath but was in no position to comment, after all, Richard was bank-rolling the show that could launch his Broadway career. In any case, he was hoping that the more inebriated Richard became, the less interested he would be in interfering with Larry's choice of dancers for his chorus line.

After the head start he had given her, Gina had been phenomenal all morning and he was pretty sure that there would be no problem in having her in his final line-up but he was a little concerned about the slightly plump blonde girl she had pointed out to him. There was no doubt that the girl was a fabulous dancer, and there was something special about her that made her incredibly watchable, but he'd employed curvy girls before and despite their promises to lose weight they usually ended up putting it back on once they had signed a six-month contract. She would have to be outstanding in the tricky final routine to be considered.

The two men pushed through the double doors and were once more enveloped in the dungeon-like gloom of the auditorium, illuminated only by the desk lamp on the table from where Richard had wielded his axe that morning. The twenty-four remaining candidates were already standing around in groups on the stage, and the air was thick with nervous tension.

'Right, we'd better get started,' Richard said, slumping heavily into one of the velvet-covered seats. 'You go and teach them the routine Larry and I'll make a few notes on the most likely looking girls. We have to be out of here by five so they can set up for tonight's performance, and I'd like to get this done and dusted today.'

Larry clapped his hands together as he made his way towards the orchestra pit.

'Okay, girls. I hope you've all had a decent lunch because you're going to need a lot of energy for this final routine. Form yourselves into three lines of eight and no talking,' he said, nimbly taking the steps leading on to the stage two at a time, noticing as he did that Gina had sensibly lined up in the middle row alongside her protégée. Wise move, Larry thought, not exposing yourself to too much scrutiny from Richard by being on the front row, but not hiding away at the back either. He stood facing the dancers to give them some final words of encouragement. 'Right, this is it. Your big chance: don't blow it. I'll take it slowly to start, and I'd advise just marking it until we do it to the music,' he said before turning to face the auditorium, 'and five, six, seven, eight…'

Reducing the numbers from twenty-four to sixteen had been fairly simple. The girls who struggled to pick up the intricate steps quickly were thanked and asked to leave, as were the girls whose body language suggested they were getting fed up with repeating the routine over and over again.

'I don't get it,' Richard said, after releasing a girl who had marked the routine in the previous round because she was getting tired. 'She was top of my bloody list too. Pretty and with a great figure, but her attitude stinks. I can't be doing with that.'

Larry had checked Richard's list a few times. Gina had been in the top half throughout, but her newfound friend had constantly been languishing near the bottom.

'I think we just need to make our minds up on who is going to make the best and most matched chorus line. All these girls are excellent dancers and performers; it just has to be down to how they look as a unit. Do you agree, Larry?'

Larry had the feeling that the next girl to go would be the voluptuous blonde. All the other girls were of a similar slight build. She looked heavy alongside them, but Larry had found his eyes drawn to her time and time again. She had something indefinably special about her.

'Suggestion. Why don't we agree jointly on our best eight and then each have two favourites join the line-up? If anyone looks really out of place, you will have the casting vote.'

Larry was banking on the fact that the day had dragged

on rather more than Richard had hoped. In fifteen minutes, they would have to vacate the theatre, and he was probably hoping to get back to the pub for a couple of drinks before being picked up and driven home.

Richard shrugged, a definite signal that he was beginning to lose interest.

'These are my top eight. Have you got a problem with any of them?'

Larry was relieved to see that Gina had made the cut.

'No, I'm absolutely fine with all of them. I'll call those girls forward, and then we can each add our two favourites.

CHAPTER 8

Maybe Dad was right; I shouldn't have brought so much stuff with me, Alice thought, dragging her heavy suitcase up the final flight of stairs to reach Linda's bedsit on the top floor of a once grand Victorian villa. It had been a long, exhausting day, both physically and emotionally, and the last thing she needed was to be accosted by the ground-floor tenant as she tried to creep up the stairs without attracting attention, having collected the spare keys from under the rock which Linda had thoughtfully marked with a splodge of pink nail varnish.

'I hope you're not going to be trouble,' the neighbour, Ruby, had said. 'Linda knows the rules. These flats aren't meant to be sub-let, and I won't hesitate in telling the landlord that you're here if you're always going to make that kind of racket going up the stairs.'

Stupid woman, Alice thought, fumbling to get the key in the lock of Linda's door before the timed lights on the stairwell and landings went out. As if I'm always going to be lugging a heavy suitcase up here; and it wouldn't have hurt her to offer a bit of help. The door opened with a squeak and Alice pushed her suitcase the final few feet before closing the door and collapsing in a heap on the two-seater Parker Knoll sofa that had seen better days.

Despite the saggy springs supporting the seat cushions and the wooden arms, Alice was very tempted to curl into a ball and go to sleep, but that wasn't going to happen. She had promised her mum and dad she would ring as soon as she got to the tiny flat in West Kensington and they would probably be going frantic by now as it was almost 9 p.m. As if to remind her of how late it was, her stomach rumbled. She hadn't eaten a thing since the salad and cappuccino at Joe's café over six hours ago. What a good job I didn't bin the cheese and pickle sandwiches Mum made for me, she thought, reaching to the bottom of her shoulder bag and retrieving the now decidedly squashed package. She could imagine the look of horror on Gina's face as she sank her teeth into the thick white bread, stuffed with chunks of cheddar and generous amounts of tangy brown pickle, but she didn't care. She was hungry, and there would be nothing in Linda's cupboards to eat as she had already been on tour for the previous two weeks.

The first sandwich was demolished in five bites with Alice barely chewing her food before swallowing. She reached into the greaseproof paper for another and was surprised when a tear dropped on her hand. She touched her face; it was wet with tears. The whole day had been totally overwhelming, and the taste of home had clearly been the final straw. I'm not sure I'm ready for the cut-throat world of London's West End, she thought, pressing the heels of her hands into her eyes to stem the flow before taking a much smaller bite of the second sandwich and chewing thoroughly to savour the taste. Then why are you here, the more positive side of her brain asked?

You could have just got on a train back to Nottingham, with your tail between your legs, when you went to the station to fetch your case.

'I have to give it a chance,' Alice announced to the empty room, 'or I'll always wonder what might have been.'

Sandwich number three in hand, she grabbed her coin purse and door keys and headed down to the first-floor landing, where the pay phone was, and dialled home. It was answered on the second ring, and she could hear the anxiety in her mum's voice as she struggled to push the coin into the slot.

'Mum, it's me. Can you hear me?'

'Alice. Thank God. I've been worried sick for hours. You were supposed to ring the moment you got to the flat. Alice? Are you okay? Are you crying? What's wrong, didn't you get the job? Don't worry, love; there'll be other auditions. Oh, I wish I was there so I could put my arms around you.'

'I – I'm okay,' Alice said, swallowing hard to try and stop her tears, 'it was just hearing the worry in your voice. I'm sorry it's so late but the audition went on forever, and then I had to go and get my case from the station in rush-hour traffic and the buses were all so full I couldn't get on with my case. I only just got to Linda's, and I guess I'm just exhausted.'

'You don't have to do this, Alice. You can come home if it's all too much for you. You know we love you and think you are the best dancer in the world, even if those stuck-up Londoners can't see it.'

'Mum, I can't come home.'

'Yes, you can. You'll never be a failure in our eyes.'

'No. I really can't come home. Rehearsals start on Monday. I got the job!'

'Oh my!'

Alice could hear her dad and sister in the background saying, 'What? What's happened?' Then the beeps signalled that she needed to put more money in to continue the call. By the time the money had gone through, it was her dad's voice on the end of the phone line.

'Clever girl, Alice. I told you you'd show them Londoners a thing or two. We're so flaming proud of you. Tell us all about it – I'll hold the phone out so Mum and Mary can hear too.'

Alice related the day's story, occasionally interrupting her flow to push another coin into the slot, telling them all about meeting Gina and how she was sure she had helped her get the job because she already knew the choreographer, Larry. She missed out the bit right at the end of the hours of auditioning where the show's producer had asked her to step forward from the line-up of the final twelve.

'What's your name?' Richard had asked.

'Erm, Alice.'

'Well, "erm Alice", the choreographer and I are having a bit of a disagreement about you. He thinks you are one of the best dancers here, and you are, but aesthetically you are spoiling my perfect chorus line because you're a bit on the chunky side.'

Alice was aware of the sharp intake of breath from some of the girls on the stage behind her and the sniggers of others. How humiliating. She could feel her face colouring up like a beetroot. I will not cry, I will not cry, I will not cry, she repeated silently in her head.

'So, "erm Alice", you've put me in a difficult position. Do I over-rule my choreographer and choose somebody slimmer or do I ask you to lose weight and then trust you that you will? What would you do in my position, "erm Alice"?'

This was more brutal than Alice could ever have imagined when she had stepped aboard the train in Nottingham that morning. To be judged on dancing ability was one thing but to be singled out for being one size larger than the rest of the girls was something else entirely.

'I'm waiting, and my patience is running out.'

This man is a bully, Alice thought. I don't care if he's a West End impresario, at the end of the day he's only another human being, exactly like me. She had raised her chin a fraction of an inch in defiance, trying to keep the wobble out of her voice.

'All I can promise is that I will try my hardest to lose weight. I've loved the routines that we have learnt today and I think I would be an asset to the show but you are the producer and if you think someone else is better suited than me aesthetically, then, of course, I understand your decision.'

There had been total silence. You could have heard a pin drop to the floor from the wardrobe mistress's mouth in her little sewing room on the fourth floor of the building. All the other dancers dropped their gaze to the stage, but Alice kept her eyes on Richard's. Eventually, he spoke.

'All right. I'll give you a chance, but I'll be watching you, "erm Alice". Step back in line. For the ladies who have not been called into the line-up, thank you for your efforts today. Please give your details to Larry as there is a strong possibility we may need to replace one of our chorus if she can't keep her promise. Congratulations to the rest of you. Rehearsals start at 9 a.m. sharp on Monday morning, and we will have your contracts ready for you to sign then.'

No one had moved until Richard left the auditorium through the double doors at the back of the stalls and then Gina was the first to put her arm around Alice's shoulders.

'The girl from the provinces has done good. It seems your skin is already growing thicker. I'll help you shed a few pounds one way or another.'

Alice wasn't sure what Gina meant, but she had thanked her anyway. She was shell-shocked. She had her toe on the first rung of the ladder of her childhood dream, and she wanted to climb right to the top.

'Don't let me down, Alice,' was all Larry had said to her when she gave him the address of the West Kensington flat.

'Dad, I'm on my last 10p and the beeps are going to go any minute. Thanks for believing in me.'

'We love you, Alice...' was the last thing she heard before the phone line went dead.

A voice from the foot of the stairs startled her.

'About bloody time too,' Ruby said. 'We all have to share that phone you know, and the bathroom, so don't go thinking you can spend hours in there.'

Alice was too tired to respond with anything other

than a weak smile. She dragged herself back up the stairs to the top floor, undid the fastenings on her case, removed her pyjamas and cassette player and went to bed, serenaded by Barry White and his Love Unlimited Orchestra.

CHAPTER 9

Soot and stale perspiration combined to create a noxious aroma that invaded Alice's nostrils as she shuffled forward along the crowded platform of Piccadilly Circus tube station, hemmed in by hundreds of other commuters, heading for the exit. On the first morning of rehearsals, she had felt claustrophobic, afraid that the sooty smell was a fire and panicking that she would be trapped underground. It was a fear she had developed at a very young age once she understood what her father's job entailed.

Sheila Abbott had taken her two young daughters to the pit-head one sunny, summer morning to show them where their daddy worked. They had both waved to him happily as the miners, wearing their protective helmets with flashlights on the front, crowded into the lift to take them down to the coalface. As the gate closed and the lift began its descent, Alice had started to scream uncontrollably. She cried relentlessly throughout the day and had flung herself at her father's legs the moment the back door of their terraced cottage opened that evening. The nightmares of being swallowed up by the ground went on for months with Alice waking in the night drenched in sweat and gasping for breath. Eventually, after dozens of nocturnal visits where Sheila stroked her four-year-old daughter's forehead and uttered soothing words, they stopped only to return a few years later after the Aberfan disaster.

Alice's family had stared at the black-and-white images on their tiny television set, watching in horror as the primary school was engulfed by a deadly slag heap. 'Those poor little mites must have been terrified,' Sheila had said, wiping the tears from her eyes with a pristine white cotton handkerchief, 'drowning in that filthy stuff.' The panic was instant. 'Mummy, I can't breathe,' Alice had said, falling dramatically to the floor, clutching her throat. Once again, the nightmares faded in time, but death by suffocation was still Alice's biggest fear.

She eased forward onto the bottom tread of the towering wooden escalator that would carry her up to street level. In the four weeks since rehearsals had begun, she had developed a coping mechanism. By breathing slowly and deeply she could control her fear of travelling on the tube in such overcrowded conditions to a degree, but only when she stepped onto the escalator did the tension that held her shoulders in a vice-like grip begin to melt away. Only another two weeks until the show opens, she thought with relief, and then I won't be subjected to the crush of London's rush hour twice a day.

Despite her anxiety, there was a lightness to Alice's step as she fed her ticket through the machine at the barrier and emerged into the hustle and bustle of central London. For the past month, the dancers had been using a rehearsal studio on Floral Street, near Joe's café, while the principal characters were learning songs and running lines in a practice room in south London, away from the prying eyes of show-business journalists. Richard was building the hype surrounding the new show by keeping his stars a secret, but today they were due to be unveiled to the press. The whole cast was required for a photo-call at the theatre, in full make-up, followed by the start of an intensive two-week rehearsal period before the first preview shows started.

'Here, let me get that,' a male voice said, as Alice reached her hand out to push open the stage door.

'No need,' Alice replied, without a backwards glance, 'Women's Lib and all that.'

'You don't strike me as a Women's Libber,' the voice persisted.

'Why? Because I'm wearing make-up and high heels?'

'Sorry. I didn't mean to offend.'

'No offence taken. I just think it's funny how people get stereotyped. I'm blonde, but I'm not dumb.' Alice looked back over her shoulder as she held the heavy door open for the man she had been verbally sparring with. He was wearing a khaki-coloured wide-brimmed beanie hat that was obscuring half his face. He looked vaguely familiar. 'Have we met before?'

'Trust me, I would have remembered if we had.'

'Peter, there you are,' Larry said, approaching them. 'Richard's getting a bit tetchy. He wants everyone on stage as soon as possible for the big reveal, and that includes you, Alice. The auditorium is teeming with press. I have a feeling in my bones that this is going to be the best show ever. Nice disguise, by the way, Peter. I doubt that even your mother would recognise you wearing that.'

Maybe his mother wouldn't recognise him but Alice had. No wonder he seemed familiar; those twinkling blue eyes that had made her go weak at the knees since she was fourteen years old and the cheeky grin that had been the last thing she saw before closing her eyes at night. Peter was the former lead singer with Moot Point and posters of his face were plastered all over her bedroom wall in Cotgrave.

'Move it, Alice, or you'll be late. Don't give Richard an excuse to have another go at you.'

Blushing furiously, Alice rushed past Larry, and headed for the sanctuary of the dancers' dressing room, her shoes clattering loudly on the concrete corridor.

'Great body,' Peter said, half under his breath.

Larry followed Peter's gaze. True to her word, Alice had stuck to her diet and, combined with all the extra exercise during rehearsals, had lost a stone in weight since her audition. She still had curves in all the right places, but her waist was now as tiny as Gina's. Larry had been so wrapped up practising the routines, until the girls worked together like a finely tuned engine rather than a bunch of misfiring spark plugs, he had barely noticed the physical transformation. Alice was truly stunning.

'Down boy,' Larry warned, 'your playboy reputation precedes you. She's just a kid. Don't spoil things for her.'

'Reputations are created by the press, and in my case, they've got it totally wrong,' Peter said, pulling off the cloth hat to reveal shoulder-length blonde hair. 'Besides, I don't think you need to nursemaid that one, she seems perfectly capable of looking after herself. Right, let's get this show on the road.'

Alice burst through the dressing room door, her eyes doing a quick scan as she searched for Gina's distinctive auburn hair.

'Over here, Alice, I've saved you a place next to me. What's up? You look all flushed. Have you been running?' Her friend had commandeered a place furthest from the door to the corridor and closest to the sink and was busy arranging her make-up on a white cloth.

'You'll never guess who the male lead is,' Alice said, unable to conceal her excitement.

'Peter Flint?'

'You knew?'

'Yep. Larry told me a couple of weeks ago.'

'You knew and you didn't tell me? I thought we were supposed to be friends.'

Gina tapped the side of her nose.

'We are friends, but Larry swore me to secrecy, and I've known him longer than I've known you. If it had somehow leaked to the press and got traced back to you, Richard would have fired you and probably me too. You really pissed him off when you stood up to his bullying at the audition. So, you see, I was being a true friend by not telling you and not jeopardising your big break.'

'Honestly, Gina, you've got an answer for everything. I'm glad we're friends, I wouldn't want to get on the wrong side of you.'

'Very wise. Anyway, what's with the flushed face and the hyperventilating?'

'Are you kidding? I've just been talking to Peter Flint – *the* Peter Flint whose picture I've had stuck on my bedroom wall since I was fourteen and who I could only ever dream of meeting – and I've only gone and blown it.'

'Blown it?'

'He offered to hold the door open for me, and I made some smart-arse remark. I wish I could rewind the last fifteen minutes,' Alice groaned.

'Don't worry, he probably won't remember. These stars are so full of their own importance they rarely pay much attention to us chorus girls. Anyway, he's married, isn't he?'

'Girlfriend actually, and I read in Cosmo that they're going through a rocky patch. But you're right; he wouldn't be interested in me.'

Gina looked at her stunningly beautiful friend, who now had a figure to die for, and shook her head slightly.

'Be careful, Alice. If he did show an interest in you, it would just be to get in your knickers and after he's got what he wants things could get awkward. Trust me, I've been there. Have you heard the saying, "Don't shit on your own doorstep cos the smell lingers"? You'd do well to remember that because a successful West End show can have a very long run.'

'You're right, Gina,' Alice said, feeling deflated, 'I guess I'm just a bit star struck.'

'I'll always look out for you, Alice, you're like the kid sister I never had. Come on, plaster your smile on and let's do some posing.'

CHAPTER 10

'You look like the cat who got the cream. I take it the photo call went well?'

'Well? That doesn't come close to describing it. I can hardly believe that we managed to keep Peter Flint and Tammy Dixon headlining a secret! You should have seen the jaws drop, even among that bunch of hard-nosed journos. Of course, there were one or two raised eyebrows as well, doubting that two pop stars could hack it on the West End stage, but they haven't heard them in rehearsal. Honestly, Anita, this really is the show that is going to confirm my status as an impresario rather than a producer. Be a love and get me a scotch on the rocks.'

Anita surreptitiously checked her watch. It was 4.15. At this time of day, most people would be drinking tea rather than scotch but then her husband wasn't most people. The charms on her bracelet connected with the cut lead-crystal decanter but for once Richard seemed oblivious.

'When do the tickets go on sale?'

'First thing tomorrow morning. The London papers are running the story tonight and the nationals tomorrow.

The guy from the *Evening Standard* reckoned his editor would put it on the front page. This is the one, Anita. I'm finally going to have a show that everyone wants to see. It could run for years.'

'I hope so. It will take at least six months of full houses before we break even,' Anita said, emphasising the word 'we' as she handed him his drink.

'Thanks for reminding me that it's your money bank-rolling the project. You couldn't let me bask in a bit of well-deserved glory for just a few moments, could you?' he said, downing his scotch and crossing to the sideboard to pour himself another.

Anita bit her lip.

'I know it's all down to you finding the right script and taking a chance on two unproven leads, but you could give me a bit of credit for having the faith to back you when no one else was interested.'

The knuckles on Richard's hand were white as he gripped his whisky tumbler hard, struggling to control his anger. For a split second, he imagined himself spinning round to face his wife, eyes blazing, smashing the glass in the brick fireplace, and telling her he hated her guts.

'Of course, I mean you too, love. We're a team, aren't we? Come here and give me a hug.'

There was a moment of hesitation before Anita crossed to where her husband was standing with his arms outstretched. She rested her face against the softness of the expensive cashmere suit jacket she had bought him for Christmas, which now bore the distinct aroma of cigars.

'You do mean that, don't you? You still want it to be us? It's just that sometimes you make me feel as though you don't want me in your life any more.'

'Don't be silly. Look,' he said, taking her face between his hands, 'I know it hasn't been easy for you since losing your mum, but it will be all right if you'll let me help. Why don't we go upstairs for a while, before Miriam gets home, and show each other how much we still care?'

Anita couldn't hide the flash of panic in her eyes from her husband.

'We could, but I was going to suggest going into town for dinner to celebrate. Maybe Langan's? And you could tip off the press. It would be more good publicity for the show, but I wouldn't want to be seen out in public with my hair looking such a mess. Why don't I ring Sharon at the salon to see if she can squeeze me in for a quick wash and blow-dry and you could ring the restaurant?'

Richard dropped a kiss on to the top of his wife's perfectly coiffured hair.

'Great idea. Wear the red dress with the ostrich feathers around the neck and the hemline. I like that on you, and maybe when we get home we can carry on where we've left off,' he added, revelling in her discomfort.

CHAPTER 11

'Hi Mum, it's me. I'm ringing to see how Mary's exam went today?'

'I'll fetch her for you in a minute. Are your rehearsals still going well?'

'Today was a bit full-on. It was the photo-call for the press. You may even catch a glimpse of me in the *Sun* or the *Mirror* tomorrow. How weird is that? Little old me in the newspaper. And, you'll never guess what?'

'What?'

'Well, it's more of a who really. Guess who the leading man is?'

'I don't know, love. I'm not really up on West End stars.'

'Not a West End star, Mum, more of a pop icon.'

'Erm…? Give me a clue. Is he English?'

'Yes. And he used to be the lead singer in a band I like.'

'Oh, er… do you mean the chap that was in Manfred Mann? He's moved into musicals, hasn't he? What was his name? Was it Paul something?'

'You're thinking of Paul Jones, Mum, but no, it's not him. They were a bit before my time. Here's another clue. There's a poster of him on my bedroom wall, unless

Mary's taken it down of course.'

'Oh, I know the one you mean. He left the band to pursue a solo career a couple of years ago, and broke millions of young girls' hearts – yours included if I remember rightly. I can't remember his name though so it probably wasn't a wise move.'

'Peter Flint, and trust me, soon everyone is going to know his name. It was the first day of rehearsing with the whole cast today, and he is incredible. I can't wait to tell Mary.'

'She's been outside in the garden on a sun lounger since she got back from school. It's been so hot again here today, but I don't suppose you've had much chance to get outside. Hang on a minute, I'll just give her a call.'

Alice could hear her mum calling her younger sister as she leant against the faded wallpaper, twiddling the cord of the pay-phone around her fingers. At least it was a little cooler on the lower landing than it was in Linda's top floor bedsit. Alice hadn't dared leave the windows open for fear of burglary so when she had got home, it was not only hot but also stuffy. She had wanted to take a cool bath, but there was already someone in the bathroom. How nice it would be not to have to share the bathroom with five other flats, she thought, and then immediately felt guilty, realising how lucky she was to have somewhere half decent to stay. One of the other dancers – Diane – was living in a hostel for girls in Earls Court. She regaled the rest of them with horror stories about sleeping eight to a dormitory and breakfasts of soggy white bread and jam. Alice pulled a face at the thought. Mind you, I'm going to need to start looking for somewhere else to stay soon, she thought. Linda's back in four weeks, and that will fly if the past month is anything to go by.

'You've got to be kidding,' Mary squealed down the phone. .

'I take it Mum told you about Peter Flint then.'

'Can you introduce me? Oh my God, wait until I tell the girls at school. Have you spoken to him yet?'

Alice cringed at the memory of their brief exchange that morning.

'Just a few words. He seems really nice, though. How was your exam? It was geography today, wasn't it?'

'It was all right. A bit boring, if I'm honest, but at least I'll know where you are in the country if your show goes on tour. Last one tomorrow, thank goodness, and then I'm freeeeeeee!'

'Any ideas about what you're going to do?'

'Come to London to see you?'

'I meant about a job.'

'The careers teacher organised an interview for me in a travel agent when I told him I wasn't interested in the bank but, to be honest, I'm not that keen. It must be horrible arranging for other people to go on fabulous holidays while you're stuck behind a desk.'

'A bit like being ground staff at an airport. That's my last 10p so when the beeps go, I'm off. Good luck tomorrow and I'll have a word with Mum and Dad about you coming to visit for a few days, although there's no point until the show opens cos I'm never here.'

'I don't mind hanging around the theatre. I might accidentally bump into the gorgeous Mr Flint.'

Saved by the beeps, Alice thought, as she replaced the receiver. Peter hadn't spoken to her again that day, but there had been a few times when she'd felt his eyes on her which left her feeling weak at the knees.

A shadow appeared behind the frosted glass of the bathroom door, and Alice nipped around the turn in the stairs just in case it was grumpy Ruby from the ground floor. The last thing Alice wanted was anyone bursting her happy bubble.

CHAPTER 12

'My office. Now.'

Gina's head shot upright from the position where her chin had been resting on her chest. Franco was towering above her, his face like thunder, and the podgy, balding American, whose business selling greetings cards had made him a millionaire, but not a very interesting one, was drumming his fingers in an aggravated manner on the table. As Gina eased out of the private booth, she could hear Franco apologising profusely and offering the customer a bottle of Moët on the house.

Shit, Gina thought, I'm in for it now. Momentarily she debated whether or not to make a run for it, but what would be the point? Franco knew where she lived and he would have no hesitation in sending the boys round to rough her up a little. Imagine if I turned up to rehearsals tomorrow with a black eye or worse, she thought.

Four and a half weeks of burning the candle at both ends had finally caught up with Gina. She was up each morning at 7.30 to get to rehearsals for nine, getting home at seven for a couple of hours' sleep before cabbing it into the Ostrich Club for 10.30. Even on quiet nights she wasn't allowed to leave until half past two, which meant crawling into bed an hour later for four hours sleep before the whole routine started over.

It was little wonder that she had dozed off as the boring American droned on and on about the global expansion of his company, which meant he was constantly travelling away from his wife and family. Earlier in the evening, he had shown her a photo of his wife wearing a swimming costume, crown and a sash with the words Miss Idaho on it. As a successful local businessman, he had been one of the judges in the beauty pageant and the newly crowned Miss Idaho, who must have been thirty years his junior, had fallen head over heels with the dashing and scintillating Mr 'Cards R Us'. It clearly had nothing to do with his millions of dollars, Gina thought, as she perched on the edge of her chair, waiting for Franco to finish trying to sort out the mess she had caused.

'You'll pay for that bottle of Moët out of your wages,' Franco said from behind her, his voice laced with ice. 'I don't know what's been wrong with you this past couple of weeks, Gina. You used to be one of my best girls but carry on like this, and I'll have to get rid of you.'

Gina sat perfectly still, not daring to even blink. What did he mean by 'get rid of you'? she wondered.

'All it takes is for a sleazeball like that to bad mouth the Ostrich to his cronies and I'd soon be out of business. The Americans are big spenders. I can't afford to lose their custom. What have you got to say for yourself?'

'I'm sorry, Franco. It won't happen again.'

'You're damn right, it won't,' he said, moving his face inches away from Gina's so that she could almost taste the garlicky tomato pasta he had for his supper, and gripping her wrist so tightly she thought it might snap. 'You've never stepped out of line before so I'm giving you a warning. But you only get one warning. Do you understand?'

'Yes, Franco. Thank you.'

'I'm also giving you a week off, unpaid of course. When you come back, I expect you to look a bloody sight better than you do tonight. Now get out, before I change my mind and have one of the bouncers teach you a lesson you won't forget.'

Gina was shaking as she pulled the office door closed behind her. Franco wouldn't have been so lenient with one of the less popular hostesses, and she knew it. Glancing across at the booth she had vacated ten minutes earlier, Mr 'Cards R Us' didn't seem to be missing her too much. He currently had his hand up her friend Pamela's dress and his tongue down her throat. How the hell did I ever get into this? Gina thought, picking up her handbag and jacket from the tiny cloakroom near the entrance and heading up the carpeted staircase to the street. More importantly, how am I going to get out of it? Maybe if the new show is as successful as Larry predicts, I'll take him up on his suggestion of going to Broadway with him, far away from Franco and his heavies.

She flagged a black cab almost instantly.

'Barnes, please. Riverside Mansions.'

'Right you are, miss.'

Gina rummaged in her handbag for her powder compact, wincing in pain as her wrist caught the hard edge of the frame. She checked her face. Franco was spot on, she thought, I look a state, but nothing a couple of decent nights' sleep won't sort out. I'll be right as rain by the weekend, which is just as well considering my plans. Her eyelids were drooping again.

'Wake me up when we get there, please.'

'Will do, miss.'

CHAPTER 13

A lice shook water from her hands and then ran them through her hair to mop up the last droplets of moisture. There's no way I'm touching that, she thought, looking at the stained, soaking wet roller towel that needed changing. It didn't dampen her mood. She had been singing at the top of her voice in the echoey toilets, loving the way it made her sound, and not merely to cover the noise of her peeing. Alice was happy. The first week of the full company run-throughs was coming to an end, and she had received nothing but praise from Larry. Even Richard hadn't singled her out for undue attention. A knock on the door startled her.

Who would knock on the outer door to the loos? she thought, unless it was the cleaners checking to see if there was anyone in there. Maybe they're finally going to change the towel. She smiled at her freshly applied lip gloss in the mirror and dropped it into her bag before pulling on the handle of the door.

'Are you in there alone?'

Peter Flint was standing in the doorway. Alice felt like a rabbit caught in headlights. Why would Peter be knocking on the door of the ladies' toilets?

'Erm, yes, I think so.'

Peter advanced towards her, causing her to step back into the room, and closed the door behind him before leaning on it.

'W–what are you doing? You shouldn't be in here.'

A mix of excitement and fear was causing Alice's heart to beat faster. She was alone in a room with the man she had been fantasising about all week, but she couldn't help recalling Gina's warning.

'Was that you singing just now?'

'Yes. I'm sorry, was it disturbing you?'

'You have a great voice. Have you thought about going for the understudy auditions on Monday morning?'

'No. I wouldn't want to draw attention to myself because the producer really doesn't like me. I'm only in the show because Larry spoke up for me. Anyway, I'm not good enough.'

'You can't really believe that? Are you fishing for compliments?'

'Not at all,' Alice protested. 'I like singing, but I've never had any lessons or anything.'

'All the more impressive; a natural talent. Trust me, I think you should audition. I'm pretty sure Richard won't let a personal dislike colour his professional judgement. All he will be looking for is someone with the ability to stand in for Tammy if she was off sick, which will probably never happen because everyone in this business has the attitude, "the show must go on". Would you like me to have a word with him?'

'No, please don't. I've never even appeared on the West End stage before. I'm not sure I could do it. And besides,

I don't have an audition song prepared.'

Peter looked thoughtful.

'I have a plan. "A Time for Taking Chances", that you were singing just then, crops up twice in the show, once as Tammy's solo but later it is reprised as a duet with me. How about you and I practise singing it together and then on Monday, at the auditions, you could start it on your own, and I could walk on stage and join you? What do you think?'

Alice didn't know what to think. Peter was offering her a fantastic opportunity to stand out from the crowd and eventually that was exactly what she wanted, but it had all come too soon. She could feel his eyes boring into her.

'I think it's a terrible idea. I'm not very popular with the other girls as it is and this would just make things worse. Besides, if I do this – and I'm only saying if – I would want to get the role on my own merits.'

'Well, won't you at least let me help you practise?'

'Why are you doing this? What do you want in return? I don't believe in the casting couch as a way of getting on.'

'I agree. It never pays off in the end. Look, I'm not going to lie, I think you're a really attractive girl, but I've only just split up with my nightmare of a girlfriend and I'm definitely not looking to get involved with anyone else anytime soon.'

'Then, why?'

'Because there is something special about you. People's eyes are drawn to you like a magnet when you're on the stage. You have star quality, which in some respects is distracting in a chorus line of girl dancers. The fact that you also have an amazing singing voice means you can step out from the crowd and fulfil your destiny. And what's so refreshing, is that I don't think you have any idea just how talented you are.'

'Do you really mean that? You're not just saying these things to get me into bed with you?'

'Listen. I don't know what you've heard or read about me, but I'm not the guy the press have made me out to be. I don't go around sleeping with every girl that throws herself at me; I have more self-respect than that. I want a girl to like me for who I am, not what I am. Who do you think I am, Alice?'

'I think you're the former lead singer in a band whose poster I've had on my bedroom wall since I was fourteen. I think I've gone to sleep dreaming about meeting you but never believing I actually would. I think I'm star struck and in danger of succumbing to sweet talk. I think all of these things, but I have no idea who you are because I don't know you.'

'Well, let's put that right. Come and have a drink with me in the pub over the road and we'll make a start on getting to know each other. There is one proviso, though.'

Here we go, Alice thought, disappointment flooding through her just as she was beginning to trust him.

'What?'

'You have to promise to at least give some thought to the understudy auditions on Monday. Deal?'

'Deal,' she said, visibly relaxing, 'but I'm only stopping for one drink.'

'So long as it's a double,' Peter said, holding the door open to let her pass, much to the surprise of the cleaning lady, armed with a fresh roller towel.

CHAPTER 14

Gina closed her eyes, took a deep breath and slipped slowly beneath the surface of the water until she was completely immersed. How long will I be able to stay like this, she wondered, before I need to come up for air? The warmth of the water mixed with two capfuls of the expensive bubble bath that Edward had brought her as a birthday treat, created a creamy lather that would cleanse her body but not, unfortunately, her mind. She parted her lips slightly, allowing a tiny amount of the fragranced water to enter her mouth, moved it around a little and then expelled it, imagining the bubbles rising to the surface and forming a dome before collapsing in on themselves. The phrase 'wash your mouth out with soap' sprang into her head. Goodness knows I need to after what I've just done, she thought. It wasn't the sex, she had long since got past the shame of taking money in return for allowing men to have her body, it was what she had said to her oldest, most considerate client.

Edward had been visiting Gina twice a month at the Riverside Mansions apartment since she had taken over the tenancy two years previously. They had met at the

Ostrich Club when he came in for a late-night drink with some of his colleagues from the Admiralty. As a former sailor, he could hold his liquor better than most of the rest of his party, who had spent their naval careers chained to a desk, so was able to hold a lucid conversation with Gina while the rest of his crowd had resorted to groping some of the other hostesses. They had got on really well, and as it approached closing time, he asked her if she would like a lift home. Gina had refused. Unlike some of the girls, her job ended the moment she stepped outside the Ostrich and besides, she was too embarrassed to allow him to see the humble surroundings she called home. Edward persisted. He suggested a nightcap at the apartment he owned in Barnes, which was currently being renovated and, somewhat reluctantly, Gina had agreed.

The moment she walked in through the door Gina fell in love with the place. It was a long way from the damp, cramped basement bedsit in Chalk Farm where she found refuge after her mum had started dating Ronnie, a nightclub bouncer who was also her drug dealer. Gina always felt uncomfortable when he stayed over in their council flat, conscious of the lascivious glances aimed in her direction, but the day he 'accidentally' walked in on her having a shower, was the last day that she lived with her mum. She had packed all her stuff into two canvas bags, helped herself to the rent money from the tin in the kitchen and left while her mum was sleeping off the excesses of the previous night and Ronnie was out dealing. She got on the number 68 bus in Croydon and stayed on it until it reached its final destination.

Gina had never been to Chalk Farm before and knew no one in the area, but she didn't care. It was a chance for a new start and luck certainly seemed to be on her side. Fifteen minutes after getting off the bus with all her worldly possessions, she was standing on the pavement outside the Post Office, reading the job vacancy cards in the window, when one of the counter staff removed the board to add a new card.

Bedsit To Let
No DSS, no pets, no children

Gina scribbled down the address, asked the shop assistant for directions and thirty minutes later handed over two months' rent in advance. It had been her home ever since.

'I've always dreamed of living somewhere like this,' she said to Edward, moving between the rooms and delighting in the touch of smooth walnut and mahogany as she stroked the console table in the hallway and the backs of the dining chairs in the large lounge.

'Once the decorating is finished it's going to be sold. My wife and I used to come up to town regularly from our house in Cheltenham to go to the theatre or meet up with friends for dinner, but she's not so good on her feet nowadays. It hardly seems worthwhile keeping it if we're only staying here a couple of times a year. Brandy?'

'How could you bear to part with it? Look at those windows and the view of the river. It's perfect.'

Edward had followed her across the room, handed her the drink and was gazing out at the lights twinkling on the far shore of the River Thames.

'I know. This was my bachelor pad before we got married, and I always thought I'd be passing it on to our children one day, but we never had any. It's funny how life doesn't always work out the way you think it will.'

'You can say that again,' Gina agreed, unable to keep the sadness from her voice.

'I hope you don't mind me asking, but how did a smart, beautiful girl like you end up working in a place like the Ostrich?'

'Simple, really. I needed the money. I was between dancing jobs, they call it resting, and couldn't afford to pay my rent. My landlord was threatening to throw me out. My best friend, Joanna, was working there and always seemed to have plenty of cash to spend, so I asked her to have a word with Franco, the boss. It's one of the worst decisions I've ever made. I hate having to be nice to men who struggle to keep their hands to themselves and are usually as dull as ditch water; present company excepted, of course.'

'Then why don't you leave? Are you afraid it would spoil your friendship with Joanna after she helped you get a job there?'

'Joanna died. She fell out of the second floor window of her flat onto some railings. They said it was an accident but I've never been convinced.'

'I'm sorry.'

'So am I. She was a good person. Without her I may never have had a dancing career. But, to answer your question, I stay because it pays the rent and these days I spend more time than ever resting between jobs. It's a cruel industry. Once you hit thirty, you really are over the hill, and most choreographers couldn't care less if you're a better dancer than the eighteen-year-old fresh out of Bush Davies. I suppose I should think about starting something new but dancing is all I've ever known.'

'What if you didn't have to pay rent?'

'What do you mean?'

'What if I said you could stay here rent free?'

'I would say that there must be a catch.'

'I like you, Gina. Maybe we could come up with a mutually beneficial arrangement. My wife and I are no longer intimate, but I still have sexual urges. I think she knows that I occasionally visit prostitutes but if she cares, she doesn't say as much. I don't like using call girls. I'm always worried about picking up a venereal disease. I think you know where I'm going with this?'

'You think I'm a hooker because I work at the Ostrich. True, some of the girls go back to hotel rooms to have sex with clients they have met in the club, but I'm not one of them. I've never crossed that line because I choose not to. In fairness, I suppose me coming here with you might have given you the wrong impression about me. I think I'd like to leave now.'

'I'm sorry if I've overstepped the mark. I just thought… oh, never mind.'

'What did you think?'

'I just thought that if I wasn't twenty-five years older than you and married, you are the sort of girl I would like to spend time with. Is that so wrong of me?'

Gina had taken a long hard look at Edward, really seeing him for the first time, despite having been in his company for the previous four hours. He had clearly been very handsome in his youth and still had a boyish air about him. Unlike most men in their mid-fifties, he didn't have a paunch around his middle and he still had a full head of hair, albeit predominantly grey. She had

had worse-looking boyfriends, and most of them had only been after her for sex, so what was the difference? She hesitated, aware that what she said next may alter the course of her life.

'It will have to be on my terms.'

'Which are?'

'I want my name on a tenancy document which will have a peppercorn rent on it. That way you can't just throw me out if you get bored of me. We'll have to reach an agreement on how often you can visit, and it would always have to be pre-arranged. I want to be able to have friends over without being nervous about you turning up out of the blue and expecting "payment" for me living here.'

'I'm okay with those conditions. I can just tell my wife that I've decided to keep the flat for the time being because the property market isn't buoyant. A peppercorn rent is better than no rent at all, and I think a visit once a fortnight wouldn't arouse my wife's suspicions. From my side, I would ask two things. You wouldn't be allowed to have any other paying clients, and I would want to know if you started seeing someone, romantically. If it got serious, our little arrangement would have to end. Agreed?'

'What do we do now? Spit on our hands and shake on it?'

'I think this is more appropriate.'

He had leant towards her and kissed her gently. It hadn't been unpleasant.

Gina surfaced, reached for a small towel for her hair and

a larger one to wrap around her body, then pulled the plug out to allow the foamy liquid to drain away. She patted herself dry and slipped into her cotton robe before settling on the sofa with a white wine spritzer. Damn, she thought, why now? Just when I'm getting back on my feet in theatreland with Larry's new show, I have a falling out with Franco and Edward voices his suspicions about me sleeping with another man for money.

She hadn't denied it, how could she? It was true. But his accusation, following an energetic session of sex the previous evening, had taken her by surprise.

'Gina, I need to ask you something and I want you to be honest with me,' he had said. 'I was out with some former Admiralty colleagues a couple of nights ago and one of them, who is now a member of parliament, got very drunk. He started talking about getting a cab to Barnes to go and visit a friend of his called Gina who gives fantastic blow jobs. I managed to dissuade him but it set me thinking. Was he talking about you?'

Her silence had spoken volumes.

'I'll take that as a yes then. We had a deal. I told you I'm not prepared to share you with anyone else. I've risked destroying my marriage by keeping this apartment on and allowing you to live here. I trusted you, Gina, and you've betrayed that trust.'

Realising that Edward only knew about the tip of the iceberg and anxious to prevent him delving any deeper, Gina went on the attack as her best form of defence.

'But your wife doesn't need to find out about any of this, unless of course you're thinking of evicting me in which case she might receive an anonymous letter.'

Edward's shocked face had upset Gina. She had grown

fond of him but she had to protect herself. He dressed in silence with her watching from the rumpled bed then strode across the parquet floor of the living room and turned to face her before letting himself out.

'I've misjudged you, Gina,' he had said and then was gone.

She hated having to threaten Edward, but he had left her with little choice. If he tried to evict her, she would go to his wife and tell her about their little love nest, she thought defiantly, taking a sip of her spritzer. It suddenly tasted very bitter, but she downed it anyway and padded through to the kitchen to pour herself another. One step forward, two steps back, she thought, the story of my bloody life!

CHAPTER 15

'Hi, Fred.'
'Morning, Alice,' the stage door keeper responded. 'I take it you're here for the understudy auditions unless you've forgotten that the rest of the company have been given the morning off.'

'No, I hadn't forgotten. Someone persuaded me to come along and try out, but I'm probably wasting my time.'

Fred raised his eyebrows. He liked the blonde dancer who always had a cheerful greeting for him.

'That's not the right attitude. Everyone has to start somewhere. Can you sing?'

'A bit, but I've never been trained or anything.'

'It's sometimes better that way. I've often heard producers say that raw talent can be moulded more easily into a style without having to unlearn bad habits. If you can hold a tune, you've as much chance as anyone else.'

'Thanks for the vote of confidence, Fred. Do you know where I have to go?'

'They're holding the auditions on stage. Fran's in the wings compiling a list. Just pop your name on it then sit in the auditorium until she calls you up. Good luck, Alice.'

'Thanks, Fred, I'll need it.'

There was no one in the wings apart from Fran as Alice approached. She didn't dislike the stage manager, but she wasn't the easiest of people to get to know. She had a complicated job, making sure all the cast members were in the right place at the right time for entrances and exits, and also co-ordinating the stage-hands with scenery changes, props, flying backdrops in and out and bringing the curtain down. Today Fran's podium, which normally held her script with every action noted down to the second, held a sheet of paper with half a dozen names on it.

'Are you here for the understudy auditions?' she asked, without looking up.

'Yes.'

'Name?'

'Alice Abbott.'

'Someone's already put you on the list. Go and sit in the stalls with the others until I call you. Have you got your sheet music for the pianist?'

'Erm, no. I was just going to sing "A Time for Taking Chances".'

'Don't you have a second song?'

'No. I didn't know I needed to. Is it a problem?'

'Maybe not. It's usual to have a couple of songs prepared to show variety, but that's a pretty difficult song to sing, so they should be able to judge if you're any good just from that,' Fran said, a dismissive tone to her voice.

Alice made her way on to the apron of the stage and down the steps into the auditorium just as the doors at the

83

back of the theatre opened, heralding Richard's arrival. She slipped into her seat, nerves jangling, wondering how on earth she had been persuaded by Peter to attend.

There were only six girls auditioning to be Tammy's understudy and her friend Gina wasn't among them. When Alice had asked her if she had ever wanted to do something other than dancing in the chorus, Gina had said, 'I stick to what I'm good at. I sound like a strangled cat when I sing, and as though I'm reading from a script when I try to deliver lines, so the only possible next step for me is to move into choreography'. Alice hadn't had the chance to tell Gina she was auditioning this morning, as the meeting with Peter in the ladies' loos had taken place after her friend had left on Friday and the decision to attend had not been reached until late the previous afternoon.

It had been another gloriously hot and sunny week as the heat wave gripping the UK continued, so some of the girls suggested meeting up on Sunday afternoon in Hyde Park for a picnic and a bit of sunbathing. Alice and Gina were as thick as thieves, but Alice's relationship with most of the other dancers was still a little prickly. Gina thought it would be a good idea for her to try and mingle a bit while declining herself, saying she hated sunbathing because it turned her lily-white skin pink. 'Yet another of the joys of being a red-head,' she had said. 'Look, I know you're not overly keen on some of them, particularly the ones who have been so bitchy about your weight, but there is a saying, "keep your friends close and your enemies closer".' Gina had lots of sayings for a variety of different situations and, in this instance, Alice thought her friend might be right.

She had packed a towel, her cassette player, some apples, which were her contribution to the picnic, and a brown glass tub of coconut oil she had bought from the chemist the previous day to apply as sun lotion. She got on the tube at West Kensington and off again at Earl's Court to change lines and also to meet up with Diane, for whom anything was preferable to hanging around the hostel.

It had been a fun afternoon. The girls started with a game of rounders, which Alice's team had won despite her deliberately dropping an easy catch from a hit that Hannah, one of the girls she was struggling to get along with, had looped up in the air. Exhausted by the exertion in the soaring temperatures, they had flopped on to their towels to relax. Some of them had stripped down to their bikinis, but Alice was too self-conscious about her body to reveal that much flesh in public so kept her shorts and vest top on.

At 6 p.m., as they were packing up to leave, Hannah had said, 'You'd better hope those tan lines fade before the dress rehearsal on Friday or Richard will have another go at you.'

Overnight, the pinkish-tan colour on her skin had developed, making the lines where her clothes had been even more obvious. Alice sensibly decided to hide beneath bell-bottom trousers and a long-sleeved cotton smock when she got dressed that morning. No point in advertising my sunburn, she thought.

The first three girls who Fran had called up on to the stage to sing had all been very good, in Alice's opinion, making her slide further down into the velvet upholstery and question once again the wisdom of her decision to audition. Despite being the last to arrive, her name was next on the list, and she could already feel the dryness at the back of her throat. At least I'll only embarrass myself in front of two of the other dancers, she thought, but what a shame one of them had to be Hannah.

'Alice Abbott, please,' Fran called.

Right, well, this is it, Alice thought, unfolding herself from the plush chair and climbing the steps onto the stage, her legs shaking with trepidation. She blinked as the spotlight was trained on her, unable to see out into the auditorium momentarily.

'Well, well, if it isn't "erm Alice". I hope that baggy top isn't to hide the fact that you haven't fulfilled your promise about losing weight.'

Damn, Alice thought, why didn't I wear a more fitted long-sleeve top?

'Erm, no, I've been doing really well on my diet.'

Her eyes were starting to adjust so she was able to see Richard waft his hand as if swatting a fly as he said, 'Whatever, all will be revealed in the dress run-through on Friday. So, you think you can sing?'

Richard hadn't spoken to any of the other girls in this manner. Gina was right: he still hadn't forgiven her for answering him back at the first audition. Maybe I shouldn't have come today. I should have kept a low profile and not given him the ammunition to pick on me, she thought, wishing that the stage would open beneath her feet and swallow her up.

'This feels like a re-run of your first audition. You're keeping me waiting for an answer, and you know I'm not a patient man.'

Trying her best not to antagonise him further, she said,

'Someone overheard me singing and suggested that I try out, but I don't want to waste your time if you'd rather I didn't.'

'You're here now so you may as well have a go. I can always stop you when I've heard enough. Have you given your sheet music to the pianist?'

'I haven't got any.'

'For God's sake. Is this a joke? You've come to a singing audition without any music?'

'I – I was just going to sing "A Time for Taking Chances".'

'Really? You're going to attempt the biggest number from the show at an audition?' Richard said, his voice laced with sarcasm. 'This I must hear. When you're ready...'

Alice closed her eyes to compose herself, then turned to the pianist and nodded slightly for him to begin. The first few notes were a little shaky but as she grew in confidence it came through in her voice, and before she knew it she had performed the whole song ending with a perfectly pitched top C. There was a moment of silence broken seconds later by applause from the back of the orchestra stalls. Richard turned to see who had gate-crashed his closed auditions. His male lead was walking down the aisle towards him.

'What the hell are you doing lurking back there?' Richard demanded.

Ignoring the question, Peter said, 'She's good, isn't she? It was me who persuaded her to come. It would be such a shame to let your dislike of her cloud your judgement.'

'Sit down,' Richard hissed, 'I'll deal with you in a minute.' He cleared his throat. 'Alice, that was a surprisingly good audition. Take your seat back in the auditorium while I listen to the remaining two contenders.'

Fran called out, 'Hannah Middleton.'

As the two girls passed each other at the bottom of the steps, Hannah whispered, 'Cheers, Alice. How am I supposed to follow that?'

All the bridge building from the previous afternoon in Hyde Park had disappeared out of the window in a three-minute performance. In terms of making friends, Alice was back to square one.

CHAPTER 16

If relationships with the other girl dancers were on the cool side before the auditions, they were decidedly icy after Richard announced to the gathered company, at the end of rehearsals on Thursday afternoon, that Alice would be Tammy's understudy. He held her back for a few minutes, after releasing the others, to give her times for the additional voice-coaching sessions she would need to attend, emphasising that it was highly unlikely she would ever need to stand in for his leading lady.

Alice could barely believe her good fortune, and it was all thanks to Peter having faith in her ability. It would be her turn to buy the next round of drinks in the pub over the road, and she would be able to afford it with the additional ten pounds a week in her pay packet. The extra money will also come in handy in my search for somewhere to live, she thought.

When Alice had moved into Linda's flat five weeks previously, the eight weeks until she returned from tour seemed to stretch out endlessly. I'll have plenty of time to find a place to call home, she had thought, maybe I'll even be able to share with one of the other girls. She had quickly realised that sharing with anyone in the show was highly unlikely. Her only real friend was Gina, and she liked to keep herself to herself once rehearsals had finished for the day. Alice had checked the *Evening Standard* and *Evening News* advertisements and the local newsagents' windows for something to rent on her own, but everything was so expensive, and that was without factoring in the cost of travel and food. At a particularly low point, Alice had asked Diane about the hostel she was staying in, even though it sounded like hell on earth. Now she would be able to renew her search with enthusiasm, knowing that she could afford to pay a little more for somewhere nice and, after tomorrow, the weekend stretched ahead for her to focus on her search.

Alice had gone looking for Gina to celebrate the good news. Maybe we could grab a bite to eat, she thought, bounding up the stairs to the second floor, feeling on top of the world. As she approached the dancers' dressing room, she could hear Hannah's voice. She paused with her hand on the door knob.

'I mean, there's no denying that she has a decent voice, but it's got to have helped that Peter Flint appeared from nowhere applauding her performance. What's that all about?'

Alice could hear the other girls murmuring before one of them said, 'She's obviously dropped her drawers for him. That's how some people get on in this business.'

More mutterings, then Gina's voice.

'But it's a bit risky getting into bed with the star rather than the producer. Everyone knows Richard's the one that ultimately makes the decisions. He could just have easily fired her for shagging Peter, particularly as he dislikes her so much.'

Alice's face was flaming red as she stood rooted to the spot, not wanting to hear anything else but unable to move. How could the girls be so nasty about her and why was Gina going along with them?

'You shouldn't eavesdrop, you'll rarely hear anything nice.'

Alice spun round and was face to face with Peter Flint.

'What are you doing here?' she hissed. 'Please go. If any of them come out and find us together, it will just add more weight to their suspicions.'

'What do they suspect?'

Alice blushed furiously.

'Oh, I see. They think that you allowed me to have my wicked way with you just to get the understudy role?'

'Something like that,' she muttered.

'And would that be so terrible? Maybe we should start seeing each other just to spite them?'

'That's hardly a good reason to start dating,' she said, unable to meet his eyes for fear of what he might read in hers.

'I was joking. You need to lighten up a bit. I only came up to congratulate you. You really were outstanding on Monday, better than Tammy, if truth be told. You sang it like you meant every word. I would never wish Tammy ill, but I hope we get the chance to perform together on stage. I think we would have great chemistry.'

There was something about the way he said the word chemistry that turned Alice's insides to jelly and rendered her unable to speak.

He shrugged.

'No need for thanks,' he said, turning on his heel and

heading back down the stairs to the stars' dressing rooms on the floor below.

Alice rested her flaming cheeks against the cool brick of the corridor walls. Great, she thought. Not only have I alienated all the dancers, including Gina by the sound of things, but I can never go out with Peter now, even if he were to ask me, because they would all think they were correct in their assumptions. Things aren't turning out quite how I'd hoped, she thought miserably, battling to hold back tears. I can't face them, she decided, heading along the corridor to hide in the toilets until they had all left for the day.

'You can come out now, the coast's clear.'

Alice unlocked the cubicle door and emerged, her eyes red and swollen.

'How did you know I would be in here?'

'Where else would you be? I knew you hadn't gone home because your clothes and bag are still in our dressing room.'

'I might have been in Peter's dressing room. Isn't that what you all think? I only got the understudy role because I'm "shagging" the star.'

'You were listening then?'

'Not intentionally, but I heard what you said to the others. I thought we were friends, Gina.'

'Trust me, Alice, what I said was the best way of diffusing the situation. Hannah has really got the knives out now, and nothing I could have said would make her change her opinion that you have slept with Peter. I was merely pointing out that if you were employing the casting-couch method of self-advancement, you would be better doing it with the producer than the star.'

Alice shuddered. The thought of allowing Richard to touch her made her feel physically sick.

'I've got your back, Alice. You need to start trusting me.'

'I do. It just seemed as though everyone was ganging up on me and I haven't done anything wrong.'

'Really? So, you didn't go for a drink with Peter after rehearsals last Friday?'

'Who told you that?'

'Let's just say you were seen. Look, it's none of their bloody business, or mine for that matter, who you choose to sleep with but don't expect to keep it quiet in theatreland. The walls have ears, and Peter should have realised he was putting you in a difficult position.'

'We just had a drink. Nothing more. He'd overheard me singing and thought I should try out for the understudy role. I should never have listened to him.'

'Why? He was obviously right that you have a great singing voice. You can't be a dancer for ever, as I know only too well, so it's brilliant that you've already been recognised as having another talent. You're special, Alice. One day your name will be up in lights. Come here; it looks to me as though you could do with a hug,' Gina said extending her arms and pulling her friend into an embrace.

'That's what I've always dreamed of, but now I'm not so sure. I know I'm a long way off, but people say it's lonely at the top, and I'm not sure I can handle that. I don't like being on my own. I miss my sister and my mum and dad. Maybe I should just pack it all in.'

'You'll do no such thing. You're far too talented to throw it all away because of a bunch of jealous nobodies. "What doesn't kill you makes you stronger", you should remember that.'

Another of Gina's sayings, thought Alice, the beginnings of a smile playing at the corners of her mouth.

'I don't suppose you're free for dinner, are you? I know you usually have to rush off after rehearsals, but it would be my treat. Maybe I could stretch to a couple of brandy and Babychams, and we could celebrate in style.'

'You know what? That would be lovely. There's nowhere I need to be, and it would be good to spend a bit of time with you talking about normal things. You can tell me all about your family in Nottingham.'

'And you can tell me all about yours,' Alice said, leading the way out of the toilets thus missing the pained expression that clouded Gina's face.

CHAPTER 17

'For Christ's sake. Please tell me that this is a sick joke.'
'What's wrong, Daddy?' Miriam asked, appearing at the top of the stairs, wiping the sleep from her eyes.

Richard was in the hallway, his silk dressing gown tied loosely at the waist, gripping the telephone receiver in his hand, his face a dark shade of puce. He placed his other hand over the receiver, 'Go back to bed sweetheart. It's nothing for you to worry your pretty head about.'

Anita appeared behind her daughter.

'Who is it, Richard? Who telephones at half past four in the morning?'

'Get her back to bed and then come down and make me a coffee,' he snapped, before turning his attention back to the telephone. 'Where is she now?' he demanded.

He listened, his face contorting more and more with each revelation.

'So, has she checked herself in yet?'

More intent listening.

'Well, I suggest you get dressed, get in your car and get over there. She's your bloody client. You said she could handle the pressure. Go and sort her out and for God's sake keep the press out of this,' he said, slamming the receiver back into the cradle. 'Anita, where's that bloody coffee?' he growled, pushing through the door into the living room and slumping in his armchair.

'Coming,' said his wife's voice, from the kitchen.

Richard leant forward in his chair and rested his head in his hands. What the hell am I supposed to do now? he thought, fear gripping his stomach.

'Here,' Anita said, handing him a mug of strong coffee with three sugars in it. 'Are you going to tell me what's wrong?'

He sighed deeply as he took the mug from her.

'We're screwed.'

She waited patiently.

'I should never have trusted that lying bitch of an agent. I knew Tammy had had a problem with booze before, but Lynette assured me she was on the wagon. Well, she just fell off it, spectacularly!'

Anita's face was white and pinched.

'Are we talking about Tammy Dixon?' she asked, fearing the answer. She had questioned her husband repeatedly about the wisdom of casting the pop star with a known alcohol problem in the lead role of their production, but he had been adamant that Tammy was the right fit.

'Please don't say I told you so or I won't be responsible for my actions.'

'What's happened?'

'It would seem that she was so delighted with the way the dress rehearsal went yesterday that she decided to go out to a nightclub with a few friends to celebrate. An hour ago, she rang her agent, in floods of tears, from the clinic where she spent six weeks last year drying out, threatening to check back in after consuming half her weight in alcohol. Apparently, they are talking about a three-month stay this time as the six weeks, last time, was clearly not enough. I've sent Lynette over there to try and dissuade her but she seems to think Tammy's unlikely to change her mind. What the hell do we do now? The press previews are due to start on Monday, and it looks like we have no leading lady.'

Anita was quiet. If she had noticed the use of 'we' rather than 'I' now that the project had hit a snag, she didn't say.

'Didn't you hold auditions for an understudy earlier in the week?'

Richard's sigh was deep and patient as though he were about to explain something to a small child.

'Yes, we did. A girl called Alice was selected, despite having never appeared on the West End stage before, because she has a very good voice and because we never thought she would actually have to step into Tammy's shoes.'

'Does she know the songs?'

'Well, she definitely knows "A Time for Taking Chances" because she sang it at the audition, but I have no idea if she's learned the others. Her understudy rehearsals were due to start on Monday. Surely, you're not suggesting going ahead with the press previews with her playing Melanie? The press would slaughter her and, more importantly, me.'

'What other option is there? I've... I mean, we've invested everything in this show, and there is no money left to postpone the opening until you find someone to replace Tammy, if that's what needs to happen.'

Richard looked at his wife. She had no idea how deeply financially committed they were. He had already used some of the money from the advance ticket sales to pay this week's wages. If the show didn't open on time, they would have to offer refunds, and there wasn't enough money in the pot to do that. The last thing I want to do is re-mortgage the house, he thought, but it might come to that if that stupid bint doesn't sort her life out. I should have bloody listened to Anita when she said, 'once a drunk always a drunk', but no, as usual, I ignored her warnings. He could feel her eyes on him, waiting for his response. Could she be right about Alice? Was it really their only option?

'I think we should wait to hear from Lynette Marsh. If Tammy doesn't check herself into the clinic, there's a small chance that she could do the previews and, in the meantime, we look for a new leading lady.'

'And you're quite sure this Alice girl wouldn't be up to it?'

Richard looked thoughtful. Peter obviously had the hots for her. Maybe, just maybe, he could pull her through it if they were left with no other option.

'What time is it?'

'It must be about five.'

'Right, let's go back to bed for a couple of hours. There's nothing anybody can do until we know how the land lies with Tammy. If we are going to have to go with plan B, I'll need my wits about me in case the press get a sniff of this.'

CHAPTER 18

Alice was disturbed by a shrill ringing noise. Damn, she thought, I must have forgotten to alter my alarm. She reached her arm out in the general direction of the clock and managed to knock it on the floor. At least the ringing stopped. She rolled over in bed and pulled the covers over her head to block out the early morning sunlight which was threatening to burn a hole in her eyelids. When I get my own place, I'm going to have decent curtains, she thought vaguely, before drifting back to sleep.

Dinner on Thursday had turned into a great night out at a club where Gina knew the doorman. The girls had got in for free on the proviso that they would get everyone up on the dance floor. It hadn't taken long for the floor to fill with people and, job done, the girls headed for the bar where they were immediately approached and offered a drink, a process that was repeated several times over the course of the night. It was the first time Alice had let her hair down since arriving in London, and she was enjoying herself so much that she was shocked when the club began to close around them at three in the morning.

The girls hailed a cab which dropped Alice in West Kensington before carrying on to Barnes. 'Let me pay my share,' Alice had slurred, as she tumbled out of the taxi, but Gina shook her head. 'Don't worry about it,' she had said, 'you just get yourself to bed, we've got to be up in a few hours and on top form for the dress rehearsal. At least you can have a lie-in at the weekend to catch up on some sleep.' It would have been true if Alice had remembered to set her alarm for a later time.

She had only just fallen back to sleep when she was disturbed again, this time by a loud banging noise accompanied by a voice shouting, 'Alice, are you in there?'

'Coming,' she replied, groggily, slipping her feet into her fluffy mule slippers and pulling her cotton dressing gown on.

She opened the door just as Ruby raised her hand to knock again. Even with her eyes barely open, Alice could see she looked angry.

'What's wrong?'

'What's wrong? What's wrong?' she shouted. 'I'll tell you what's bloody wrong. That phone has been ringing constantly since eight this morning with no one bloody answering it. I knew it wouldn't be for me, but in the end, I had to come up and get it if only to shut it up.'

Even though she was not fully awake, Alice couldn't help but smile. It was no surprise that Ruby was so sure the call wouldn't be for her.

'I'm glad you think it's so funny. You are on a final warning. If you do one more thing to disturb the house, I'm going to report you to the landlord for being here illegally. I'm sure your friend, Linda, will be delighted to arrive home to discover she's been evicted,' she said spitefully, before turning on her heel and stomping off down the stairs.

Ruby is a seriously unpleasant woman, Alice thought, having no doubt that she would carry out her threat. Why would anyone be calling me at this time on a Saturday morning? she wondered, a prickle of fear starting in her stomach as she grabbed the door key and headed down to the next landing. The only people who had her number were the theatre and her parents, and the latter were under strict instructions not to call unless it was an emergency. Oh God, I hope it's not grandma. Her maternal grandmother was always complaining of aches and pains, so much so that people had started to ignore her. It was a 'boy who cried wolf' scenario. She had once rung her daughter convinced that she was having a heart attack. It had turned out to be indigestion. Another time, she was certain she had broken her ankle. It wasn't even a sprain. Maybe something awful really had happened, but no one had believed her until it was too late. Alice grabbed the phone receiver from where it was dangling.

'Mum? What's wrong? Is it grandma?'

'Good morning, Alice.'

She couldn't place the voice.

'It's Alan Rodgers here, your company manager.'

No wonder she didn't recognise his voice. He had only spoken to her once when she had signed her contract on the first morning of rehearsals. Why on earth would he be ringing her? Oh no, she thought, her heart plummeting, maybe Richard has changed his mind about me understudying Tammy.

'Richard asked me to call. We have a bit of a problem, and it means I'm going to have to ask you to come into the theatre this morning. What time can you be here?'

'Erm, ten o clock?'

'That should be fine, but if you can make it any earlier, it would be much appreciated. And, Alice?'

'Yes?'

'Please don't mention this to anyone,' he said, before hanging up.

Alice looked quizzically at the receiver before replacing it. Mention what? she thought. What the hell is going on? She noticed a shadow on the wall of the next landing down as she made her way back upstairs. Ruby had clearly been eavesdropping, and now Alice was worried that she might have said something that had been overheard when she had been sworn to secrecy.

Less than an hour later, Alice pushed open the stage door and made her way along the corridor towards the stage. Four people had beaten her to it. Richard had his back to her in the centre of the dimly lit stage and was talking in a hushed voice to Alan Rodgers, a woman Alice didn't recognise and Peter. She just caught the end of his sentence: '… so, let's not scare her with too much information.'

'I – I got here as soon as I could.'

Richard turned to greet her.

'Thank you for being so prompt, Alice, in fact,' he said, pointedly consulting his wristwatch, 'you're fifteen minutes early. We're just waiting for Larry and the practice pianist, and then we can get started.'

'Started?' Alice asked, looking from Richard to Peter.

Peter had an anxious look on his face which he tried

to disguise with a reassuring smile.

'Yes. I know we said we were going to start the understudy rehearsals on Monday, but we've decided to bring it forward. We were just wondering how many of Tammy's songs you already know.'

'All of them. Word for word,' Alice said proudly, a big smile on her face. 'I love listening to her sing; she has such a great voice.'

'Yes, she does,' Richard said, casting a sidelong look at the woman. 'That's why I gave her the role. But you have a very good voice too, Alice, and that's why I have put my faith in you as her understudy.'

It was something about the way that Richard had said the word 'you' that made Alice feel a flutter of nerves.

'Is Tammy sick?'

'Not sick, exactly. She has a little issue that we are hoping will be resolved by Monday but, just to be on the safe side, we need you to be up to speed.'

Alice's eyes opened as wide as saucers. Peter reached out his hand and rested it on her arm.

'It may be that we would have to ask you to fill in for her on one or two of the preview nights. How do you feel about that? Do you think you would be able to do it?'

Alice's head was swimming. This was not supposed to happen. She was going to practise the songs and learn the lines and the dance steps so that, maybe one day, a long time in the future, she'd have the chance to perform in a Wednesday matinee.

'Can I just have a minute with Alice?' Peter said, taking her arm and steering her towards the wings before Richard could question it. 'Look, Alice, I know this isn't ideal, but I got you into this, and I promise I'll help you through it. I know that you are capable of pulling this off but you have to believe in yourself as much as I believe in you. Do you trust my judgement?'

Alice looked into his deep blue eyes and whispered, 'I think so. But what if I mess up?'

'You won't. But even if you did, you will have tried your best and that is all anyone can ask of you. Will you give it a go?'

Alice nodded, her eyes never leaving Peter's. Behind her back, Peter raised his thumb and Richard released the breath he didn't know he had been holding.

CHAPTER 19

'How are you feeling?'

'I'm not really sure. One minute I'm excited beyond belief and the next I'm so nervous my teeth start chattering.'

'Under the circumstances, I would say that is perfectly natural. I'm nervous for you. I couldn't believe my ears when Richard made the announcement this morning. Mind you, I would have expected him to be tearing his hair out with a last-minute hitch of this magnitude but he seemed perfectly calm. He's done a complete U-turn on you. You must have really impressed him over the weekend.'

'I don't know about that. He looked relieved when I told him I already knew all of Tammy's songs so we have been able to concentrate on me learning the lines and the staging. I just think he has no other option at the moment. Me stepping in for the previews is preferable to postponing *Theatreland's* opening night. Can you imagine how much that would have cost financially, not to mention all the bad publicity?'

'True. West End shows cost a small fortune to stage

and, apparently, he's used his own money. Well, I say his, but in truth it's his wife's inheritance.'

'I met his wife on Saturday. She was at the theatre with him in the morning.'

'That's unusual in itself. Richard doesn't normally let her anywhere near his territory. What's she like?'

'She's quite short with dark hair and a bit on the plump side.'

'I know what she looks like. I've seen pictures of them together at functions. No, I meant, what is she like as a person?'

'Well, she didn't say much. She just thanked me for agreeing to give up my weekend to rehearse and said if I do well, then maybe the part could be mine permanently. But I'm under no illusions. Once Tammy is feeling better, Richard will understandably want his first choice, and he'll forget all the hard work that Peter and I have put in. I'll be back to being just another face in the chorus.'

Gina sipped her cappuccino and studied her friend. Surely, she wasn't naïve enough to believe that? If her suspicions about Tammy were true, all Alice needed to do was perform to the best of her ability and if she were as good as Gina thought she would be, she would keep the role of Melanie and be catapulted to overnight stardom. She couldn't resist a smile as she remembered the look of abject horror on Hannah's face when Richard was speaking.

'So, did they tell you what's wrong with Tammy?'

'No. They didn't say much at all really, just that she needs to rest for a few days.'

Gina was fairly sure she knew what Tammy's sudden indisposition might be. Having worked in London's West

End for the past twelve years, she had a lot of friends and contacts. The word on the street was that Tammy had signed herself back into the Melrose clinic after going on a drinking binge, which was no surprise to anyone who knew her history. The only surprise was that the press hadn't picked up the story yet.

When Larry had originally told her that Tammy Dixon had signed up for the show, Gina had kept her concerns to herself, not wanting to dampen his enthusiasm that *Theatreland* was going to be the big hit show of the year. She had also marvelled at Richard taking such a huge chance on her staying sober. He had a lot invested in the production, and there were plenty of actresses, with more experience and excellent singing voices, who would have been equally as good in the role of Melanie, but perhaps Richard didn't fancy them. He was known throughout theatreland for having a penchant for slim, young blondes, and his inappropriate behaviour towards them. Maybe he made a move on Tammy on Friday, Gina thought, and that was enough for her to drink herself to oblivion. Thank God I'm a redhead and too old to warrant any attention from him, she thought, shaking her head. He really does live up to the abbreviation of his name – a total dick – and seems incapable of keeping that particular body part in his trousers.

She glanced across the table at her friend who was reaching into her bag for her purse. I'm going to need to have a little heart to heart with Alice, she thought, because now that she has lost weight she is exactly his type.

'Thanks for getting me out of the theatre for a bit, Gina, I was starting to go stir crazy. Peter and I have been imprisoned there for most of the past forty-eight hours, not that I'm complaining, of course,' she added, blushing slightly. 'Anyway, I have to get back for another costume fitting. Sandie, the wardrobe mistress, wasn't able to come in over the weekend and although I'm the same size as Tammy, we're a different shape. When I tried her costumes on this morning they were tight on the bust and loose on the waist. I don't think I'm Sandie's favourite person, she's having to unpick seams and insert secret panels all over the place. I hope nothing bursts open on stage tonight. Can you imagine how embarrassing that would be?'

'I'm sure Sandie knows what she's doing, they have to make alterations and repairs all the time. And you can put your purse away. When you nipped to the toilet, I told Joe you were now the star of the show, and he said our coffees are on the house.'

'Really? What a kind thing to do. I hope you told him it was only temporary?'

'Why would I do that?' Gina said, blowing a kiss in Joe's direction as she followed her friend out of the café. 'Firstly, it might not be temporary, and secondly, I never look a gift horse in the mouth. Anyway, it's good for business to be able to tell his other customers that a West End star "frequents his establishment",' she said, in a pseudo-posh voice.

'Are you teasing me?' Alice asked, linking her arm through Gina's.

'Only ever so slightly and only to stop you feeling nervous about tonight. What did your mum and dad say when you told them? They must be so proud of you,' Gina said, experiencing a flash of jealousy for the first time since she had heard her friend's news. It was nothing to do with Alice taking centre stage. She was envious of her friend having a family who cared about her. Gina had discovered a lot about Alice's home life over their dinner on Thursday evening but whenever Alice had turned the tables and asked questions, Gina changed the subject or found excuses not to reveal anything about her own personal life.

'I haven't told them.'

'Why ever not?'

'I think it would just make me worse knowing that they are nervous for me.'

'I suppose, but they would probably have wanted to send you a good luck telegram and maybe even some flowers.'

'They wouldn't have been able to afford stuff like that, so it's just as well they don't know. I would hate for them to feel guilty about not being able to send anything.'

And that's why I like you, Gina thought, as the two girls crossed the road, dodging the traffic and laughing at the London cabby who was shaking his fist at them. But how long would it be before the cut-throat show business world of London's West End turned Alice's head and hardened her heart?

CHAPTER 20

There was a tap on the dressing room door. Alice quickly brushed her tears away.

'Come in,' she said.

She watched through the mirror framed with lights as the door opened and a huge bouquet of flowers came in to view, totally camouflaging the person carrying them.

'Oh my gosh, they're magnificent,' she said, her hands flying up to her cheeks. 'Are they for me?'

'No, they're for the cleaning lady,' Peter said, his head peering round from one side of the display. 'And the only thing in this dressing room that's magnificent is you. You absolutely nailed it. I'm so proud of you. Hey… have you been crying? What on earth for? The audience loved you!'

'I'm just feeling a bit overwhelmed by it all. Ten days ago, I hadn't even auditioned for the understudy role, and now I've performed Melanie in front of all those people. I have to keep pinching myself to make sure it's not just some weird dream.'

'You can pinch me too if you need any further proof,' Peter said, standing the flowers in the sink in the corner and crossing to where she was sitting at the dressing table.

'Ow,' he exclaimed, 'I didn't actually mean it!'

'Well, you shouldn't have offered then.'

'Do you always take everything so literally? Don't bother answering. I've spent so much time in your company over the past three days I think I'm starting to realise that when it comes to you, what you see is what you get.'

The previous evening, after rehearsals had finished, Peter had insisted on taking Alice for a drink to help her relax and unwind. They had walked down to a pub he knew on Victoria Embankment, arm in arm, and had managed to find an outside table in the beer garden overlooking the river, to enjoy the warm evening air. It was exactly what they both needed after spending the day in the stuffy theatre. True to her promise, Alice had bought the first round of drinks. As Peter sipped his beer, he watched her from beneath his eyelashes. There was something so natural about her that appealed to him. She seemed at ease in his company, totally unaware of the envious glances of other girls who had recognised him. He asked gently probing questions, desperate to know more about the girl who had got under his skin from the first minute they'd met.

Drinks had turned to dinner as daylight began to fade and a glorious orange sunset cast its glow across the murky River Thames. The waitress passed through the tables lighting candles housed in empty rosé Mateus bottles and, feeling emboldened by their soft flickering light, Peter had reached his hand across the table to touch hers. The electricity shot through him like a bolt of lightning. He had always laughed at people who said you know when you've met 'the one', but he wasn't laughing now.

'Is that a bad thing?'

Peter was jolted out of his reverie. Alice was watching him through her dressing room mirror.

'Is what a bad thing?'

'What you see is what you get?'

'Not at all. It makes a refreshing change. Most people in this industry are fake. They put on a show of who they think you want them to be but, in the end, they let their guard drop and the real person is exposed.'

'You mean Lisa?'

'It's not just her. I've had the same problem with every girlfriend since our first single went to number one in 1968. It's the fame and fortune most girls are interested in, not the person. Sadly, you're about to discover that fame really isn't all it's cracked up to be.'

'Don't say that. Can't you just let me enjoy my five minutes in the spotlight before I'm unceremoniously dumped back in the chorus?'

'You don't get it do you, Alice? After that performance, tonight, there is no way that you're going to disappear back into obscurity. Mark my words, there will be dozens of offers from agents clamouring to represent you, and if Richard does decide to side-line you when, or should that be if, Tammy comes back, there'll be no shortage of auditions for other leading roles. You really have been given the lucky break that everyone dreams of.'

'But I couldn't have done any of it without you.'

'Don't be silly, of course you could. I knew you had an outstanding voice but your acting ability took even me by surprise. You could have heard a pin drop when Melanie told Frenchie that she'd loved him from the first moment she laid eyes on him. It was so intense.'

'I wasn't acting.'

Peter's heart skipped a beat and his eyes fixed on hers through the reflection in the mirror.

'Sorry, I shouldn't have said that. Very unprofessional. I just got caught up in the moment.'

Before Peter could respond, there was a loud knock on the door, and Richard burst into the room. 'I hope you're decent.' He stopped in his tracks. 'I'm not interrupting anything, am I?'

'I was just delivering your bouquet of flowers.'

'Oh, erm, thank you,' she said, unable to keep the surprise out of her voice.

'Anita's idea, and thoroughly well deserved. I hope Peter didn't pretend they were from him. You were pretty good out there, "erm Alice". Obviously, there's room for improvement but for a first preview, and after so little rehearsal time, it was an impressive performance, wouldn't you agree, Peter?'

'I was just saying as much when you came in. Do you want Alice and me to do the press interviews together? It might be easier for her first time. The journalists can be pretty tricky customers, and they could twist her words.'

'Interviews?' Alice said, a look of panic in her eyes.

'All part and parcel of the job, dear. You're right though, Peter, I don't think we should throw our debutante to the wolves just yet. Get changed, Alice, and we'll meet you front of house in five minutes, and it's probably best to say as little as possible if you can do it without appearing like a half-wit.'

Alice kept her eyes lowered as the two men left her dressing room. How could I have been so stupid to think that Peter would buy me flowers? she thought. And then to virtually tell him that I love him? How am I going to face him tomorrow? I need to speak to Gina; she'll know how to handle this.

Alice quickly changed into her trousers and crocheted top, hoping that she was suitably dressed to meet the press, then made a quick detour to the dancers' dressing room on the floor above. The lights were already off. She hurried down to the stage door.

'Fred, have you seen Gina?'

'She's gone love, but she left you this note,' he said, handing her a folded piece of pink writing paper. 'And I hear congratulations are in order. Everyone says you were brilliant.'

'Oh, I don't know about that, Fred, but at least I didn't forget my words,' she said, taking the note from him and feeling ridiculously disappointed that Gina had left without congratulating her in person.

CHAPTER 21

'I hate to admit it, but you were right,' Richard said, perching on the edge of the bed to undo his shoelaces.

For once he had been pleased to see a crack of light from under the door to the bedroom that he and his wife shared, indicating that she was still awake. He was still buzzing from the audience reaction to the first preview of *Theatreland* and wasn't ready for sleep but, uncharacteristically, he hadn't gone out drinking for fear of accidentally letting slip the real reason for the stand-in leading lady.

Anita folded the corner of the page over on the book she was reading to keep her place, and lowered it on to the gold-coloured satin eiderdown.

'You're early. When I heard the front door, I thought maybe things hadn't gone as well as we'd hoped, but I take it Alice did okay?'

'She was so much more than okay. She was utterly spellbinding. We knew she could sing but what a bonus that she can act as well. Mind you, it has to help in the love scenes that she is totally besotted with Peter. Poor kid.'

'From what I saw on Saturday, he seems pretty smitten with her too.'

'I wouldn't say smitten. You know what these pop stars are like. Girls fall at their feet and they string 'em along until they've had enough of them. I'll give it a month, tops, before he dumps her and moves on to the next gullible victim.'

'Oh, Richard, you're such a cynic. Maybe Peter has had enough of the pop star lifestyle? Perhaps he's ready to settle down and was waiting for the right girl to come along.'

'And perhaps the moon is made of cheese,' Richard sneered. 'You read too many of those romantic novels with their "happy ever after" endings,' he said, indicating her discarded paperback. 'Real life isn't like that.'

Before the silence that had fallen between them lengthened sufficiently to darken Richard's ebullient mood, Anita said, 'So, how did you handle it with the press? Did you tell them earlier in the day that it wouldn't be Tammy performing?'

'No. I avoided going front of house at all before the show and then, when they were in their seats waiting for the performance to start, I went up on stage, announced that Tammy was indisposed and had Fran dim the house lights immediately. There were a few mutterings, as you might imagine, but no one called out any questions and, more importantly, no one got up to leave. Funny, isn't it? I cast big names from the pop world as a hook to get bums on seats, but the show is so good it doesn't matter who is starring as long as they do it well. Hindsight's a wonderful thing. I could have avoided all this mess with Tammy and saved myself a fortune in salaries to boot.'

'What's happening with Tammy? Is she still at the Melrose?'

'No. She stayed in over the weekend to sober up, but she discharged herself this morning. Lynette said her mother is staying with her for a few days until she's back on her feet and she's assured me she will be fit enough for opening night.'

'Which presents you with a new problem, doesn't it?'

'What do you mean?'

'Alice, of course. Surely, you're not just going to send her back to the chorus?'

'What else would you have me do with her? She was given a wonderful opportunity to step into the limelight for a short period and, judging by tonight's performance, she has a fantastic future ahead of her, but she signed a six-month contract to be part of my chorus line, and unless the show folds or someone wants to buy her out of it, that's exactly where she'll stay. Don't look at me like that, Anita, the girl was fully aware from the start that filling in for Tammy is only a temporary situation.'

'Isn't it going to be awkward for her? I'm pretty sure some of the other girls will be terribly jealous.'

'That's as may be, but Tammy is also under contract, and technically she's off sick. Even though it was self-induced, Lynette pointed out this morning that as long as she is willing and able to work, I have no choice but to keep her until the end of the contracted period. I think someone must have tipped her the wink about how well Alice was doing. Anyway, she threatened to sue if I tried to terminate Tammy's contract early. Alice will just have to grow a thick skin. It's a tough world out there.'

'Well, I think you should find a way to show how much

you appreciate the effort she has made. Did you say her family live in the provinces?'

'Nottingham, I think.'

'How about inviting them on an all-expenses paid trip to see Alice in one of the remaining preview shows?'

'You know, that's not such a bad idea. Let me sleep on it,' he said, climbing into bed and switching off the bedside lamp. 'Night, dear.'

CHAPTER 22

'Hello?' said the voice on the other end of the line.
'What happened to answering the phone with our phone number? Mum would be cross if she knew you weren't doing as instructed.'

'Alice!' Mary squealed in delight, 'it's so good to hear your voice. Is everything okay?'

'What is it with my family? Can't I ring home to say hello?' Alice replied, detecting a note of anxiety in her sister's voice.

'Of course, it's just that you usually ring in the evening because it's cheaper and that must cost quite a lot judging by the number of coins you have to keep pressing into the slot.'

'Fair point,' Alice said, glancing at her wristwatch. It was just past midday, but she wanted to ring home immediately after her meeting with Richard. She had initially felt sure that he had called her into his office to tell her Tammy was well enough to perform that evening, so it had taken her by surprise when he had made his generous offer. 'As it happens, I'm more than okay. Are Mum and Dad there?'

'No. Don't faint, but Dad got an interview for a job and Mum went with him for moral support.'

Alice felt a pang of something. She wasn't sure if it was jealousy because her sister was there to support their dad, who had been out of work for so long, or disappointment that they hadn't told her anything about it last time she had phoned.

'Don't be mad, Alice. Mum wanted to tell you, but Dad didn't want you worrying about him what with all the added pressure of being the lead understudy. Was it yesterday you started your extra rehearsals?'

'It was supposed to be, but actually, I had to start a couple of days earlier. What sort of job is Dad interviewing for?'

'It's for a school caretaker at the Rushcliffe School. Please don't let on that I told you. If he doesn't get the job he'll be mortified and, if he does, he'll want to tell you about it himself. So, why did you have to start rehearsing early?'

Alice lowered her voice, to make sure that she wasn't overheard in the echoey backstage corridor where the theatre payphone was situated.

'Tammy, the leading lady, is sick so they called me in on Saturday morning. Guess what?'

'What?'

'I had to perform the role in the first preview show last night.'

'You're kidding!'

'No. I was terrified before the show. I kept thinking I would forget the words or something, but once I got on stage, Pete made everything so easy.'

'Pete, now, is it?'

Alice could kick herself for her slip of the tongue.

'I said "Peter". It must be a dodgy line. Anyway, as a thank you for standing in at the last minute, the show's producer has invited the three of you up to London to see one of the preview shows and stay in a posh hotel overnight.'

More squeals from the other end of the phone line.

'That's unbelievable! When?'

'Well, there are four more preview shows before opening night on Saturday, but I'm not sure how many of them I will be doing so, I guess the sooner, the better. Obviously, it's too late for tonight but maybe tomorrow? Do you think Mum and Dad will be up for it?'

'You are joking, right?'

'They would have to buy the train tickets up front, but Richard says he will reimburse the cost.'

'Is this the same Richard who gave you such a hard time about your weight? He'd better stay out of Dad's way, or he'll give him a proper clout, free trip to London or not.'

That was something Alice hadn't considered. Her dad didn't stand on ceremony for anyone, and he had been furious that anyone should suggest that his precious daughter needed to lose weight.

'I'll have to trust you to talk Dad out of landing one on Richard and anyway,' she said, smoothing her free hand over her trim waist and flat stomach, 'he was right.'

'I'll try, but you know how overprotective Dad is. I'm so excited, Alice, I want to run down the street shouting about it. I am so proud of my big sis, and I'll get to meet Peter Flint. My friends are going to be so jealous.'

'I think you're more excited about meeting Peter than

coming to watch me, not that it matters. Look, I've got to run, I'm meeting my friend Gina for lunch, not that I can afford to eat much after the cost of this call. Tell Mum and Dad all about it, and I'll ring back tonight just after six, when it's cheaper, to finalise the arrangements. I can't wait to see you all and, who knows, maybe Dad will get this job he's gone for too.'

'I hope so to, but remember, you don't know anything about his interview.'

'Yes, ma'am. Speak later, bye.'

Gina was already seated at their usual table in Giuseppe's when Alice pushed the door to the café open. She had felt terrible having to leave the theatre directly after the show the previous evening when all she wanted to do was congratulate Alice on the brilliant job she had done. Even Hannah had expressed grudging admiration at the speed with which Alice had learned all the songs, although she stopped short of praising the actual performance. At least she saw my note about meeting here for lunch, Gina thought, as she watched her friend pause for a few words with the café owner, so she knows how proud of her I am.

There had only been a few customers in the Ostrich Club when Gina arrived at 10.30, but she was good at her job and had persuaded the gentleman she was with to buy a bottle of champagne, which she hoped would put her back in Franco's good books. A little after midnight, Pamela had come over to their booth and whispered in her ear. She had raised her eyebrows in question at her friend but was met with a slight shrug of the shoulders. 'I'm so sorry,' she had apologised, 'my manager wants to speak to me, but Pamela will look after you.' The man was already halfway to drunk and didn't seem to mind the change of escort. She tapped timidly on Franco's office door, remembering only too well the last time she had been summoned there.

'Come in.'

Gina pushed the door open.

'You wanted to see me?'

Without looking up, he said, 'There's a guy at table 24 asking for you. I told him you were with someone else, but he was most insistent, says he knows you. He's been drinking already but doesn't look the violent type, although you never can tell. I don't want any trouble, Gina. Go and sort him out.'

Relief flooded through her as she closed the door behind her. Franco was a bully, and he scared her. The relief was short-lived as she approached table 24 and realised who the insistent gentleman was.

'What are you doing here?' she hissed, edging into the seat opposite Edward. He had given the Ostrich a wide berth since the night they had met.

'That's no way to speak to the man who has been letting you live in his apartment virtually rent-free for the past two years,' he said, in a voice that was just a little too loud.

Gina looked over her shoulder, nervously.

'Please, Edward. Why have you come here? Why didn't you just call me to meet up at the flat?'

'Didn't know who I might find you there with, you little slut,' he spat.

'That's not fair.'

'Isn't it? I had a nice long chat with Alf, the doorman, before I came here. You might have thought you and he had a good understanding, the soul of discretion and all that, but he's been there since I bought the place and I know how to loosen his tongue. It's amazing what information twenty quid can buy.'

Gina could feel beads of perspiration forming on her forehead under her thick stage make-up.

'I can explain.'

'I doubt it. We had a deal, Gina. You can't have your cake and eat it. I've got the names of some of the politicians and other high-profile people you have been entertaining at my apartment, some of who mix in the same social circles as me. I don't think any of them would relish the idea of their sordid sex lives being released to the press and some of them employ people to make sure that doesn't happen. Am I making myself clear?'

Gina nodded. She could feel the blood draining from her face.

'You picked the wrong person to threaten. I may not have sex with my wife any more but I still love her, and I'd do anything to protect her and our way of life.'

'What are you going to do?'

'Nothing. It's you who's going to do something. I told you, I want you out of the flat. You've got three months which, under the circumstances, is pretty generous.'

'And if I refuse?'

'Let's just say, if I were to mention to any of your clients that you had been shouting your mouth off about who you screw, you probably wouldn't make it to the end of a week. Barnes is right on the river, very convenient for disposing of a body.'

'You're threatening me?' she asked, trying to sound braver than she felt.

'It's not very nice, is it? Now you know how I felt.' He pushed his chair back and got up to leave, then leant forward taking her hand in his. Slowly he began to squeeze it.

'You're hurting me,' she said, acutely aware of the attention they were starting to attract from Franco who had come out of his office and was now leaning on the bar, right in her eye line.

'Just reminding you not to try and contact my wife, or I may have to take things into my own hands.'

'Is everything all right here, Gina?'

She locked eyes momentarily with Edward; kind, thoughtful, caring Edward. All she could she see there now was hate and disgust.

'Yes, everything's fine, Franco. This gentleman was just a bit surprised by the high price of the drinks so he's leaving.'

Franco watched Edward's retreating back, thoughtfully.

'He looks familiar. Has he been in here before?'

Gina shook her head.

'I don't think so,' she said, biting her lip to try and hold back tears. She desperately wanted to go home and cry herself to sleep but she didn't dare ask Franco if she could leave early.

'I'm surprised you couldn't persuade him to have a drink. Maybe giving you that week off was a mistake. You seem to have lost your touch.'

Gina pushed all thoughts of the previous evening to the back of her mind and plastered a smile on her face as Alice approached the table.

'Sorry I'm a bit late. I had to phone home. You'll never believe what Richard has done. He's only offered my parents an all-expenses paid overnight stay in London so that they can come and see me performing in the previews. How nice is that? Are you okay? You look a bit pale. Is that why you had to rush off last night?'

'No. I had to be somewhere when I'd much rather have been celebrating with you. I'm fine, probably just a bit tired. You were so amazing last night. Here, give me a hug.'

Gina clung to Alice for a few moments wondering how their two stars could be moving in such polar opposite directions. There was no doubting Alice's talent, but she seemed to attract a huge helping of luck too. If only some of it would rub off on me, she thought, as Giuseppe approached with two frothy cappuccinos.

CHAPTER 24

'Fancy a nightcap?' Peter asked, sticking his head around Alice's dressing-room door.

'Just a quick one. I need to get some sleep if I'm going to be at the top of my game tomorrow.'

'What's so special about tomorrow?'

'Mum, Dad and my baby sister are coming to London. I spoke to them before the show tonight, and they are all so excited. I wouldn't want to let them down. It's going to be a pretty busy day. Their train gets in just after eleven, so I'm going to meet them and maybe have a bit of lunch with them before rehearsals. Richard's booked them a suite at the Dorchester. It's on Park Lane. Can you believe that? I've only heard of Park Lane because of Monopoly, and now my family are going to be staying in a posh hotel there, overlooking Hyde Park.'

'Did you say Richard organised this?'

'Well, one of his people I expect, he's far too busy with all the stuff to do with the show to spend time on my family, but it was his idea and he's paying, meals and everything.'

Somehow Peter doubted that any of it was Richard's

idea. He was known in the industry for being tight with money, as his agent had discovered when they were negotiating his fee. The only person Richard liked spending money on, apart from himself, was his pampered daughter. Peter flinched at the thought of her. She wasn't unattractive, far from it in fact, but the way she had thrown herself at him when Richard had brought her to rehearsals on Sunday was disgraceful, and she was only fifteen. Peter was surprised her mother had allowed her out of the house in a skirt so short that it only just covered her underwear and wedge sandals so high that she could barely walk. Maybe Anita wasn't allowed to have much of a say in disciplining her daughter. She came across as a bit of a doormat, although Peter was pretty sure that the trip to London for Alice's family, like the flowers the previous night, would have been her idea.

'That's very generous of him, but no more than you deserve. Come on, grab your jacket. I'm taking you to Joe Allen's, where all the theatre crowd hang out after their shows. It won't hurt to introduce you to a few people. Richard's being nice now because he needs you but he could easily turn on you again. It would be good to have a backup plan.'

'I don't know if I feel up to it, Pete. I'm so shattered with all the rehearsals and now the performances as well. I could barely get up this morning when my alarm went off at 10, and tomorrow I'll have to be up much earlier to get to St Pancras to meet up with my family. Don't let me stop you going, though.'

Peter was trying to read Alice's body language. Was she giving him the brush off or was she actually tired and in need of an early night?

'You're right about Joe Allen's,' he said, 'we can do that another time. Let's pop across the road for a quick one before they call last orders.'

'Are you sure you don't mind? I could murder a cider. It was so hot under the lights tonight.'

'Only when you're in the spotlight,' Peter teased.

'Are you making fun of me,' Alice asked, flicking the switch on the lights framing her mirror and locking the dressing room door behind her.

'As if,' he replied, leading the way downstairs and heading towards the stage door.

'Night, Fred,' Alice said, tapping on the window of the small cubicle that served as his office and dropping her key on the counter.

'Night you two,' he responded, 'don't do anything I wouldn't do.'

'That gives us plenty of scope,' Peter said, grabbing Alice's hand and darting out into the busy street filled with theatregoers spilling out of the numerous theatres, and the cabs that had arrived to transport them home or to the nearest railway station.

'What do you mean?'

'Surely you must have noticed Fred's tattoos? He used to be in the navy, and you know what they say about sailors… a girl in every port.'

Alice started to follow Peter into the pub and then stopped, forcing him to stop too. It was packed to the rafters with late-night drinkers. There was a fog of cigarette smoke, and the smell of it, blended with sweat and stale beer was overpowering. People had to shout to each other to be heard, and there wasn't a single inch of spare floor space, let alone a table.

'What's up?' he said, raising his voice above the din.

Alice shook her head, indicating the packed pub over his shoulder.

'Too busy.'

'You're right,' he said, noticing the fear in her eyes. 'I know a café that stays open to the wee small hours. We can get a soft drink instead if you like?'

'Much better idea. You don't mind, do you?'

'Of course not. We wouldn't be able to hear ourselves think in there, let alone talk. Are you all right? You look a bit shaken.'

'It's nothing. I'm not that keen on crowds in confined spaces is all.'

'Do you want to talk about it?'

'Not really. Something happened in my childhood, and it comes back to haunt me in similar situations. I'm just being silly.'

'No, you're not, and one day, you'll tell me all about it and then maybe it won't be such a problem in the future.'

'I wouldn't want to bore you.'

'You could never bore me, Alice,' Peter said, pulling her into the doorway of a shop, to move out of the way of people hurrying to get their last train home. 'I don't want to rush things but, from the moment I laid eyes on you, I felt like I had found my soulmate.' He could almost hear his heart thumping in his chest, and as he pulled Alice closer, he could swear he heard hers too. 'You're just perfect, Alice, everything I've ever wanted in a girl.'

Her eyes were closed as he softly placed his lips over hers. He felt an initial resistance for half a second before she relaxed and kissed him back. It lasted only moments but was enough to send messages of desire to the depths of his being.

'Come on,' he said, his voice croaking slightly, 'let's go and get that drink to cool off.'

One of the strip lights above the counter in the café was flickering as Peter and Alice ordered their drinks before moving towards a table near the back. Of the dozen or so tables, only two others were taken, and their occupants only had eyes for each other. As they placed their glasses of Pepsi Cola on the Formica-topped table, it wobbled and some of the fizzy brown liquid spilt over. They both reached for the paper serviettes at the same time, causing a shot of electricity to run through Peter and, judging by her reaction in withdrawing her hand quickly, Alice had felt it too. She mopped up the spill on the table while Peter folded the serviettes in half and pushed them under the table leg.

'My dad does that,' Alice said, attempting to break the tension.

'Tell me about your dad.'

'What do you want to know?'

'As much as you want to tell me.'

'He's forty-six, eight years older than my mum, but she wears the trousers. He left school at sixteen to become a miner like his dad and granddad before him. He's an honest, hard-working man with a heart of gold but, since being made redundant three years ago, he hasn't been able to get a job and not for the lack of trying. He's very protective of me and my sister Mary, so you'd better watch out if I introduce you to him tomorrow.'

'Why would I need to watch out?' Peter said, fiddling

with the glass sugar dispenser on the table. 'I want the same thing as him; for his daughter to be looked after and loved.'

Alice ignored the comment.

'My mum was a "stay at home" mum until Dad lost his job. Lots of families in my village were in the same situation, so the wives had to go out looking for work. Mum could have taken a full-time job in a shop or something, but she prides herself on making home-cooked dinners for us all. She took an office-cleaning job instead so, although she has to get up really early, she is home by nine in the morning. She reckons it pays just as well as if she were full-time in a shop, but most people would feel affronted by having to clear up other people's dirt. Mum just gets on with it. I think she enjoys the freedom and camaraderie of going out to work, so she'll probably keep doing it even if Dad does get the job he interviewed for today. Don't say anything, will you? I'm not supposed to know, but Mary let it slip when we were chatting on the phone earlier.'

'That's easily done. I don't know why people tell young kids stuff if they don't want it repeated.'

Alice looked at him questioningly.

'Who said Mary was a young kid?'

'You did. You said earlier, my "baby" sister.'

'Oh, that's just our joke. There are only thirteen months between us, but I like to wind her up by calling her the baby of the family.'

'Wow, that's close. You're almost like twins.'

'In looks maybe but, that apart, we're totally different.'

'In what way?'

'She's much more social than me for a start. While

I was at dancing school every evening, Mary would be at the local youth club. She's completely at ease being chatted up by members of the opposite sex while I'm painfully shy.'

'You've been okay with me.'

'It's different somehow. Maybe it's because we're working together and we've spent so much time in each other's company while we've been rehearsing. I feel like I've known you my whole life rather than a few weeks.'

'I feel that way too. Do you believe in fate?'

'Yes, I do. If Tammy hadn't got sick, we wouldn't be sitting here now.'

'You really are an innocent, aren't you?'

'What do you mean?'

'Tammy's not sick in the normal way – you know, a cold or laryngitis. She's an alcoholic. She promised to stay on the wagon for the duration of the show, but she couldn't keep her promise.' Peter might have found Alice's shocked expression quite comical if it hadn't been for the seriousness of the subject. 'She went out last Friday and got pissed as a newt, and then some, and ended up back at the clinic where she spent time last year. I'm amazed you haven't heard any of the gossip in the theatre.'

'I don't pay much attention to gossip, and besides, the other dancers don't speak to me much apart from Gina.'

'Oh yes, your red-headed friend. There are rumours about her too.'

'I don't want to know. She befriended me at the first audition, and she's been there for me ever since. I'm not interested in hearsay.'

'Fine,' Peter said, raising his hands in submission, 'but she may not be who you think she is. Just be careful.'

'Can we change the subject, please? I don't like talking about Gina behind her back.'

'Okay, okay. Don't get mad. I'm only trying to look out for you. So, what does your sister do when she's not being chatted up by boys?'

'Nothing at the moment. She's just finished her A levels and is waiting for her results. If they're not too good, she'll have to get a job, but if they are as good as I think they'll be she's going to university in Sheffield.'

'She must be really clever. Some of my friends went to university but only because they had rich parents.'

'I think all that's changing. Quite a few of the upper sixth from our comprehensive end up going to university. But you're right; she is clever, much cleverer than me. I think it's because I was born in August so I was always the youngest in my class and struggling to keep up, whereas she's a September birthday so one of the eldest.'

'August, eh? That's only a few weeks away. We'll have to organise something special for your birthday. What date?'

'The thirty-first. You see I'm not making it up, I have an excuse for not being the brightest—'

'You are bright in other ways. You pick up steps and melodies and words really quickly. It's not that you're not bright, you're not academic is all.'

'Thank you for that vote of confidence,' Alice said pushing her chair back with a scraping sound on the tiled floor, 'and for the Pepsi. I really must go, though, or I'll be good for nothing in the morning.'

'I'll walk you to the Tube, unless you'd rather me flag you a cab.'

'The Tube's fine. The walk from the station will do me

good especially as it's not so hot and sticky now.'

They walked along hand in hand through the streets of London's West End, heading for Leicester Square tube station.

'One day, your name will be up there in lights. Starring Alice Abbott,' he announced to bemused passers-by.

Alice gazed up at the canopy above the Duchess of York's Theatre, the glow of the lights illuminating her skin and sparkling in her eyes.

'Do you really think so? It's what I've dreamed of since I was a tiny child.'

'I know so. And I'm pretty sure it will be sooner than you think. The stars are smiling on you, Alice. Grasp your good fortune with both hands.'

At the underground station, Peter went as far as the ticket barriers, where he planted another kiss firmly on Alice's lips, before heading back out to the street and hailing a black cab to take him home to his mews cottage in Knightsbridge. If it had been anyone else, he thought, I might have tried a bit harder to get them to share my cab home, but not Alice. She's different. Now she knows how I feel, I'll simply have to wait until she feels ready to take things to the next stage.

CHAPTER 25

Alice had lain awake in bed for a long time listening to the dulcet tones of Barry Manilow singing 'Could It Be Magic', repeatedly touching her lips and reliving the sweetness of the kisses she had shared with Peter. It was nothing like the animalistic attempts of the few boys she had allowed to come near her previously. Always before, it had felt as though they were trying to eat her face, forcing their tongues into her mouth despite her attempts to push them away. She had never allowed anyone to go beyond a few gropes of her breasts. None of the kissing and fondling had ever aroused her at all, and she had begun to wonder whether she may indeed be a lesbian, as one of the Romeos had suggested upon being rebuffed. It was crystal clear to her now that she simply hadn't met the right man.

Eventually, she had dozed off at around two in the morning only to be woken by a ringing sound a few hours later. She reached for her clock but quickly realised that it was not her alarm. It was the payphone. Anxious to avoid another run in with Ruby, she leapt out of bed to answer the phone even though she had no idea if the call was for her. She grabbed her dressing gown and door key and ran barefoot down the flight of stairs, picking up the receiver just as she heard the door to the ground-floor flat being wrenched open with enough force to pull it off its hinges.

'That had better not be for you, Alice,' Ruby's voice thundered, 'or I'm definitely reporting you to the landlord.'

'Hello,' she whispered into the phone.

'Alice, is that you?'

It was her mum's voice but she sounded strange.

'Mum? What's wrong?'

'I'm so sorry, Alice, I'm afraid we won't be able to come,' she sobbed on the other end of the phone line.

'Don't cry, Mum. Did you miss your train?' Alice asked. 'It's not a big deal, you can get a later one.'

There was a slight pause.

'The train's not until eight thirty. It's only seven.'

Jesus, Alice thought, no wonder Ruby is so annoyed at being woken by the phone.

'Then, what's wrong?'

'It's your grandma. She's had a suspected heart attack. Your dad and I are leaving for the hospital. We can't leave her, Alice, you do understand, don't you?'

'Of course, Mum. Do you need me to come home?'

Alice was wondering how on earth this would be possible with another preview tonight and Tammy still a no-show.

'No love, not unless… unless they think she's not going to make it. I don't know what I'll do if she doesn't pull through. There are so many things I've never told her.'

'Come on, Mum. Try not to look on the dark side. Hospital is the best place for her. Lots of people survive heart attacks these days. Granny's tough as old boots, it'll take more than this to keep her down.'

'I want to believe that, really I do, but I've got a bad feeling about it. She's only sixty, that's no age.'

'Mum, you're getting yourself all worked up. Just take a deep breath a minute. Is Dad there?'

'Yes.'

'Let me speak to him.'

'All right love?' Ted Abbott's voice sounded tense.

'Dad, just answer with yes or no. Is it really bad?'

'Yes.'

Alice's heart sank.

'Have they said if they think Granny is going to survive it.'

'No.'

'Do I need to get a train home today.'

'No.'

'You can answer this one properly, Dad. Why wouldn't I come home?'

'Because there's nothing you can do. Your mum and I will be with her at the hospital. We'll let you know if there's any change. I'm so sorry about not being able to come and see you in your show.'

'Don't be silly, Dad. There'll be other chances and other shows. Look after Mum and give Granny my love when she wakes up.'

'Will do, love. Thanks for being so understanding.'

Alice replaced the receiver and leant back against the wall, the tears she had managed to hold back while she was on the phone now spilling down her cheeks. She loved her grandma, but she loved her mum more, and it felt dreadful not to be able to comfort her in person. She wanted to go home, surely Richard would understand?

she thought. Then she remembered how vile he could be. There was no way she wanted to get on his bad side again. However much she wanted to get the next train to Nottingham, it simply wasn't going to be possible. She heard a noise from the ground floor as if a Yale lock had clicked in place. Ruby had been eavesdropping. Alice had been planning on going downstairs to apologise about the early call but the nosy bitch had just crossed the line. Normally mild-tempered, Alice could feel anger bubbling in her chest as she marched down the stairs and knocked loudly on Ruby's door. It was answered almost immediately.

'I'm sorry the phone woke you up but it was an emergency. As no doubt you heard while listening in on my conversation, my grandma has been rushed to hospital and may not survive. I don't abuse use of the areas we all share, but I repeat, this was an emergency. If you want to tell the landlord that I've been living here without his permission, then go right ahead. Right at this moment, I couldn't give a damn.'

Alice stormed up the stairs to the top-floor flat, jammed her key in the lock and slammed the door behind her, beyond caring what any of the other residents thought. She flung herself on her bed and sobbed, for herself, for her grandma, but mostly for her poor mum. She eventually fell into an exhausted sleep only to be woken by the unnecessarily early alarm she had forgotten to turn off. More sleep seemed unlikely, so Alice got up and padded through to the kitchen to make herself a cup of tea. As she waited for the kettle to boil, she noticed a piece of blue writing paper pushed under the door.

Alice,

I will not be reporting this morning's incident to the landlord, although I can't speak for any of the other tenants you disturbed.

I hope your grandma will make a full recovery

Ruby

Alice screwed the piece of paper into a tiny ball and started to cry all over again.

CHAPTER 26

'Well, the good news is, as you can see, Tammy is feeling much better and will be rejoining the cast from tomorrow. She will sit in on this afternoon's rehearsal and make notes about the minor changes we have made and she will also watch the performance tonight. Please join me in welcoming her back.'

There was a smattering of applause.

Alice looked across at Tammy. She looked pale with big dark shadows beneath her eyes but nothing that some heavy-duty stage make-up couldn't hide.

'I'd also like to take this opportunity to thank Alice who has done a magnificent job of standing in for Tammy. She will resume her position in the chorus from tomorrow and will continue in her role of understudy in case Tammy should feel "unwell" again. Rehearsal starts in ten minutes. Thank you, company.'

Richard left the stage en route to his office with Alice in hot pursuit.

'Richard, have you got a moment please?'

'What is it, Alice?' he asked, trying to weigh up her mood. Was she going to go all prima-donna on him and make demands that he had no intention of giving in to? The Equity rate for understudies was a standard figure in the West End, and he wasn't going to raise it merely because she had done a few preview performances.

'It's about my parents and sister.'

He relaxed a little.

'Ah, yes. They're coming to see the show tonight, aren't they? Just as well they didn't leave it until tomorrow eh?'

'Erm, well actually, I'm afraid they won't be coming after all.'

A flicker of annoyance flashed across Richard's face. He had gone to a lot of trouble for this girl's family, having to promise freebies to his pal at the Dorchester in order to get them an upgrade from a standard room to a junior suite with a view over Hyde Park.

'It's my grandma, you see, she's had a heart attack and been rushed to hospital. My mum and dad can't leave her.'

'Well that's a shame, Alice, but these things happen.'

His tone was dismissive, giving no opportunity for her to ask if it might be possible for her to take a couple of days off, which wouldn't have been such a big deal as she would be back in the chorus from tomorrow and they had managed pretty well without her so far. She would have to wait until her day off on Sunday and risk the dreaded Sunday rail service.

'Was there anything else?' he asked, glancing pointedly at his watch.

'No, I just didn't want you to think they were ungrateful by simply not showing up.'

The rehearsal ran very smoothly, and Alice was getting

ready for the evening performance when there was a tap on her dressing room door.

'Come in.'

It was Fred, which was most unusual as he rarely left his post.

'Who's overseeing the stage door, Fred? I thought you never left it.'

'Fran said she'd mind it for five minutes. I wanted to come up and tell you myself.'

'Tell me what, Fred?'

'I've just received a phone call from your dad.'

Alice gripped the arms of her chair.

'He wanted me to pass on that your grandma has regained consciousness. She's still a bit groggy, but she's sitting up in bed having a cup of tea. It seems the heart attack wasn't as serious as they had at first feared, probably brought on by this infernal heatwave. Just as a precaution, they're keeping her in the hospital overnight for observation.'

A huge weight lifted off Alice's shoulders. For the whole day, she had been burdened with guilt.

'Oh, Fred. You have no idea what a massive relief that is. And thank you so much for coming up to tell me personally.'

'That's all right, Alice. I wanted you to know before the show, particularly as it's your last one in the lead role for a while. Right, I'd best get back.'

What did Fred mean, 'for a while'? Alice thought. She turned back to the mirror to continue applying her lipstick, and the thought went out of her mind, replaced with relief.

There was another knock at her dressing room door

and Peter's head appeared around it.

'Can I come in for a minute?'

Alice pressed her lips together to smooth her lipstick. 'Of course.'

'It's a shame you've just applied your lipstick, I was hoping for a good-luck kiss.'

'Good luck?'

'Yes. Richard asked me if I would accompany Tammy to Joe Allen's after the show tonight. He thought it would be a good idea for us to be seen out in public together and has arranged for a few photographers to be there. To be honest, I can't think of anything worse than babysitting Tammy, but I had already agreed to it before I knew about your grandma. I thought you would want some time alone with your family as you haven't seen them in a few weeks. Any news on your gran?'

'Fred just popped up to tell me my dad rang and Granny's conscious.'

'That must be a load off your mind. It means you can enjoy being Melanie in your final performance for now.'

'What do you mean, for now? Fred said something similar.'

'You don't really think Tammy's going to hold it all together for the next six months, do you? I'll give her two months tops, although it wouldn't surprise me if she didn't make it past two weeks.'

'Poor thing. Addiction is a terrible thing. I've never been a big drinker. I can just about manage a couple of glasses of cider and one or two Bacardi and Cokes before I start to feel tingly. Any more, and all I want to do is go to sleep.'

'Cheap date.'

'Oi – there's nothing cheap about me, apart from my clothes and shoes of course.'

'Then that's what you must do when you get your pay cheque with the extra money for your understudy performances.'

'What?'

'Treat yourself to a new pair of shoes. You've earned them.'

There was another tap on the door.

'Five minutes, Miss Abbott.'

'Oh, Miss Abbott is it,' Peter said, pretending to tug at his forelock.

'Don't worry. It'll be back to plain old Alice tomorrow.'

'There's nothing plain about you, Alice Abbott. You are the most gorgeous creature I've ever seen,' he said, pulling her into an embrace and dropping a kiss on to her forehead. 'Come on. We don't want to be late for curtain up.'

Alice gathered up the few remaining bits of make-up in her towel, forming a parcel, to move everything back upstairs to the dancers' dressing room. She slipped her bag over her shoulder and looked over the room once more to make sure she had removed all traces of having been there, apart from her costumes which Sandie would deal with the next day. Tammy had been very sweet, coming around to see her after the show and thanking her for doing such a good job as understudy, before heading off to Joe Allen's with Peter. Alice had to admit to a pang of jealousy as she had watched them go.

Balancing her silver dance shoes on the top of the make-up parcel, she flicked off the dressing-room lights and headed upstairs. The dancers' dressing room was empty and, not for the first time, Alice wondered where Gina was always in such a rush to get to after the show. She must have a boyfriend, she thought, reaching for the light switch and dropping a shoe in the process. I'll have to ask her about it next time I see her. She crossed the room to her place next to Gina. Scrawled on the mirror in bright red lipstick was the message, 'back where you belong'. Oh, that's sweet of Gina, Alice thought, at least she left me a message.

'That's not a very nice thing to say!'

Alice let out a small scream. She hadn't heard Richard come into the room.

'Sorry Alice, I didn't mean to startle you. I heard a noise up here as I was locking my office and thought I'd better come up to check we haven't got any tramps sleeping rough. It must have been this falling that I heard,' he said, handing Alice her silver shoe, 'these corridors and floors are so echoey.'

'Thank you. What did you mean by that's not a very nice thing to say? I presumed it was Gina welcoming me back.'

'Maybe you're right, but if it were, I would have thought she would have signed it with a kiss as you two are so chummy. Looks more to me like one of the other girls being bitchy. I'll make an announcement before rehearsal tomorrow afternoon. I won't tolerate that sort of thing in my company.'

'Please don't. It will only make things worse. Gina told me at the first auditions that I would have to grow a thick skin if I wanted to get on in this business and I think I'm toughening up a bit.'

'If that's what you want, Alice, but any other bullying and you report it directly to me, understand?'

'Yes, Richard.'

'I don't suppose you've got much planned for this evening after your family cancelled their trip?'

'No. I'll just head home and get some sleep. The call about my grandma came through at seven this morning, so I'm pretty shattered.'

'Any more news?'

'Yes. She's conscious and sitting up in bed drinking tea. At least she was earlier when my dad rang the stage door.'

'Well, that's good news. You must have been worried sick all day, and I'll bet you haven't eaten.'

Alice realised she hadn't had anything solid to eat all day, only a cup of tea at breakfast and a cappuccino at Joe's.

'You're right. I'll pick myself up a Chinese takeaway on my way home.'

'I can do better than that. Look, it's not your fault your family couldn't make the trip down to London, but I am quite a bit out of pocket for the suite I organised at the Dorchester. Why don't we have a slap-up dinner and afterwards my driver can take you home. What do you say? It would also be my little thank you to you for doing such a good job standing in for Tammy.'

Alice hesitated. She wasn't sure she could sustain a conversation for the hour and a half or so it would take for them to eat dinner.

'Steak and salad would be a lot better for your waistline than a greasy takeaway, and we want to keep you in good shape in case Tammy should get "sick" again. You would like to play the role of Melanie again, wouldn't you?'

There was something vaguely threatening about his words, but Richard was smiling. Come on, Alice, she thought. Pull yourself together. He's just being nice. It's only dinner and then a chauffeur-driven ride home. It beats the Tube and waiting for twenty minutes on the orange plastic chairs of the "Happy Garden" for a takeaway that would be lukewarm by the time I've walked back to Linda's.

'Thanks, that would be lovely.'

'Good. Let's go.'

Alice had never ridden in a chauffeur-driven car before. The closest she had come was a taxi from the centre of Nottingham to her home in Cotgrave once, when she had missed the last bus after a trip to the cinema. That had smelled of an overpowering air freshener that had caused her to have the windows wide open, despite it being the middle of winter, but the Mercedes smelled of leather. At first, Alice was self-conscious, letting Richard do most of the talking, but in the short drive to the Dorchester she started to open up a little about her life before coming to London.

As the car pulled to a halt, Richard said, 'Thank you Max. Please be back here in a couple of hours to take Alice home. Did you say you had something for me?' he added, locking eyes with his driver in the rear-view mirror.

'Oh, yes sir,' Max replied, reaching into the breast pocket of his jacket and handing a small square envelope to his boss.

The doorman in his smart attire stepped forward and opened the door of the Mercedes for Alice to get out and she followed Richard into the magnificent reception area, resplendent with marble floors and velvet-covered bench seats.

'Wait there a moment, Alice, and I'll just discuss with Trevor on the desk what he can do for us at this time of night.'

Alice watched as Richard approached the desk. The two men clearly knew each other. There was a lot of head nodding and smiling before he turned and signalled for her to join him.

'Trevor is going to organise room service in the suite I booked for your family if that's all right.' Richard didn't wait for an answer. 'I thought we could have a prawn cocktail to start, followed by steak with chips and salad, unless you'd like something different? How do you have your meat cooked?'

Alice wasn't sure. Her mum did all the cooking at home, and she just ate what she was given. Her family rarely ate out in restaurants, and when they did, there was no way they could afford to eat steak.

'Erm, what would you suggest?'

'Do you want it bloody, pink or charred to death?'

Bloody sounded awful to Alice, so she opted for the safety of the middle.

'Pink please.'

'So, one rare and one medium rare please, Trevor. How long will it be?'

'About twenty minutes, sir. Would you like to go straight up to your room or would you care for an aperitif at the bar first?'

'I think we'll have a martini before heading up,' Richard said, taking the key from the desktop and steering Alice past the entrance towards a pair of glass doors.

'Have you tried vodka martini before, Alice?'

'I've had vodka with lime. I didn't like it much; I thought it tasted like hairspray. I've had Martini and Cinzano Bianco, but I've never had vodka mixed with martini before. I'm not much of a drinker. I usually stick with cider.'

'So, that could be another of your weight issues, not

JULIA ROBERTS

that there's anything wrong with your weight at the moment. I'm pleased to see you stuck to your word about getting in shape.'

Alice felt uncomfortable knowing that Richard had paid such close attention to her figure.

'Beer and cider have lots of calories, and I should know,' he said, patting his rounded stomach. 'My doctor advised me to switch to wine and shorts in preference, and thankfully I'm allowed champagne, which we'll be having a bit later.'

Richard ordered at the bar, and the two of them settled at a table near the window. When the waiter came over with their drinks a few minutes later, Alice was surprised to see some sort of green vegetable, skewered with a cocktail stick, rolling around in the bottom of her glass.

'What's that?'

'It's an olive. They grow them in Mediterranean countries. Have you ever been abroad?'

'No. We mostly go to the east coast for our holidays because it's not too far to drive. I think my dad's worried that our old car wouldn't make a long journey. Mum's always dreamed of going to Cornwall, and I'm going to treat them to a week there, if I'm ever rich and famous. My old dancing teacher has travelled a lot, though. Austria, Switzerland, Germany... I don't think she's ever mentioned olives, though. Do you eat it?'

'You could, but I'm not sure I'd recommend it. Probably best to wait for your prawn cocktail. Have a sip of your martini.'

Alice did as instructed; it burnt the back of her throat a little and didn't really taste of much.

'What do you think?'

'I think I prefer Bacardi and Coke, to be honest.'

Richard shook his head.

'Oh dear, oh dear, so you've got a sweet tooth as well. Next you'll be telling me how much you like chocolate.'

Alice decided it was best to keep quiet about her near-addiction to chocolate-covered peanuts. She took another small sip of her drink while Richard downed his and signalled to the waiter for another. She could already feel the alcohol having an effect on her body which was not surprising as there was no food in her stomach to soak it up. Small sips Alice, she thought, or I'm going to get drunk.

After his third martini, Richard pushed the club chair backwards and got up.

'I reckon our dinner should be ready.'

'Good. I could eat a horse, not that I would, of course.'

'Nor me, although they do in some parts of the world, along with dogs and cats and all sorts.'

They crossed back across the marble floor of the reception and waited for the lift. Alice couldn't help thinking what a marvellous treat it would have been for her parents and her sister. I'll have to make it up to them somehow, she thought, as the doors closed and the lift rose to the top floor. As they approached the suite, the door opened, and a waiter pushing a trolley came out.

'I've laid your table next to the window, sir. Your main course is under the silver domes on the sideboard, and your champagne is on ice. Would you like me to open it for you, sir?'

'No, I can take it from here thank you,' Richard said, pressing a five-pound note into the man's hand.

'Thank you, sir.'

'Well, what do you think, Alice? Would your mum and dad have liked this?'

'They would have loved it,' she said, taking in the opulence of the room. There was a huge stone fireplace to her right and next to that a desk with a green leather inlay top. Across the other side of the room was a chesterfield sofa next to the sideboard, and in the window the table was laid with their starters. 'Just one thing. If this is a hotel bedroom, where are the beds?'

'It's a suite which means you have a relaxing area with the bedrooms off it. This one has two bedrooms and two bathrooms through that door.'

'It's incredible. I think if the two levels of my parents' house were laid side by side this would actually be bigger.'

Richard had been fiddling with the champagne cork, and it popped as she finished speaking, spilling some of the froth on to the carpet. He filled two champagne bowls and handed one to Alice.

'Cheers. You deserve this. Without your willingness and hard work, the previews would have had to be cancelled, and the press would have wiped the floor with me. You saved the day, Alice, and, when the time comes, you will be justly rewarded. For now, though, let's celebrate your achievement in style.'

The bubbles tickled Alice's nose as she took her first sip of Moët & Chandon.

'Oooh, I like that. It's a bit like grown-up lemonade.'

Richard pulled her chair out for her to sit down and shook the damask napkin onto her lap, casually brushing her breast in the process. If Alice noticed, she didn't react, she was far too intent on getting some food inside her before she started to feel dizzy.

CHAPTER 28

Peter had stuck to Tammy's side like a limpet all evening, vigilant that the only liquid passing her lips was tonic water. In some respects, she was decent company, but he would much rather have been with Alice, particularly in light of the shock she had had earlier regarding her grandma's heart attack. At least it looked like she was on the mend, but it had been awful timing. It was such a shame that her parents hadn't been able to watch their daughter performing Melanie. She had been good on the first two nights, but tonight she had been brilliant. Anyone who has seen the previews is probably going to be disappointed if they come back for a second viewing once the show has opened properly, he thought. Vocally, Tammy was virtually as good, but she was missing the raw innocence of youth that made Alice a better candidate for the role. The character of Melanie was falling in love for the first time, and the sheer wonderment of it all had been portrayed to perfection by Alice. Peter hoped that what she was feeling for him was the real thing and that she was not just star struck.

'So, Peter, looking forward to having your proper

leading lady back?'

Gerard Snape, the show business reporter with the *Evening News*, was a weasel at the best of times but if he sniffed a story, he was intolerable.

'Of course. It's good to have Tammy back and firing on all cylinders.'

'What exactly has been the problem? Everyone's been very tight-lipped about it.'

'That's none of my business. I know as much as you, Gerard, and that's not very much. She's been off sick, and now she's back, that's all that matters really.'

Gerard was not going to be put off that easily.

'So, it wasn't a lover's tiff then?'

'What are you talking about?'

'Rumour has it that you and your leading lady have been seen out socially.'

Shit, Peter thought. This stupid moron has obviously received some information about me being seen around with my leading lady, and he's put two and two together and come up with five. I don't want to scare Alice off with all the press attention she'll get if I correct him and say that I've been seeing her but, on the other hand, I don't want this jerk printing some half-arsed story about Tammy and me, and Alice getting the wrong end of the stick. That's the trouble with being famous: you can't even go for a late-night Pepsi without somebody recognising you although kissing her in a brightly lit doorway probably wasn't the smartest thing to do.

'Check with Tammy if you like Gerard, but she'll simply confirm there is no love interest between us.'

'So, why was she off then?'

Gerard was starting to get on his nerves. What he really

wanted to say was 'mind your own bloody business', but he knew that would just make the journalist dig deeper and potentially be negative about the show.

'Let's ask the lady, shall we?'

Tammy, was deep in conversation with some actors and actresses she knew from other West End productions.

'Sorry to interrupt folks but Gerard here is very keen to know why you've been off for the past few days, Tammy. He seemed to think it might be because you and I have been dating and had a lover's tiff.'

Peter's remark was met with peals of laughter from the rest of the group she was chatting to, but Tammy herself looked like a rabbit in the headlights. Maybe putting her on the spot like this wasn't so bright, Peter thought, but it's too late now. Say something, anything, Peter willed.

Tammy didn't say anything; instead, she burst into tears. Oh, that's just bloody great, Peter thought. All eyes were on him now.

'What? This is nothing to do with me. Come on, Tammy, I think it's time we got you home,' he said, putting a protective arm around her shoulder and moving her towards the exit.

'Have you got anything to say, Tammy?' Gerard persisted.

'Only that Peter and I will work it out,' she sniffed.

Out on the street, Peter hailed a cab, bundled her into the back of it and climbed in.

'Where to, mate?' the driver asked.

'Where do you live?'

'Clapham. Broomwood Road.'

'And then back to Knightsbridge please.'

'Will do, mate.'

Peter knew that cabbies weren't keen on going south of the river, but the return fare to Knightsbridge had prevented him from kicking up a fuss.

'What the hell did you say that for?'

'You put me on the spot. I didn't know what else to say. Don't be mad at me, please,' Tammy said, still sniffing into her paper hankie.

'Okay, okay, just stop crying. Let's get you home, and I'll try and sort it out tomorrow. But don't be surprised if you see some crazy headline about us in the *Evening News* tomorrow.'

'I'm sorry, Peter.'

So am I, Peter thought. I just hope I can get to Alice to explain things before she sees the papers.

CHAPTER 29

Alice tried to move her head, but it was too painful. Every inch of her body felt uncomfortable, and a thousand hammer drills were pounding her skull. Through her closed eyelids, she could tell it was daylight. She reached out for her clock to see what time it was but was met instead by a pillow. Why did I put my pillow on my bedside table? she wondered. Maybe it was to deaden the sound of my alarm. I don't remember doing that; I don't even remember how I got home.

She tried to think, but her head was spinning. This must be what Mary calls the whirling pits. She tried to remember what she had advised Mary to do when she had come home rolling drunk from her Christmas party. Breathe. Yes, that's it, take deep breaths. It didn't help; it simply made her feel even more light-headed. I must remember that for the next time Mary comes home drunk. Perhaps if I open my eyes I won't feel so dizzy, she thought. Slowly she eased her eyes open, the flood of bright light blinding her momentarily, but, as they adapted, she realised why she couldn't remember how she got home. Alice wasn't at home; she was lying in the king-size bed of the suite at the Dorchester.

With trepidation, she moved her hand to touch her body. It connected with skin. A gasp caught in her throat as she reached for the sheet to cover her nakedness. Very gently she turned her head to the side, fearful of what she might find. The other side of the bed was empty and didn't look as though it had been slept in. Momentary relief was replaced with two questions. Why am I naked and who removed my clothes?

Her mouth was as dry as the Sahara Desert; I need water, she thought. Turning her head to the other side, she could see a bottle of mineral water on the bedside table. Next to it was a drinking glass and tucked under that was a sheet of paper. Moving as slowly as she could, Alice eased herself up onto her elbow and reached for the bottle of water. With an unsteady hand, she poured some into the glass and took several small sips allowing the water to wash around her mouth before she swallowed it. Although she felt sick, Alice was determined not to vomit. If she could get past the first couple of hours of wakefulness, she knew she would be okay. A few sips more and her sandpiper-dry tongue that had felt too large for her mouth started to feel more normal. She reached for the note and sank back onto the pillow to read it. As she unfolded it, two ten pound notes fluttered on to the bed covers.

Dear Alice

I hope you enjoyed what you can remember of last night. It seems you were more tired than you realised, falling asleep before you finished your steak. Rather than waking you up to drive you home, I thought you

*might as well make use of the bedroom as it was paid
for. I took the liberty of undressing you as I thought
you would sleep better.*

Alice cringed at the thought of Richard seeing her naked.
How could I have allowed myself to get so drunk that I
passed out over dinner? she thought.

*I've left you some money to get yourself a taxi home
when you wake up. You can order room service if
you're hungry, again it's all paid for. You just need to
leave the key at the front desk when you go.*

*I think it's probably best if we keep this between
us. We don't want the other girls thinking you receive
preferential treatment especially as this was a one-off
occasion. I will expect you at rehearsals at 2 pm, sore
head or not.*

Richard

Alice wanted to curl up in a ball and go back to sleep, then
wake up later in her floral pyjamas in her own bed to find
that everything had been a terrible dream. How will I
ever face Richard again, she thought, after making such a
complete fool of myself. It must have been the champagne
on an empty stomach; I can't remember anything after
that. Right on cue, her stomach grumbled, protesting
the lack of food and the excess of alcohol. If I'm going to
make it to rehearsals, I need to pull myself together. I'll
order some dry toast and have a shower while I'm waiting
for it to arrive. She picked up the telephone receiver and

dialled 4 for room service as instructed on the phone.

'Hello, room service,' said a voice that was far too bright and loud for Alice's current condition.

'May I order some toast, please.'

'Yes, ma'am, and what would you like to drink with that, coffee or tea?'

'I don't mind. I probably won't drink it anyway.'

'Would you prefer fruit juice?'

'No, tea will be fine.'

'And what newspaper would you like?'

'You choose,' Alice said, just wanting to get off the phone.

'Very good ma'am. And what time would you like this for?'

'What time is it now?'

'Eleven fifteen, ma'am.'

Alice stared at the receiver. It couldn't be. How could she have slept so long?

'As soon as possible please, and just leave it outside my door as I may be in the bathroom.'

'I will do my best to have it with you in fifteen minutes, ma'am.'

'Thank you.'

Alice dropped the receiver back on to the base and eased herself into an upright position. Her head was still pounding, and she couldn't imagine how on earth she was going to be able to dance in a few short hours. With a gargantuan effort, she pushed herself into a standing position and gingerly padded across the plush carpet to the door opposite which she presumed must be the bathroom. If only I didn't feel so lousy, she thought, glancing around at the splendour of the marble surfaces and gilded mirrors, I could have truly appreciated this. Her heavy stage make-up was badly smudged, with one of her false eyelashes creeping down her face like a rogue spider. She pulled it off and gently unpeeled the other one placing them on a tissue so they could be re-used. Without her specialist cleanser to remove her make-up, soap and water would have to do, but at least there was some body lotion which she could use to moisturise her face afterwards.

Tempting as the bath tub looked, Alice knew that a shower made more sense. She tied her hair into a knot on top of her head and put the plastic shower cap on before stepping into the cubicle and pulling on the lever to release the water. The treat of showering in total privacy did not escape Alice having previously only showered communally at the swimming baths. How the other half lives, she thought, reaching for the bar of soap and unwrapping it from its paper covering. The needles of water felt good. Not too harsh but releasing enough water to get properly wet. She rolled the bar of soap over in her hands to produce a creamy lather and moved her hands efficiently over her body before tackling her make-up with small circular movements. The emulsified eyeliner and mascara seeped into her eyes, making them smart, but it was nothing compared to the persistent pain in her head. That I can understand, she thought, but why does the rest of me hurt so much? As soon as I've had some toast, I can have some Panadol. Mum always says you shouldn't take painkillers on an empty stomach. The thought of her mum brought tears to Alice's eyes. She would be so ashamed of me if she knew what a state I let myself get into. I'm never drinking champagne again if that's what it does to me, she vowed.

Stepping out of the shower, Alice heard a tap on the outer door of the suite. She wrapped herself up in the fluffy white towelling robe and headed towards the sitting room to collect her breakfast tray. The table was still set up in the window from the previous evening. That's odd, she thought, I'm sure Richard's note said I fell asleep over my steak and yet the prawn cocktail glasses are still on the table. Intrigued, she lifted the silver domes covering the plates on the sideboard. The sight of the remains of Richard's steak, oozing blood, made her gag, so she quickly replaced the covers but not before noticing that her plate of food was completely untouched. How odd, she thought, retrieving the heavy wooden tray from the hallway outside her room.

She carried it through to the bedroom and placed it on the end of the bed, before rummaging in her handbag, which was sitting on the pile of her neatly folded clothes, for her painkillers. I wonder if anyone will notice that I'm wearing the same clothes as yesterday if I go straight to the theatre from here instead of going home. Probably not, she decided, and it will save me a journey in a smelly diesel taxi, the thought of which made her feel even more sick. If I can just finish this toast and maybe a few sips of tea, I can take my tablets and then lie down for another hour or so before I need to leave for the theatre. That's a good plan, she thought, lifting the heavy silver teapot and pouring some of the deep brown liquid into a cup. She could almost hear her mum's voice admonishing her for pouring the tea before the milk but in her fragile state that was the least of her worries. She added three spoons of sugar, wondering if it might be as effective for a hangover as it was for shock and took two of her headache pills. I wonder how long they will take to work, she thought, lifting the tray onto the floor and pulling back the bed covers.

'Oh my God, that's all I need.'

On the lower sheet was a bright red stain. She quickly undid the towelling robe and dropped it to the floor and was relieved to see that there were no marks on it. Thank God, she thought, searching frantically in her bag for her Lil-lets. Her period wasn't due for another couple of weeks, so the search drew a blank. Damn, now I'm going to have to go back to the flat. I can't risk any of the other girls having tampons with them, or being willing to let me have one for that matter, and the stupid machine in the toilets is always broken. What a shit day this is turning out to be, punishment for getting so drunk last night.

She got dressed as quickly as her thumping head allowed, stuffing toilet paper into her pants to try and soak up any flow. She attempted to clean the blood stain off the sheet using a face flannel without much success, leaving a big pinkish wet patch instead. I just want to get out of here before the chambermaid turns up, she thought, this is too embarrassing for words.

Alice grabbed the money Richard had left and stuffed it in her purse, checked the room to make sure she had everything and left as quickly as she could, tucking the *Evening Standard* newspaper from her breakfast tray into the top of her bag.

CHAPTER 30

'Well, this is a surprise,' Anita said, as the waiter pushed her chair in and laid the napkin across her lap. 'We haven't been here for years and you know I love this view,' she said, gazing out of the window at Hyde Park. 'What's the occasion?'

'We're celebrating. Tammy's back and raring to go after her little mishap. Ticket sales have been excellent following the previews and the critics' reviews. Everyone seems to think we have a winning show on our hands. I think champagne's in order.'

'You know I never say no to champagne.'

Richard did know. His wife had expensive taste which didn't stop with champagne. She had enough shoes and handbags to open a small shop, and she kept the local hairdressing salon in St John's Wood in business, single-handedly. When he had suggested going out to lunch over breakfast that morning, her first reaction had been to ring the salon for a wash and blow dry. If it keeps her happy, it suits me, Richard thought, thumbing through the menu.

'So, how was Alice last night?'

For a split second, Richard's heart stopped beating. How could his wife possibly know what had gone on between him and Alice at the Dorchester?

'Her parents were down, weren't they? They must have been so proud of their little girl.'

Richard released his breath. He didn't want to outright lie to his wife but this gave him a convenient excuse for getting home at two in the morning, and she would never find out that they hadn't been able to come.

'That's why I was so late getting home. After the show, we had a small celebratory dinner at the Dorchester.'

No lies there; he thought, smugly.

'And back to the chorus for her today. You'll have to keep a close eye on her, Richard, to make sure there's no bullying.'

For a moment, he wondered if his wife was toying with him. Keep a close eye on her? Did she know more about last night than she was letting on? A vision of Alice's limp body as he laid her on the bed and slowly undressed her, filled his mind. Now that she had lost the puppy fat she had an amazing figure. A flat stomach, narrow hips and beautiful full breasts. He could still taste the sweetness of her skin as he had flicked his tongue over her nipples. It was a shame that the powder Max had given him that he had slipped into her champagne had been so effective. He had hoped it would make her very drowsy and unable to resist his approach, like the previous times he had used it, rather than knocking her out completely. It had almost been like having sex with a corpse, albeit a very beautiful one. He was pretty sure she wouldn't remember a thing, but leaving the note would explain any questions she may have, while making it clear that it wouldn't be wise to tell anyone about their private dinner. She may be stunning, but she's also either stupid or naïve, he thought. Going to a hotel room with a man was only ever going to have one outcome.

'I'm pretty sure her friend Gina will look out for her. She's been around the block a few times and won't take any nonsense.'

'Well, that's good. The West End needs fresh new talent like her, and it would be a shame to lose her because of stuff that's not performance-related.'

Again, Richard wasn't one hundred per cent sure what his wife was driving at. She always appeared to be totally oblivious to the rumours that surrounded him and his penchant for young blondes, but maybe she had her suspicions after all. Was she warning him off? he wondered. Well, he'd got what he wanted from Alice, and he had a strict rule never to drug the same girl twice, so her warning, if that's what it was, was irrelevant.

'Are you ready to order dear? Max is picking me up at one forty-five so it's only a quick lunch for me. You can stay longer if you like and enjoy the sweet trolley.'

And that way she'll be picking up the bill for my guilt-inspired lunch treat, he thought.

CHAPTER 31

Alice was glad to be out on the street. She had dropped her key off at the front desk, fully expecting them to say that the chamber maid had called down reporting the stained sheet and that she would not be allowed to leave the hotel without paying for a replacement. The doorman had offered to hail her a taxi, but she had declined, saying she wanted to get some fresh air. The last thing Alice wanted to do was walk, and the London air in the sweltering midday heat was anything but fresh, but she was anxious to put as much distance as possible between her and the hotel. Once she had rounded the corner, she spotted a taxi with his yellow light on and waved her arm around manically for him to stop.

'Where to, miss?'

'West Kensington, please. Do you know how long it will take?'

'Difficult to say. The traffic's not too bad so probably about fifteen minutes.'

'Would you be able to wait for me for a few minutes and then bring me back to the West End?'

'I'd have to leave my meter running.'

'How much do you think it will be?'

'It depends on how long you keep me waiting.'

'Not long. I need to fetch something from my flat. It won't be more than twenty pounds, will it?'

'No, I shouldn't think so. You just keep your eye on the meter though if that's all you've got. I can always pull over, and you can go the rest of the way on the bus.'

'I haven't got time for a bus; I have to be at work by two.'

'Sit back and relax, we'll get you to work on time.'

The traffic was crawling through Knightsbridge, but it was nothing compared to High Street Kensington where it was at a virtual standstill. Alice glanced anxiously at the meter and then at her watch. She pulled both the windows down in the back of the cab to let some air circulate, but the noise of angry drivers tooting their horns was too much for her fragile head, so she had to close them again. She gazed up at the iconic Biba store as the cab inched forward. Maybe Peter and I can go shoe shopping there when I get my bonus payment, she thought, a smile finding her face for the first time that day. She still found it hard to believe that the pop star she had idolised for so many years was so nice in real life and was such an amazing kisser. She blushed at the thought.

'So, what is it you do love? I mean, two o'clock is a bit of an odd time to be starting work.'

'I'm in a West End show.'

'Matinee today, is it?'

'No, final rehearsals. It's our last preview show tomorrow and our opening night on Saturday.'

'Oh, is that the one with them two pop stars starring?'

'Yes, Tammy Dixon and Peter Flint,' she answered,

butterflies dancing around her tummy at the mere mention of his name. It was so tempting to tell this complete stranger that she and Peter were seeing each other.

'That's them. Shows are not really my thing, I'm more of a football man, but I remember reading about them in the paper this morning.'

It must have been another review of the preview shows, Alice thought. How funny that this cabby is completely unaware that he's got the stand-in Melanie in the back of his cab.

'Yes, apparently, they've got over their little lover's tiff and are back together.'

Alice felt like she had been punched in the stomach. What was this man talking about? He must have got it wrong.

'It's all over the front page of the early edition of the *Evening News*. I've got a copy here if you fancy a read, we're not going anywhere for the next five minutes or so,' he said, handing his crumpled copy of the paper through the glass partition that separated them.

Alice could feel that her cheeks were flaming red as she took the paper. Just moments earlier she had been about to tell this man that she and Peter were dating. Just moments ago, she had still been under the delusion that Peter loved her; the same Peter that was staring up from the front page of the paper with his arm around Tammy. A big fat tear rolled off the end of her nose and landed right between his eyebrows, spreading slightly as blood would do if he had been shot. What an idiot I was to trust him, Alice thought, why didn't I listen to Gina? She folded the paper closed without reading the story.

'Looks like we're on the move. I should have you home in five minutes, and it looks much clearer going back into town.'

'I'll be as quick as I can,' Alice said, closing the door to the cab and heading up the tiled path to her front door.

'Doesn't matter to me, miss. Like I said, the meter's running.'

Alice pushed the door open, but before she could reach the foot of the stairs, Ruby appeared in the hallway blocking her way. Oh no, Alice thought, what have I done now?

'Where the hell have you been?' she demanded. 'I've been banging on your door all morning.'

'I didn't come home last night.'

'I can see that,' she said, 'you look like shit.'

'I'm sorry, Ruby, but it's none of your business if I choose to stay out with friends. And I don't have time for this, I've got a cab waiting to take me into the theatre.'

Ruby's voice softened, 'You may not be needing that. I'm afraid I've got some bad news for you. You'd better come inside my flat.'

Can this day get any worse? Alice thought. Someone must have complained about me to the landlord, and I'm being thrown out. She fully expected to see her bags packed and cluttering Ruby's front room but there was no sign of them, just an overstuffed burgundy-coloured sofa with an equally overstuffed tabby cat asleep on it.

'Move, Mr Tibbles,' Ruby said, ushering the cat out of the way. It jumped down, stretched lazily and ambled off hopefully in the direction of the kitchen. 'Sit down, Alice.'

'What is it, Ruby, you're scaring me.'

'I'm so sorry, love. Your mum rang this morning. It's your grandma; she had another heart attack last night and never regained consciousness.'

Alice could feel the blood draining from her face.

'No, that can't be right. The hospital said she was making a good recovery. You must have got it wrong. Are you saying this to punish me because the phone disturbed you again?'

'What kind of monster do you think I am? That would be plain cruel.'

'Noooo,' Alice wailed, sinking on to the sofa, 'no, she can't be dead.' The tears came then, huge racking sobs as Alice rocked herself backwards and forwards. 'I want to go home,' she cried, 'I need my mum.'

'I know you do, but we need to calm you down first. I'll go and get rid of your taxi and then make you a cup of sweet tea, that's good for shock.'

CHAPTER 32

'Afternoon, Fred. Is Alice in?'

'I haven't seen her yet, Peter. It's not like her to be late,' he said, glancing at the clock.

'No, it's not. Would you give me a knock when she gets in? I need to speak to her before rehearsal starts.'

'Will do. Is everything okay?'

The question fell on deaf ears. Peter was already halfway up the stairs to his dressing room. Fred had a pretty good idea what the problem was. Spending many hours a day cooped up in his tiny stage door office, he was an avid reader of newspapers and had seen the front page spread in the early edition of the *Evening News*. He knew how journalists liked to embellish the truth if they thought it would sell more papers, and he was pretty sure that was what had happened in this case. Fred was a people-watcher. There was no chemistry at all between the couple photographed on the front page, but it was a different story between Peter and Alice. He had watched the romance flourish from their first meeting in the corridor outside his office. 'Poor kid,' he muttered to himself, 'she's got a lot to learn about the world of show business.'

Fifteen minutes later, the whole company was assembled on the stage, but there was still no sign of Alice. Richard marched up the aisle from his seat in the centre of the stalls.

'Larry, where the hell is Alice? Part of the reason for this rehearsal is to integrate her back into the chorus. A tiny stint in the spotlight and she thinks she's a bloody star. I've a good mind to dock her wages for keeping everyone waiting.'

'There must be an explanation, Richard, I'm sure Alice wouldn't be deliberately late. I'll go and ring her digs; maybe she's not well.'

'Take fifteen everyone and, if she's still a no-show, we'll have to start without her. Larry, I'll be over the road,' he said marching back up the aisle and crashing through the double doors at the back of the auditorium heading for the pub.

Shit, Peter thought. Alice must have seen the paper and can't face me. I should have thought to ask Fred for her phone number and called her myself to explain how the press works in this town. He couldn't help feeling a twinge of disappointment that Alice would take the story on face value but, at the same time, it illustrated her depth of feelings towards him that she would allow it to jeopardise her job.

'I hope you're satisfied?'

Peter spun round. Gina was glaring at him.

'Hold on a minute. I didn't ask them to print that story. There is nothing going on between Tammy and me.'

'Is that right? You just happened to be out at Joe Allen's with her, and your arm fell around her shoulders? Do me a favour. Alice might be wet behind the ears, but I'm not. I warned her not to get involved with you, but she didn't listen. You do realise she could lose her job over this?'

'Gina, I swear there is no truth in the story at all. Richard asked me to accompany Tammy to Joe Allen's as publicity for the show. It was a pissed-off hack trying to keep his editor happy by inventing a story when neither of us was forthcoming about the reason for her absence. I didn't even know they had a photo of us until I saw the paper this morning. I was going to try and explain things to Alice when she got in, but she must have already seen it. I would never do anything to hurt her; she's the best thing that has ever happened to me.'

'Well, if that is true, I suggest you interrupt Richard's pint, or whatever he drinks these days, and tell him your suspicions. If she loses this job because of you, you'll have me to answer to.'

Wow, Peter thought, as he watched Gina storm off into the wings, I wish I had a friend who was as fiercely protective of me as that. And she's right; I have to speak up for Alice before Richard does something rash. It's all his fault in the first place for forcing me to babysit Tammy, he thought, tracing the producer's footsteps.

Richard was ordering his second scotch on the rocks when Peter approached him at the bar.

'Can I get you one, Peter?'

'No thanks, I just wanted to have a word about Alice. I think she may be upset because of the front cover of the *Evening News*.'

'Ah, yes. Nice bit of publicity for the show but I don't see why that would upset Alice.'

'Well, we've sort of been seeing each other.'

Richard raised his eyebrows.

'I've seen you flirting with her, but I didn't realise it was getting serious.'

'It's early days, of course, but I think she may be "the one".'

'You've only known the girl a month. It's a bit premature for wedding bells, isn't it?'

'Sorry to interrupt,' Larry said, hurrying towards them. 'I've just got off the phone with someone called Ruby. It seems Alice had some bad news this morning: her grandma died.'

'Oh no, that's awful. Did you speak to Alice? She shouldn't be alone at a time like this. Could you run the rehearsal with my understudy this afternoon and I'll get back for the show tonight?'

'She's not there. Ruby told me Alice has gone back to Nottingham to be with her family.'

'And she didn't think to ask, or at the very least, inform us?' Richard said.

'Bloody hell, Richard. She's obviously not thinking straight. She's just lost her grandma after being told yesterday she was on the mend.'

'Don't you dare speak to me like that. She might be your bit of skirt but I'm your boss, and you'll show me some respect.'

Before the situation could escalate, Larry interrupted, 'Apparently Ruby promised to ring the theatre to notify us, but Alice was in such a state that she forgot to tell her which theatre. The woman's been working her way through all the West End theatres in alphabetical order since Alice left.'

Richard and Peter glared at each other.

'She gets a maximum of two weeks' leave, Larry. If she's not back after that, you'll have to bring in one of the reserves. I told you she was trouble from the start. I can smell 'em,' he said, downing his scotch. 'Well, don't just stand there, we've wasted enough time already, the show must go on!'

'Arsehole,' Peter said under his breath, to Richard's retreating back.

Larry raised a finger to his lips to signal him to shush until Richard was out of earshot.

'Leave it. I've seen Richard like this before. He's totally irrational when he's angry. He'll take Alice back with open arms; she's far too talented to let slip through his fingers.'

'Have you got a contact number for Alice in Nottingham?'

'No, the only address and phone number she gave us was her London digs and, if I remember rightly, that was only for a few weeks. Poor kid, when she does come back, she may not have anywhere to live. What a turnaround for her in the space of a few days.'

'Doesn't the theatre have a digs list?'

'Good point, although I've just had a better idea. Gina has a spare room at her flat, maybe Alice could stay there temporarily.'

'Would you ask her? I think it would be better if Alice weren't living on her own,' Peter said, following Larry into the dim auditorium.

'Will do. Right, ladies,' he said, clapping his hands together, 'opening positions please.'

CHAPTER 33

The train journey seemed interminable. Alice stared out of the window with unseeing red-rimmed eyes, the countryside rushing past in a blur of greens and browns punctuated only by scheduled stops in characterless stations. She was dreading what lay ahead. It had taken all her willpower to get on the train that morning and then only after a serious amount of cajoling from her mum. 'Your grandma was so proud of what you've achieved, Alice,' she had said, 'she wouldn't want you to throw it all away on account of her. She's gone now, we can't change that, but we can honour her memory by continuing to do things that would have made her happy.'

Sheila Abbott surprised everyone with the calm and controlled way she had dealt with her mother's unexpected death two weeks previously. Alice had arrived home to a house full of tears and hushed whispers, no one quite able to comprehend what had happened but, after a visit to the Chapel of Rest to say her goodbyes, Sheila had seemed at peace and had switched to organisation mode. She was determined that her mother should have the best send-off they could afford and now that Ted had finally been offered a job, she had no reason to feel guilty for some of the small extravagances she knew her mother would have appreciated had she been there in person.

She hired the community hall in the village and decorated each table with a framed photo of her mother at different stages of her life. The budget didn't run to caterers, so Sheila spent a large part of the day before the funeral baking cakes and scones and, on the morning itself, she roused the family at 6 a.m. to help her prepare the sandwiches. They had quite a production line going. Sheila made the fillings, Alice buttered the bread, Mary filled the sandwiches, and Ted cut them into triangles before wrapping them in greaseproof paper to keep fresh. There had been a few tears at the graveside, but the family returned home after the wake, tired but content that they had celebrated a life rather than mourned a death.

Alice had clung to her mum on the station platform earlier, willing some of her mother's strength to transfer to her. Not all the tears she had cried in the previous two weeks were for her grandma, a fact that made her feel guilty and selfish. Part of her reluctance to return to London was having to face Peter, knowing that he had been stringing her along. She felt such a fool to have fallen for his sweet talk. Attending her grandma's funeral had put distance between them, but it would still be awkward the first time she ran into him backstage.

At least one of her problems now seemed to have a solution. Alice had rung Fred the previous day to ask him for a list of digs. Linda was returning from her tour on Sunday, giving Alice only two days to find somewhere else to stay. She dreaded the thought of moving into the hostel in Earl's Court, but it seemed there would be no choice. Fred had genuinely sounded pleased to hear from her. 'We're all missing you,' he had said. Somehow Alice doubted that. 'Gina has kept asking me for a contact number for you, but we've only got your London details. Do you want me to pass your Nottingham number on to her?' he had continued. Less than ten minutes later, the phone had rung.

'Alice? It's me, Gina. Are you okay?'

'I've been better,' Alice said, 'but we're coping. Mum's been amazing. She's helped Mary and me through it, even though her heart must be broken.'

'You're lucky to have such a close family.'

'I know, and I'm lucky to have a caring friend like you. Thanks so much for ringing.'

'That's what friends are for. Listen, Larry spoke to me a week or so ago. He said he thought you were going to have to move out of your flat soon. Is your ballerina friend back off tour?'

'On Sunday. That's why I rang Fred. It looks like I'll have to move into Diane's hostel for a week or two until I can find myself somewhere else to live.'

There was a slight pause on the other end of the line.

'Are you still there, Gina?'

'Yes. Look, it's not a long-term solution because I've got to find a new place soon myself, but I've got a spare room, and you're welcome to come and stay until you find somewhere.'

'I don't know what to say. Do you mean it?'

'I wouldn't offer if I didn't.'

'Thank you so much. I'll never forget this kindness.'

'Let's just say you owe me one. Have you spoken to Peter at all?'

'No, and I don't intend to. You were right, Gina, I should have kept my distance.'

'You shouldn't always believe what you read in the papers, you know. They have a nasty habit of twisting the facts. Maybe you should give him a chance to explain when you get back.'

'Pictures don't lie. How is Tammy, by the way? And how is the show going? I can't believe I missed opening night.'

'The show is as fabulous as Larry told me it was going to be. We're playing to packed houses and multiple encores every night. And just for the record, and don't go getting all big-headed, but Tammy is not a patch on you.'

Alice allowed herself a smile. Tammy might have won Peter's attentions, but at least Alice had the satisfaction of knowing that her friend thought she was better in the role of Melanie, and Gina always told it straight.

'Thanks. That means a lot.'

'What time is your train in tomorrow?'

'Eleven thirty.'

'Lunch at Joe's?'

'Sounds good. I've missed his cappuccinos. Are we rehearsing?'

'Just the chorus and entirely for your benefit, as Richard made a point of saying. He has returned to being a great big dick, although, if rumour is to be believed, his anatomy doesn't match his personality.'

'Gina, you're awful.'

'I know, but you like me, as Dick Emery would say. Next time he's reading you the riot act, just think "little finger", if you get my drift. Look, I'd better go, I've been on Fred's phone for ages. See you at Joe's at twelve thirty.'

The lift in mood Alice had experienced after the phone conversation with Gina had all but evaporated by the following morning. The double shock of losing her grandma and finding out that Peter had been stringing her along had made her forget how badly she had disgraced herself at the Dorchester. Not only had she got to face the embarrassment of running into Peter with his girlfriend, she would also be seeing Richard for the first time since the incident, knowing that he had seen her naked. Alice shuddered. It's little wonder that I was so reluctant to get on the train this morning, she thought, miserably.

CHAPTER 34

'I never thought I'd be saying this to you, but I think we're going to have to fatten you up a bit.'

Alice smiled at her friend's bluntness. She hadn't had much of an appetite over the past couple of weeks and stress had also played a part in her dramatic weight loss.

'I wouldn't recommend it as a diet.'

'Some people suit being thin, but you definitely don't. Joe, can you make cappuccino with full-fat milk?'

'Not successfully, bella, you can't get enough air into the milk so it is not so frothy. How about I get Alice a bowl of spaghetti for her lunch instead of a salad.'

'I'm not that hungry—' she began to protest.

'That sounds like a good idea, and then maybe an Italian ice-cream for dessert.'

'I probably won't eat it.'

'You'll have to. Giuseppe would be insulted, and we'd never be able to come here again. Seriously, though, your face is way too thin. You'll have to stuff cotton wool balls in your cheeks or Richard will be moaning at you.'

'That's one piece of advice I think I'll ignore. I could choke on them while I'm jigging around.'

'That's better.'

'What?'

'A bit of the Alice I know. You looked so sad when you walked in. I mean, I know you are but don't let it defeat you.'

'I'll be all right once I've got today out of the way. I'm actually looking forward to being back in the chorus. It feels like wiping the slate clean and starting over.'

'Good girl.'

'So, when can I bring my things over to your flat? You know, I don't even know where Barnes is.'

'About that. There is something I have to tell you.'

'Have you changed your mind? Look, it's okay, I can go into the hostel like I was planning.'

'No, I haven't changed my mind, but if you're going to be living with me, you need to know something that I'm going to ask you to keep secret. Have you never wondered why I always rush off straight after the show?'

'Of course, but that's your business. Have you got a boyfriend? Does he stay at the flat too?'

'No, that's not it. I don't think Richard would be too pleased to find out that I double at a venue called the Ostrich Club.'

'Double?'

'I work two jobs. When I finish at the theatre, I grab a cab to Swallow Street ready to start my job as a hostess at ten thirty. I don't usually get home much before three, but I promise I'll be as quiet as I can.'

'Why don't you want people to know?'

'Hostesses don't have a very good reputation. People think they are glorified hookers, but no one makes you go off with the clients. Mostly it's just encouraging people to buy exorbitantly priced drinks,' Gina said, being deliberately vague.

'Can't you quit now you've got the show?'

'It's not that easy. I've been there for years, and it kept food on the table when I didn't have any dancing work.'

'So, it's a loyalty thing?'

'Not exactly. I'm a bit scared of the boss, if truth be told. Seriously,' she said, noticing Alice's doubtful expression. 'I wouldn't be surprised if he had connections with the mafia.'

Alice's only knowledge of the mafia was from the film *The Godfather*. The scene with the horse's head in the bed had given her nightmares for weeks.

'Can't you go to the police?'

'It's not that simple. Franco pays us cash so I would probably end up in all sorts of trouble for not paying tax on it. Look, don't worry about me, I've got an exit plan. Larry seems to think the show may transfer to Broadway and, if it does, I intend to go with him. Maybe you could come too as the star. I can see it now, "Alice Abbott in *Theatreland*", in lights almost as tall as we are.'

'Wouldn't that be amazing? But I don't think I'm ready for that kind of attention. You warned me I would need to toughen up to be a success in this business and it's been a pretty steep learning curve. The chorus will do just fine for the time being.'

'We'll see. You can't escape your destiny for ever.'

'*Bon appetito*,' Giuseppe said, placing a mountainous bowl of spaghetti carbonara in front of Alice and an egg salad in front of Gina.

Alice's eyes widened.

'You're going to have to help me out with this lot, Gina.'

'I've done enough helping you out,' Gina teased. 'You're on your own with that.'

Alice stuck her fork into the pile of pasta, twisted the strands round it with the aid of a spoon and popped it in her mouth. The creaminess of the sauce mixed with the saltiness of the bacon and the aromatic garlic awakened her taste buds.

'Oh my,' she said, rolling her eyes, 'this is really good. It's the first thing I've had in two weeks that hasn't tasted like cardboard. Go on, try a bit, your secret's safe with me.'

'I'll pass on the pasta, but I hope my other secret is safe with you?'

'Mum's the word. I won't tell a soul.'

'Good. So, how does Sunday morning sound to you?'

CHAPTER 35

'Can I help you, miss?' Alf asked, observing the pretty blonde girl struggling through the double doors, a large bag slung over one shoulder and a suitcase in her other hand, but making no attempt to move from behind his desk to help her.

'You must be Alf,' Alice said. 'Gina's told me all about you.'

'I wish I could say the same,' he replied, grumpily.

'I'm going to be staying with Gina for a few weeks until I can find myself something more permanent,' she offered, by way of explanation.

'Right. Well, I'll buzz up and let her know you're here. Press the button for the lift. It's a bit creaky, but it will save you dragging your case up two flights of stairs.'

Alice did as instructed. She wasn't a fan of lifts, but her case was heavy, and it was clear that Alf had no intention of helping her with it. Gina's description of him had been spot on. 'Think Henry the Eighth,' she had said, 'but without the crown and the ginger beard.' The lift trundled into view. It was tiny and had a double retractable gate-like closure.

'Close the outside gate first and make sure it clicks in place or you won't be going anywhere. Then press 2. And don't forget to close both gates again when you get out, or the lift will be stuck up there.'

'Thanks for your help, Alf,' she said in a cheerful voice, employing Gina's strategy for dealing with him: smile and be pleasant. 'He must be bored stupid sitting at that desk from eight until midnight every day,' she had said. 'What happens when he's not there?' Alice had asked. 'The front door operates with a code, which changes monthly for security reasons,' Gina had explained. 'Don't let me forget to give it to you or you'll be camped out on the doorstep if you go out after work.' Alice couldn't envisage it being a problem. She had no intention of going out anywhere now that she wasn't seeing Peter.

The lift bumped to a stop, and Alice slid the doors back to let herself out, making sure to close them again after her so as not to upset Alf. She glanced around the dim landing, looking for number 32 and just as she spotted it, the door was flung open. Gina was still in her pyjamas.

'Welcome to my humble abode,' she said, stepping to one side to let Alice pass. 'Here, give me your case, and I'll show you around. Jeez, what have you got in here? Bricks?'

'Shoes. It's my one weakness. Oh my God, Gina, there is nothing humble about this. Why on earth are you moving?'

'Not my choice, I can assure you. My agreement came up for renewal, and the owner decided he wanted me out. I'll miss this place.'

'I'm not surprised, it's incredible, and you're right by the river. It must be worth a fortune. Have you any idea where you'll go?'

'I told you, I'm planning on heading to New York. It's a shame I couldn't have stayed here until the show transfers, but things very rarely slot into place like that for me.'

'Is it definite then?'

'What?'

'Is the show going to Broadway?'

'Apparently so. Richard's already been in talks with a big impresario over there, so it looks like it will be a joint production. We'll have to start practising our American accents. This is your room. What do you think?'

Alice stood in the doorway barely able to believe her eyes. The room was almost as big as Linda's entire flat and had an oversized double bed which she immediately ran over to and flopped back on.

'This is like a five-star hotel.'

'Familiar with five-star hotels, are we? What haven't you been telling me?' Gina teased.

Alice immediately coloured up, memories of waking up naked in the bed at the Dorchester filled her mind. It was a night she was ashamed of, and she had no intention of ever telling a soul about it, not even her best friend.

'I've seen pictures in magazines.'

'The only thing you don't have is your own bathroom; we have to share.'

Alice laughed.

'At least it's only the two of us,' she said, remembering the daily ritual of waiting by the door to Linda's bedsit, listening out for the sound of the bolt being released on the bathroom door, before racing down the stairs to try and beat the other tenants to it. She was grateful to Linda for the roof over her head, but there was very little about Avondale Road that she would miss, although Ruby had shown a much nicer side to her personality on the day of her grandma's death. She had even poked her head out of her flat that morning as Alice was leaving. 'If you're ever back visiting Linda,' she had said, 'pop in for a cup of tea.'

'So, what do you fancy doing today? I'm working tonight, but we could go for a pub lunch by the river if you fancy it?'

'That sounds great. Don't you ever get a night off?'

'Thursdays. My favourite day of the week.'

'Then it will be my favourite day too. I'll buy us a bottle of wine, and we can sit and paint our nails and have girly chats.'

Gina couldn't help feeling a little envious of Alice's innocence. It was a very long time since she had a girly chat with anyone. Her only company was male and usually she was getting paid. She knew it was too risky to continue with gentleman callers at the flat after Edward's thinly veiled threats, but the occasional night in a hotel wasn't so bad, and it was a means to an end. One day soon I'll have enough saved to buy my own home outright, and then I'll be answerable to no one, she thought.

'Right, well I'll leave you to unpack, and we'll head out about twelve.'

Alice bounced herself off the bed, moved towards Gina and flung her arms around her.

'You're the best friend in the world,' she said.

Gina returned the hug before quickly turning away so that Alice wouldn't see the tears fill her eyes.

CHAPTER 36

Peter brought his hands down hard on the piano keys, the clash of discordant notes matching his mood exactly. He had never found song-writing easy, but with his head full of Alice and trying to work out ways of winning her back it was virtually impossible. How come some people write their best work from a position of heartbreak, he thought, but for me it's the total opposite.

Alice had been back in the show for almost six weeks, and he still hadn't been able to talk to her on her own because of Gina clucking around her like an overprotective mother hen. At least she's started to fill out a bit now, he thought.

When Alice had first returned from Nottingham, he had been shocked by her appearance. She was pale and gaunt, and Peter had a guilty feeling that it wasn't just as a result of mourning her grandma. He was desperate to take her in his arms and explain how the newspaper had twisted the truth, but she had been hurt and clearly wasn't ready to hear his side of the story. He was prepared to wait; a lifetime if that's how long it took. It also didn't help that Tammy was still refusing to deny there was anything going on between them for her own inexplicable reasons. How he wished he had spiked her drink that night in Joe Allen's, potentially triggering another drinking binge. That way Alice would have continued as his 'Melanie' and he was pretty certain their relationship would have gone from strength to strength. He didn't even get to sing with her at the understudy rehearsals. His understudy, Mike, had that pleasure and, on the odd occasion when he had snuck into the back of the auditorium just for the sheer pleasure of hearing her sing, the feelings of jealousy when they embraced were almost overwhelming.

I need to get out of here, he thought, I'm going stir crazy. He quickly changed into tracksuit bottoms and a T-shirt, put on his running shoes and pulled his cap down low on his forehead. He hoped that fresh air and the repetitive rhythmic pavement-pounding would bring some clarity to his jumbled thoughts.

One of the many benefits of living in Knightsbridge, apart from having Harrods and Harvey Nicholls as near neighbours, was its proximity to Hyde Park. He skilfully dodged pedestrians and traffic and entered the park through Albert Gate. September was usually one of his favourite months, but this year its arrival only served to underline that he had missed being able to join in Alice's birthday celebrations. Admittedly, it had been pretty low key with only a couple of the other dancers attending the dinner that Giuseppe had laid on at his café, but it had cut to the quick that he wasn't invited. At least she had been forced to speak to him. Mary, her younger sister, had come to stay for a few days and had clearly insisted on being introduced to him.

'Peter, this is my sister Mary,' she said, an aloofness in

her voice that saddened him.

Mary had almost curtseyed in response to the kiss he had dropped on the back of her hand.

'Very nice to meet you, Mary. Your sister told me how alike you look, but I wasn't expecting such a resemblance. You could almost be twins.'

They both had the same mane of thick blonde hair and a peaches-and-cream complexion, but Alice had cornflower blue eyes while Mary's were a dark green. That apart, they were identical in height and with a similar figure, now that Alice had regained her curves.

'People used to think we were when we were little. We're not much alike in personality, though. She's the annoying goody two shoes.'

'I'm sure Peter has somewhere he needs to be,' Alice said, 'and we mustn't keep Giuseppe waiting after all the trouble he's gone to for my birthday.' She locked eyes momentarily with Peter. What had he seen there? Defiance? Regret? It was impossible to say.

'Well, could you just sign my programme first, please?' Mary asked.

'Sure,' he said, depositing a squiggle on the page that housed his photograph.

'Oh my God, he's even more handsome in real life,' Peter overheard Mary say as Alice ushered her along the corridor towards the stage door.

'Looks aren't everything,' Alice had responded.

That exchange had been a week ago, and they hadn't spoken since. How the hell did she get inside my head like this? he wondered, pausing to catch his breath next to the bridge by the Serpentine. The sun was dropping lower in the sky, and he squinted over at the café wondering if it was still open. A woman with waist-length blonde hair was sitting at one of the outside tables with her back to him. His heart skipped a beat. It couldn't be, could it? He jogged over the bridge and approached her.

'Alice?'

The woman turned to face him. She was at least ten years older than Alice and what he hadn't noticed as he approached her from behind was that she was cuddling a very young baby. Her eyes were bloodshot, suggesting she hadn't slept much since the birth of her infant.

'I'm sorry,' she said. 'Do I know you?'

'My mistake,' Peter said, backing away. 'Beautiful baby.'

If she responded, he didn't hear, such was his hurry to put distance between himself and the woman. This is bloody ridiculous, he thought as he jogged towards the exit, walking up to complete strangers in the park. I need to speak to Alice and tell her what happened that night. If she still refuses to believe me, at least I will have tried. But how can I make her listen to me? Peter knew that Gina wasn't his biggest fan, believing him to be a shallow pop star with only one thing on his mind, but if he could just persuade her to hear him out, maybe she would put a word in for him with Alice.

CHAPTER 37

At first, Alice thought she was dreaming. There were voices, a man's and a woman's, and they were arguing. As she began to surface from the deepest part of her sleep cycle, Alice realised the voices were real. Without turning on her bedside light, she pressed the button on her clock to illuminate the face. It was half past three. She pushed back the covers and tiptoed as quietly as possible to her bedroom door. The voices had dropped to a much lower volume, and although Alice couldn't decipher exactly what was being said, she was pretty sure it was Gina speaking. It sounded as though she was trying to placate someone and Alice wondered if perhaps it was Franco from the nightclub. Gina had mentioned she was scared of him, fearful that he had mafia connections, but would he really hurt her? Every part of Alice's body was straining to catch the next piece of conversation. Hard as she tried, she couldn't make out anything. It had all gone eerily quiet. What if something had happened to Gina? Alice wrestled with her conscience for a few minutes, wondering what to do. I'd never forgive myself if I could have done something to help Gina but instead stayed hidden in my room, she concluded.

Acting much braver than she felt, she slowly turned the doorknob and eased her door open a crack. The lamp beside the sofa, which she always left on for when Gina got home from the Ostrich, was still illuminated, and in its dim light, she could see the room was now empty. That's odd, she thought. Gina always turns it off before she goes to bed. Noiselessly, she padded across the parquet floor towards Gina's bedroom and was about to tap on the door to make sure her friend was all right when she heard an altogether different sound. Although Alice had never had sex herself, she had occasionally been woken by her parents 'at it', as her sister would say, in the next-door bedroom and they were the same noises she could hear now. She dropped her hand back down to her side and retreated to her room.

Alice knew she hadn't been mistaken about the sound of raised voices arguing and yet Gina was clearly having sex and presumably with that same person. She was wide awake and confused. Was her friend being forced to do something against her will?

She lay awake wondering and worrying for what seemed like hours until she heard the front door of the apartment close. She checked the clock again; it was quarter past four. Gina would be shattered after the theatre and her shift at the Ostrich, but Alice knew she would be unable to get back to sleep unless she was sure her friend was all right. She crossed to her bedroom door and opened it. Gina, who was just reaching for the lamp switch to turn it off, whirled around.

'God! You frightened the life out of me. What are you doing awake?'

'I was worried about you. Are you okay?'

'What do you mean?'

'I heard arguing, it woke me up.'

'I'm sorry we woke you.'

'We?'

'Yes. I had a friend back,' Gina said, deliberately avoiding eye contact with Alice.

'It didn't sound very friendly. I thought maybe Franco had come back with you for some reason and was threatening you. I was worried.'

'Well, don't be. I can take care of myself; I've been doing it for long enough.'

'So, why was your friend shouting at you?' she persisted.

'If you must know,' Gina said with a resigned sigh, 'we were arguing about you.'

'Me?'

'Yes. That was Edward, my landlord, the one who has given me three months to get out of here. I rang him to ask if he could extend our agreement by a couple of months and he just showed up here out of the blue. Because Alf changes the door code every month, Edward couldn't get in, so he was waiting on the doorstep when I got back from work. I had to bring him into the flat, or he would have woken all the neighbours with his shouting, and then I had to tell him you were in the spare room in the hope he would keep his voice down. He went ballistic. Said I was taking the piss by having you living here. He was all for dragging you out of bed and turning you out on the street until I managed to placate him.'

'By placating him, do you mean having sex with him?'

Gina said nothing.

'I heard you, Gina. My God, I would rather have been thrown out on the street than you having to have sex with your landlord to protect me. I feel so guilty.'

'Well, don't. It's not the first time. My arrangement here has always had, how should I put it, "strings attached". Did you really think I would be able to afford a place like this on a chorus dancer's salary, even with the extra I earn at the Ostrich Club?'

Alice's jaw dropped open.

'Look, I'm tired. Can we talk about this in the morning? You were worried about me and, trust me, I appreciate that, but you can see I'm fine.'

Alice's mind was whirling. Even if Gina could go to bed and fall straight to sleep, Alice knew she would not. She had to know what her friend had got herself into.

'You don't sound fine. I just want to know what's going on.'

Gina wavered. 'Be careful what you wish for.'

There she goes again with another of her damn sayings, Alice thought.

'If I'm going to tell you the whole story, I need a drink,' she said, heading to the kitchen. 'Do you want one?' she asked, brandishing a bottle of white wine.

Alice shook her head. She was shocked by what she had already heard and dreading what was still to come. A thought flashed into her head. Peter had told her there were rumours about Gina the night he had told her why Tammy had been off from the show. She had an awful feeling that she was about to discover that the rumours she hadn't wanted to hear about were true.

'All I ask,' Gina said, returning to the lounge and slumping on the sofa, 'is that you don't judge me and you don't pity me. I couldn't bear either.'

'You're my friend. Nothing you tell me now will change that, I promise.'

'I wouldn't be so sure,' Gina said, a look of resignation settling on her features.

Gina told Alice about the first encounter with Edward at the Ostrich and how he had suggested their little arrangement and the conditions attached. She then went on to explain that once she had slept with someone for money, she couldn't see the point of turning down other opportunities.

'You become immune to the shame,' she said. 'The kind of clients I attract are willing to pay handsomely for their anonymity, and all the money I earn goes into a savings account at the bank. Living somewhere nice, for the first time in my life, made me want to own a home of my own without being answerable to anyone. I don't want to live with the fear of being chucked out because my secret lover has become bored of me. I'm nearly there, Alice,' she said, a hint of excitement creeping into her voice. 'I've found a terraced house in Mortlake that I will be able to afford to buy without a mortgage, but I just need a couple more months of clients to make it happen. That's why I asked Edward to extend our agreement by two months, but he just thinks I'm stalling. I didn't want to tell him about the house. I want my new start with no connections to my past. I don't expect you to understand, Alice, but please don't hate me.'

'You're right; I don't understand. You're clever and kind and beautiful. Why couldn't you find yourself a boyfriend, get married and settle down with a couple of kids and live happily ever after?'

'That might be your dream, Alice, but it's not mine. You come from a loving home with two parents who still love each other and a sister who worships you. You don't know what it's like to feel unwanted and unloved. My parents were never married and, after my father ran off when I was a baby, my mother turned to drink. I grew up in a damp council flat with mould on the walls and a treble lock on the front door because of the area we lived in. Instead of my mother looking after me, I had to care for her, cooking and cleaning up her mess when she threw up after bouts of binge drinking.'

Alice recoiled. Even the thought of vomit made her queasy.

'I grew up without a father figure, just a string of uncles who were all sad losers, like my mum. No wonder I flunked school. I used to go to bed at night with a chair back jammed under my bedroom door handle, too frightened to go to sleep in case one of them couldn't get what they wanted from her and turned their attentions to me. I used to fall asleep in class all the time, but no one ever investigated the reason why, they just punished me by giving me detention. The only thing I had to keep me sane was my Saturday morning dance class, which I paid for with my school dinner money. My teacher thought I showed promise and used to keep me behind for a private lesson when class had finished. I never took any exams, there was never any spare money, but Miss Donna used to move me up to the next grade with all the girls who had passed their exams.'

Alice was aware that Gina had drifted away from the point somewhat, but she had the feeling that this was the first time her friend had ever told anyone about her childhood and didn't want to interrupt.

'We were muddling along, just about, and then my mum started seeing Baxter. I never liked him,' Gina said, 'there was something evil about him. He was violent towards my mum, and on more than one occasion he drew a knife and held it to her throat. I didn't realise straightaway, but he was the bastard that started my mum on drugs and one night, when she was totally out of it, he forced my bedroom door opened and threatened to slit my throat if I didn't let him do what he wanted. I was fourteen. What an introduction to the pleasures of the flesh.'

Alice's hand flew up to her mouth, but Gina was oblivious.

'I scrubbed myself down there for an hour afterwards, but I still didn't feel clean. I've never felt clean since. The funny thing is, Baxter was stabbed to death with his own knife the next night by a dealer he owed money to, so there never seemed to be a point in telling anyone what he had done to me. I didn't want people knowing I was damaged goods. You are the only person I have ever told,' she said, finally focusing her attention back on Alice.

'But not all men are like that vile, depraved animal. Surely you've met some nicer ones?'

'There was one, when I was twenty. His name was Larry. I finally got past the revulsion I felt at the thought of a man touching me and let myself give in to physical attraction. I fell head over heels in love, and I thought he loved me too.'

'What happened?

'I must have been so good in bed that I turned him gay, although we've stayed friends ever since.'

Realisation dawned on Alice.

'Oh my God, you're talking about our Larry?'

Gina nodded.

Alice wanted to rush over and hug her friend, but she was mindful of not wanting it to seem like pity.

'I don't think that's how it works, Gina. I think people are born homosexual. I remember having a long conversation about it with a young comedian in my last summer show. You didn't do anything wrong; Larry just realised that despite loving you he didn't want to be with you in that way. There will be someone else; you just haven't found them yet.'

'It's too late for me now. When I crossed the line and started to accept payment for sex I knew there would be no going back. I'm okay with it, Alice, honestly I am. Once I've got my little house, I'll get myself a cat or a dog for companionship and it goes without saying that you would be more than welcome to move in with me if you would still want to after what I've just told you.'

'Of course I would want to. We're friends. We share the good times and the bad, and hopefully there won't be too many more bad times for you once you get your new start.'

'That's what I'm hoping too. When I leave here, I'm also planning to walk away from the Ostrich Club. If Franco doesn't know where I am, he and his bully boys can't hurt me.'

'You don't seriously think he would hurt you, do you?'

Gina took a sip of her wine, thinking back to her friend Joanna's untimely death. 'I don't know what he's capable of, but one thing's for certain, I have no desire to find out.'

Alice felt devastated for her friend. In similar circumstances, Alice wasn't convinced that she would have trodden the same path but then how could she know for sure when she hadn't had to endure the cards life had dealt to Gina?

'Don't give up on love. There will be someone out there who will make your heart contract and your knees go weak.'

'You mean the way you feel about Peter?'

'Felt, is more accurate.'

'Is it? Listen, I wasn't going to tell you this, Alice, because I'm still not sure how much I trust him, but Peter cornered me after the show on Monday. He pleaded with me to set up a meeting for the two of you so that he can tell you his side of the Tammy story. I told him I'd ask you but that I wasn't going to try and sway you one way or the other. I've changed my mind. I think you two should sit down together and try to sort this out.'

'I can't face him alone, Gina. I can't let him hurt me like that again. Surely, you understand? It's self-preservation.'

'I can see that it might be difficult with just the two of you, but what if I came along as kind of a chaperone, just to get things started? Maybe we could meet at Joe's so that you would be on familiar territory?'

'I don't know. Part of me wants to hear what he has to say but how will I know if he's telling the truth?'

'You'll have to trust your instincts, and I may just suggest to him that Giuseppe has mafia connections.'

Despite her reservations, Alice smiled.

'I'll take that as a yes. I'll set it up for lunch on Thursday, okay?'

'Okay.'

'We should try and get some sleep, Alice, it's almost

six o clock.'

'You're right, or we'll both be sacked for looking such a state. And don't worry, I won't tell a soul about anything we've talked about tonight.'

'I know you won't. I trust you more than anyone else on this planet. You are like the kid sister I never had.'

The two hugged then, Gina finally feeling unburdened after years of carrying her secret and Alice wishing she could do something to give her friend a happier future than her past had been.

"Night, Alice.'

"Night, Gina. Oh, I forgot to ask. What did the landlord say about keeping the flat for an extra two months?'

'He agreed in the end, but he said if I'm not out by then he's sending the heavies round.'

Most people used that phrase in jest but Alice was acutely aware that her friend was deadly serious.

CHAPTER 38

Alice deposited her cotton dressing gown on top of the cork-topped wicker linen basket that doubled as a stool, and climbed into the foam-filled bath. She had spent the morning shaving her legs and painting her toenails in between trying to decide on an outfit for her lunch date. Sunny September days were always tricky. You could never tell what the temperature was by merely looking out of the window and, even if it was warm in the middle of the day, temperatures could fall away rapidly as the sun lowered in the sky. Alice decided on her burgundy suede mini-skirt and matching long-sleeved silky blouse with a pink crocheted waistcoat over the top. It would also be only the second outing for the gold platform-soled sandals she had treated herself to with her first understudy pay cheque.

She relaxed back into the bath, smiling happily, allowing the warm fragrant water to envelop her. She was feeling very different from the way she had felt on Thursday prior to the lunch meeting at Joe's.

Peter was already at the café when the girls arrived promptly at 12.30. 'I told you he was keen,' Gina had whispered, as they greeted Giuseppe in the usual Mediterranean fashion, a kiss to each cheek, before making their way to where Peter was sitting toying with a glass of Pepsi. He scraped his chair backwards and jumped to his feet as they approached. Alice's heart was thundering as he waited for them to sit before resuming his seat. 'Thank you for coming, Alice,' he began, 'I know it can't have been an easy decision for you.'

'That's the understatement of the year,' Gina said.

'And thanks for organising it, Gina,' Peter said, acknowledging her presence.

'To be honest, I couldn't stand to watch the pair of you any longer. You with your pleading puppy dog eyes, and Alice avoiding your gaze at all costs. I'm surprised she didn't walk into something and do herself a serious injury. Look, she's doing it now.'

Alice had raised her glance then to meet his and instantly regretted it. His eyes bore into hers with an intensity that turned her insides to jelly. She had decided to be hard and unforgiving until he had explained his actions, but she could feel her resolve was already melting. Thank goodness Gina is here, she had thought, I knew this would happen.

'So, let's get straight to the point, shall we, Peter?' Gina said. 'Alice wants to know what you were doing in Joe Allen's with your arm around Tammy.'

'Well, she knows why I was there with Tammy, don't you Alice? I told you that Richard asked me to babysit her to make sure she didn't have anything alcoholic to drink. I only agreed to go because your parents were supposed to be coming to the show and I didn't want to intrude on family time.'

'There's a bit of a difference between making sure she stayed on the soft drinks and canoodling with her,' Alice said.

'I wasn't "canoodling", as you put it. There was a journalist asking awkward questions about her enforced absence, and I put my arm around her to usher her out of the club before she felt backed into a corner. I had no idea a photographer had snapped it.'

'Obviously,' Gina said.

'But it wasn't just the photograph, Peter, it was what Tammy said. I'm assuming the journalist quoted her accurately and didn't put words in her mouth?'

Peter sighed.

'This is the frustrating part for me. The journalist did quote Tammy accurately, but I have no idea why she said what she did. I've tried to broach the subject with her, and even asked her to retract the statement but she won't, and I haven't a clue why not. I've never shown the slightest interest in her, even in Melanie and Frenchie love scenes in the show, and I would say that the feeling is mutual. It's nothing like doing the show with you, Alice.'

'So, let me get this straight. You want me to believe that there is and never has been anything between you and Tammy, despite the fact that she refuses to deny it?'

'Yes. I want you to believe me ahead of some sleazy journalist who was pissed off because he couldn't get the story as to why Tammy had been off. Anybody can claim anything as far as the papers go and they will print it whether there's any truth in it or not. I could ring a news desk this afternoon and hint that I'm having a fling with Gina and it would be in the papers tomorrow; "Flint dumps co-star in favour of chorus girl".'

'Please don't go getting any ideas,' Gina said.

'Don't be ridiculous. No offence,' he said, seeing her wounded expression. 'It was just an example of how there doesn't have to be any truth in a story for the papers to print it. From their point of view, what's the worst that can happen? If someone objects to a story, they print a retraction three days later in a paragraph buried at the bottom of page thirty. I promise you, Alice, there has never been anything between Tammy and me. I don't fancy her at all, in fact, I don't even like her much. Please tell me you believe me.'

Alice desperately wanted to believe that Peter was telling the truth but was battling hard to keep her sensible head on. She had cried herself to sleep listening to Eric Carmen's 'All By Myself' countless times after the story appeared in the paper and she didn't want to go through it all again.

'I don't know. What do you think, Gina?'

'I think Peter may have a point. I'm not suggesting you rush headlong into a relationship, but maybe you could meet up for lunch, without me playing gooseberry, and see where it takes you.'

For a moment, Peter had looked as though he would kiss Gina but clearly thought better of it in case there was a long-distance lens trained on them through the café window.

'How about Sunday? We could have lunch and then go for a walk along the river.'

'I'd like that,' Alice said.

'If you give me the address, I can pick you up at Gina's,

if you like?'

Behind Peter's back, Gina shook her head vigorously at Alice who cottoned on immediately that the fewer people who knew about the opulent surroundings she lived in the better.

'I've got a better idea. Why don't we meet at the Barley Mow, on Castelnau, then if I'm late you can get yourself a drink.'

Peter hadn't objected. He was getting a second chance with Alice and it seemed that was all he cared about.

Alice had been floating on cloud nine since the meeting at Joe's willing the days to go faster and bring Sunday lunchtime around more speedily. And now it's almost here, she thought, lathering up her sponge to wash her feet. She wiggled her bright pink toenails then dipped her foot back in the bath to rinse the bubbles away before pulling the plug out and reaching for her towel to pat herself dry. She had decided on virtually no make-up. Peter saw her all the time at the theatre in heavy stage make-up and false eyelashes but nobody wakes up looking like that in the morning, and she certainly had no intention of being one of those women who never let her husband see her without her slap. Listen to me, she laughed to herself, I'm already marrying Peter, and we haven't been on our first date yet. She hummed to herself as she applied mascara, cream blusher and a neutral lipstick before releasing her cascade of blonde hair from the clip that had kept it clear of the bathwater.

On the way back to her room, Alice glanced at Gina's door. It was still closed, meaning she hadn't surfaced yet, but she had expressly told Alice to knock and wake her before she left on her date so that she could give her the once over. I'll leave her a few more minutes, Alice thought, pulling the silky blouse with its shirring elastic midriff area over her head. It was a good choice, she thought, admiring her reflection in the mirror, it emphasised her waist and full bust without being too obvious. Normally she would have gone for her skirt before her shoes, but the suede one she had selected was a little snug and would have made it tricky to bend over to fasten the buckles. Shoes on, she stepped into her skirt and wiggled it over her hips. Snug isn't the word, she thought, struggling with the side zip. Clearly, all those pasta lunches at Joe's to fatten me up after grandma died have done the trick and then some. I'll have to knock those on the head for a while, or I'll have Richard complaining about me being fat again.

'Let's have a look at you then,' Gina said from the doorway.

'Actually, I'm not sure I'm going to be able to wear this after all. I can't get the zip up, and I hold you fully responsible for me piling on the pounds.'

'Here, let me have a go. I'll hold the two sides together, and you pull the zip.'

After a couple more attempts the girls managed to fasten it without catching any of Alice's skin in the teeth of the zip.

'Are you going to be able to eat lunch wearing that?' Gina asked doubtfully, 'it gives a whole new meaning to the expression "skin tight".'

'Do you think I should change? Is it too tight? It certainly feels much tighter than usual.'

'To be honest, it makes your tummy look big. Have you got anything that's not so fitted that would go with that blouse? And we'd better get you back on salad lunches, pronto, no point in giving Richard the satisfaction of saying "I told you so".'

Alice rummaged around in her wardrobe for her second-choice outfit, a floral dress that fitted neatly under the bust and then fell away in an A-line.

'How about this?'

'Very pretty, just like you. Don't worry about your tummy; you're probably a bit bloated because your period's due. Enjoy your lunch with Peter; your diet can start tomorrow. You'd better hurry up and change; you don't want to keep the poor guy waiting.'

CHAPTER 39

In the end, Alice opted to change her shoes as well as her outfit. The gold sandals didn't work with the floral dress, so she slipped her feet into her favourite green wedge sandals instead. A much better choice, she thought, as she stood waiting for the lift to slowly trundle up to the second floor, particularly if we are going for a walk along the river after lunch. She opened the creaky gates to the lift and pressed 'G' for ground floor on the panel next to a large age-speckled mirror. As the lift began its creaky descent, she checked her face to make sure that her make-up was perfectly applied before turning sideways and running her hands over the contours of her slightly rounded stomach. Thank goodness this dress hides a multitude of sins, she thought, releasing herself from the cage-like confines of the lift and waving a cheery greeting in Alf's general direction.

'You're looking very pretty today, Alice. Are you off on a date?'

The last thing she wanted was to get stuck in a conversation with the nosey doorman, but she always made it her business to stay on his good side.

'Sort of. I'm meeting up for lunch with someone from the show,' she said, barely able to disguise her excitement.

'Well, he's a lucky chap. If only I were twenty years younger.'

And the rest, Alice thought, smiling.

'Enjoy yourself; it's good for you girls to get out and about. It must be hard having boyfriends when you're always working in the evenings.'

There was something about the way Alf said the word 'working'. I hope he doesn't think I have clients too, she thought, indignantly. It will be so much better when Gina buys the house, and we can come and go as we please, she thought, stepping out from the dim interior of the entrance hall into the dazzling brilliance of a mid-September day. She felt around in her handbag for her sunglasses and her fingers closed around the small container she kept her Lil-lets in. Since being caught out at the Dorchester on the morning of her grandma's death, Alice always kept a couple of tampons in her bag.

Her mind drifted back to Gina's comment. When had she last had a proper period? The accident on the hotel sheets hadn't developed into a full-blown menstrual bleed, which Alice had put down to the shock of losing her gran. That was almost ten weeks ago, and she realised that her last proper period had been two weeks before that. It's incredible the effect shock can have on the body, but perhaps I should sign up with a doctor and get checked out, just for my own peace of mind. Come to think of it, I've also been off my food first thing in the morning, maybe that's part of a physical reaction too although, clearly, I've been making up for it at lunchtime judging by my expanding waistline.

Alice, who had been bouncing along the pavement with a happy grin on her face in anticipation of the lunch date ahead, suddenly stopped dead in her tracks. No, that's not possible. The symptoms are just a coincidence, aren't they? A horrifying thought was forming in her mind. What if Richard hadn't only undressed her that night at the Dorchester? What if he had forced himself on her when she was in no physical state to resist him? No, surely, I would know if he had done something so despicable, she thought, cold fear gripping her insides and turning them to ice. Or would I? I was so drunk and then so hung over the following morning, I wasn't in any state to notice anything. Oh my God, is Richard really that depraved that he would take advantage of someone totally incapacitated by drink? She knew the answer to her question. He was an odious man and probably thought she deserved everything she got by allowing herself to get into such a state.

Alice's legs felt like jelly. I need to sit down, she thought. Castelnau lay just ahead, with the Barley Mow pub on the corner and its comfortable well-worn leather chairs and benches. She could picture Peter at the bar waiting for her, sipping a beer or cider and maybe having a glance through the menu, salivating in anticipation of a Ploughman's or scampi and chips.

I can't do it, Alice thought. I can't face Peter with the suspicions I now have about that night at the Dorchester, and I definitely can't face any food. All I want to do is go back to the flat and crawl into bed, but I can't do that either because Gina would want to know why I didn't meet up with Peter. Oh God, what a mess. What am I going to do? I need to think.

With that, Alice turned back along the way she had come and then cut down a footpath leading to a towpath along the river bank. It was filled with families out for a Sunday stroll, compounding Alice's feeling of being totally alone with no one she could talk to. Tears prickled the back of her eyes as she blundered forwards putting as much distance between herself and Hammersmith Bridge as she could before her legs finally gave out and she collapsed on to a grassy verge, almost hidden from view by one of the many bends in the River Thames. There she stayed for the entire afternoon, her feelings fluctuating between shame and utter despair, until she felt certain Peter would have given up on her and gone home.

There was a distinct chill in the air as she made her way back towards Hammersmith Bridge before crossing it and going into a pub on the Chiswick side of the river. She sat nursing a glass of lemonade, passing the time until it was safe for her to return to the flat in the knowledge that Gina would have left for work. She desperately wanted to talk to someone about her fears but, after their conversation earlier in the week, one thing Gina had said had stuck in her mind: 'I didn't want people to know that I'm damaged goods.' Only now was Alice starting to comprehend what that felt like.

At closing time, Alice dragged herself back across the bridge and was thankful to discover that the front door to the flats was locked. Alf did this when he needed to visit the toilet. She entered the code and slipped inside as quietly as she could before heading for the stairs, not wanting to risk waiting for the lift for fear of Alf returning and asking her how her date went. Once safely inside the flat, she went straight to her room without turning on any of the lights because she couldn't face the thought of catching a glimpse of herself in any of the mirrors Gina had on almost every wall. She unzipped her dress, let it fall to the floor then stepped out of it, leaving it in a heap, before climbing into bed.

The previous eleven hours had given her plenty of time to think. First thing the next morning, she would go to the chemist and buy a pregnancy test kit. If the result was positive, as she was now certain it would be, she would have to go to the only other person who need ever know about her predicament for help.

CHAPTER 40

Peter had waited at the Barley Mow for over an hour. At first, he had just thought Alice was running late but, after finishing his second half pint of cider, he began to wonder if she'd forgotten the arrangements she had suggested. Maybe she thought we were meeting for a walk by the river before lunch, he thought. He paid the bill, apologising profusely for occupying a lunch table when there were other people waiting to be seated, and briskly walked towards Hammersmith Bridge. He cast his eyes up and down the banks in both directions searching for Alice's distinctive long blonde hair. After a further thirty minutes of watching and hoping he finally gave up and walked up to the tube station to get the Piccadilly line back to Knightsbridge.

For the first time in his life, Peter had been stood up and, try as he might, he couldn't understand why. Every time he had seen Alice at the theatre since their meeting at Joe's café she had smiled at him. They had agreed to keep their lunch date secret as she had explained the other dancers were being kinder to her since they thought she had been dumped in favour of Tammy. On

Saturday night, though, she had risked whispering 'see you tomorrow' when they had passed in the corridor between routines. So why was she a no-show? Had she been toying with him, he wondered. Was this her way of paying him back?

'Women,' he said, slinging his door keys on the glass-topped wrought-iron shelf in his hallway, before grabbing himself a bottle of cold beer from the fridge and slumping down on the sofa in front of his television. He got increasingly drunk as the evening wore on and woke on Monday morning, still fully clothed, on the sofa with the mother of all hangovers to prove it.

Two cups of black coffee and a lengthy shower later, he had reached a decision. Maybe, despite wanting to believe him, Alice still had her doubts because of what Tammy had said. Peter had had enough of Tammy avoiding the issue. He was going to confront her at the theatre and get her to retract her comment once and for all, or he would feign feeling ill, and she would have to do tonight's performance with his useless understudy, Mike. As Peter gingerly rubbed his hair with a towel, before getting the hairdryer out, he realised he wouldn't need to fake it that much. His head was pounding, a state he hadn't been in since he'd left Moot Point.

In fact, that was one of the main reasons he'd left the band. Everyone thought he was being a big-time Charlie wanting to pursue a solo career but, in truth, he had never really been involved in the rock 'n' roll lifestyle of drugs, booze and sex, disapproving of his fellow band members and the way they treated women. He'd kept a low profile while searching for a vehicle to launch his West End career but the moment he heard the musical score for *Theatreland* he knew he'd found it. There was a lot of talk about the show transferring to New York, and Richard had already spoken to him about continuing in the lead role. Peter was playing it cool but had as good as told Richard that he wouldn't consider it with his current leading lady.

Richard had smirked at him. 'I suppose you'll only agree to it if I give the role to your little friend, Alice,' he had said. 'You should forget about her, Peter, she's trouble that one. Put your career first, there'll be plenty of other Alices when you get to Broadway, you mark my words.'

But Peter didn't want any other Alice. He was convinced he'd found his soul mate and all he had to do was convince her of it too.

By four in the afternoon, Peter was feeling a lot less fragile. He usually aimed to get to the theatre around 6 p.m., but today his plan was to be waiting in Tammy's dressing room when she arrived.

'You're early tonight, Peter,' Fred remarked when he showed up at the theatre an hour earlier than usual. 'I think you're the first in.'

'I've got a couple of things to do before the show tonight, Fred, and I also wanted to drop some lyrics in for Tammy. I've been working on a new song for us that she doesn't know anything about. Is it okay if I take her dressing room key?'

'No problem, she'll be in soon anyway, and I'll just tell her the cleaners must have left it open, so it won't spoil your surprise.'

'Cheers, Fred.'

Fifteen minutes later, Tammy opened the door to her dressing room, and before she'd had time to register that someone was already in there, Peter had moved behind her and closed and locked the door.

'What the hell do you think you're doing?'

'We need to have a little chat, Tammy.'

'Do we? What about?'

'You know damn well what about.'

'I've told you before, Peter, I have my reasons for wanting the press to think there is something going on between us.'

'That's as may be, but I now have a very big reason for wanting you to come clean.'

'I suppose you're talking about your little chorus girl. Well, I can't. And you can't make me,' she said, defiantly.

'You think? We'll see about that,' he said, advancing across the dressing room towards her.

'What are you going to do? Beat me up? How would you explain that?'

'I have no intention of laying a finger on you, to hurt you or for any other reason, but you are going to issue a retraction. I'm going to give you a couple of alternatives. You can ring that sleazy journalist right now, with me listening in, and ask him to print a retraction. I don't care if it's one line, buried deep in the paper, so long as it's something I can show to Alice. If you do that, we'll forget the whole thing ever happened.'

'And if I refuse?'

'I've been feeling a bit under the weather today. Maybe I'm coming down with something. Perhaps it would be better if you did tonight's performance with Mike?'

'You wouldn't. You're too much of a professional to let

your personal life get in the way of your career.'

'Try me.'

'So, I do the show with Mike. Big deal. He's not as good as you, but you can't stay off for ever.'

'True, which is why I will resort to plan C if you refuse the other two. I will ring that sleazebag myself and tell him exactly why you missed the first three preview shows.'

'You wouldn't.'

'Are you sure about that?'

'Please, Peter, that's not fair. Promise me you won't do that; my career in the West End will be over before it's properly got started.'

'I've got nothing against you but, from where I'm standing, you're the one that's not being fair. Alice isn't just any old girl; she's the one I want to spend the rest of my life with. The fact is, I love her, hard as it may be for you to comprehend when you clearly don't understand the concept.'

'You're wrong, Peter. I do understand, and that's precisely why I've let the story of you and me run.'

'I don't follow you.'

'I'm in love too, Peter, but I need to throw the press off the scent, and this was too good an opportunity to miss.'

'Oh, I see. You're dating a married man, so our "romance" is a convenient cover story for you. Well, I'm sorry, Tammy, you're going to have to find another alibi because this one has run its course.'

'Wrong again.'

'What? I'm not joking, Tammy.'

'I'm not seeing a married man.' She took a deep breath, 'I'm seeing my agent.'

Peter looked puzzled for a moment, 'I thought you

were represented by Lynette Marsh?'

'I am.'

'Then…? Oh, I get it,' he said, the penny suddenly dropping, 'you're in a lesbian relationship?'

Tammy nodded.

'But why try to hide it? There are loads of homosexual people in show business.'

'No, Peter. There are loads of homosexual men but how many openly lesbian women do you know?'

Peter thought for a moment.

'Precisely. It's just not as acceptable for women. I'm no trailblazer. I just want to get on with my career and my private life without people pointing their finger at me as though I'm a freak. The fear of someone finding out is what drove me to drink in the first place. It's bad enough for me, but Lynette is married and has kids. We've been trying to work out how we're going to handle the situation without causing too much upset to other people. Now do you understand why I latched on to the lifeline that Gerard Snape threw me?'

Peter looked at Tammy's pleading face. The press could make or break a person's career for no other reason than they wielded the power to do it.

'Please, Peter. Just give us a couple more weeks to think up a new story, then I promise I'll retract my comment in full.'

He wasn't an unkind person and certainly didn't want to be responsible for sending Tammy back to rehab.

'You have until the end of this week to concoct a new cover story and feed it to the press. If they are still talking about you and me as an item this time next week, I'll blow the whistle.'

CHAPTER 41

'Come in,' Richard responded to the tap on his office door. 'Take a seat, I'll be with you in a moment,' he said without looking up.

Alice closed the door behind her and sat on the high-backed chair on the other side of the wide desk from where Richard was sitting, clearly engrossed in paperwork.

It was a full two minutes before he stopped writing, put his pen down and looked up. He was surprised to see the subject of at least half of his paperwork sat in the chair opposite him. Since she had performed so well in the first three preview shows, Richard had had to deflect a constant stream of phone-calls and letters enquiring whether Alice was represented by an agent and, if so, who? Without her knowledge, he had been telling everyone that he was currently representing Alice, and that any and all queries regarding work should be addressed to him. As he watched her nervously fidgeting, he wondered if she had somehow got wind of the way he was keeping other impresarios and their job offers at bay. My discovery, my property, he thought, at least until I can be sure that Tammy is going to stay sober enough to complete her six-month contract.

'So, what can I do for you, Alice?'

'I–I need to speak to you about a personal matter,' she stammered in a barely audible voice.

'Well, let's hear it, girl. I haven't got all day.'

'Erm, it's about the night at the Dorchester.'

Richard hadn't been expecting that. He thought back to the last time he had been alone with Alice, her near lifeless body crushed beneath his bulk as he had given her a good seeing to. He was pretty sure she wouldn't be able to remember anything of the actual assault, seeing as the other girls he had drugged and forced his attentions on had been more alert during intercourse and yet still seemed to have no recollection of anything untoward happening to them. He smiled a bitter twisted smile. Who would have thought that having such a small penis could work so well in my favour, he thought.

Although he still occasionally had sex with his wife, there was very little feeling in it, either physical or emotional, for him. When they were first married, Anita had a tight virginal vagina and he was able to experience a small amount of pleasure, but since the birth of their daughter there was almost no sensation at all. Thank goodness for the supply of nubile young girls that my job gives me access to, he thought.

'What about it, Alice? I thought I made it clear in my note that it was something best not talked about.'

'And I was happy and grateful to go along with that. I disgraced myself by getting drunk so the last thing I wanted was for anyone to find out about it.'

Good, Richard thought. For one minute, he had wondered if Alice had guessed that she had been the victim of a date rape drug that had rendered her unconscious and was here to try and blackmail him.

'Precisely. So, back to your reason for being here?'

Alice shuffled uncomfortably on her chair.

'I—I did a test this morning. It was positive. I'm pregnant.'

Richard stared at Alice in disbelief. He had assumed that she, like most girls of her age, was taking the Pill. It had never crossed his mind that he would impregnate her. God, what a bloody mess. How the hell am I going to get out of this? Then a thought occurred to him.

'Well, I'm very shocked to hear that, Alice, but I'm not sure what it has to do with me? Shouldn't you be having this conversation with your boyfriend, Peter?'

'Peter's not my boyfriend. We've been for a drink a couple of times and had a kiss and cuddle,' she admitted blushing, 'but we've never had sex. I've never had sex with anyone, at least,' she said, looking down at her hands, 'I thought I hadn't. When I started to suspect I might be pregnant, I realised there was only one possible occasion when it could have happened. The night at the Dorchester...' she said, her voice trailing off.

Shit, shit, shit, Richard thought. Trust me to choose the only nineteen-year-old dancer in the West End of London who is not on the Pill *and* is a bloody virgin. If this gets out I'm finished. Anita will pull the plug on financing the show and I could even go to prison for rape. Think, Richard, think.

'Well, Alice, I didn't want to have to tell you this,' he said, sounding much calmer than he was feeling. 'I wanted to spare your blushes alongside the embarrassment of getting paralytically drunk, when all I wanted to do was treat you to dinner as a thank you for all the hard work you put in as Melanie. I must confess I was slightly shocked when you started to strip off your clothes and lead me through to the bedroom, but I'm a red-blooded male and you clearly wanted to show your appreciation of me giving you such a big break in show business. I wouldn't go so far as to say you raped me, but you as near as did when you straddled me and started gyrating your hips. I'm only sorry that I didn't make more effort to resist your advances.'

Alice was staring at Richard, a look of horror on her face.

'So, we have a problem,' he continued, without giving her time to react to the suggestion he had just planted in her mind, 'and it's largely of your making. The question is, how are we going to solve it?'

Alice's eyes were wide and she was blinking furiously. Bugger, Richard thought, she's going to start bloody crying.

'I take it you don't want to have this baby?'

No response.

'If you did, it would finish your career before it's got properly started. It would be a shame to see such talent go to waste.'

'But it's a life growing inside me, however it got there,' she whispered, finally, looking back down at her hands. 'It would be like murder.'

'Don't be silly, Alice. Didn't you do biology at school? It's not a proper baby yet, it's just a bunch of human cells that in time would grow to resemble a baby. You have no husband and, in a few weeks when you start to show, you will have no job, which means no money to support it.'

227

'My parents…' she started to say.

Don't give her time to come up with a plan to keep the baby, he thought.

'Your parents what? Hmmm? Do you think they would welcome you home with open arms once you've explained how you disgraced yourself, in fact, your entire family, by getting so drunk that you can't even remember throwing yourself at your employer? I don't think so, Alice, do you?'

Her bottom lip was quivering now. Press on, he thought, before the waterworks start.

'Look, Alice, I don't owe you anything. You've only got yourself to blame for getting into this mess but I'm a decent human being and I'm prepared to help you.'

He got up from behind his desk and moved around it to place a hand on her shoulder.

'You're not the first dancer who has asked for my help in this type of situation and I'm pretty sure you won't be the last. I know of someone who helps girls like you. She is very discreet and, under the circumstances, I will give you the money for her services. There is a condition though. You mustn't tell a soul about any of this,' he said, squeezing her shoulder a little harder, 'do I make myself clear?'

He released his grip on her shoulder and went back to sit behind his desk.

'So, Alice,' he said, attempting to keep his tone to that of a benevolent benefactor, 'do you want my help or will I have Larry look for a new member of the chorus to permanently replace you? It's your decision.'

He resisted the urge to tap his fingers on his desk. I should have trusted my instincts from the word go on this girl, he thought. I knew she was trouble from the start and, at the end of the day, the shag wasn't satisfying enough to warrant me having to fork out five hundred quid for a backstreet abortion. But I suppose I should be grateful she came to me first. If she had gone to the doctor's and they had started asking questions about the father, and why she wanted a termination, the stupid cow would probably have named me and then all hell would have broken loose.

'I don't want to rush you, Alice, but it is curtain up in thirty minutes and you need to get ready.'

Finally, she raised her head, her eyes exhibiting the desperation and indecision she was feeling.

Not quite there, Richard thought. I need this to disappear whatever it takes.

'And, once all this is dealt with, you and I can have a talk about *Theatreland* transferring to Broadway. Maybe, just maybe, there might be an opportunity for you to play the role of Melanie over there.' He had already been considering offering her the part but now, as well as costing him much less than an established leading lady, it would also put distance between them.

'I don't think I have much choice,' she said, her voice flat and defeated.

'I think that is a wise decision.'

'When?'

'I would suggest as soon as possible. It will be better for you, both mentally and physically. You will have to make the phone call yourself as I don't want to be implicated in helping you to have an abortion, but I will arrange for Max, my driver, to take you there and drop you home afterwards. Stop by here after the show tonight and I'll give you the number to call and also the money. After that you are on your own, although I will clear it with Larry for you to have a couple of days off once it's been done for you to recuperate. Don't worry, Alice, it's a fairly straightforward procedure that thousands of girls in your condition have been through before.'

He stood up, indicating that the meeting was over.

Alice left the room without saying a word.

'Ungrateful little bitch,' Richard muttered under his breath.

CHAPTER 42

Alice shivered. It was a beautifully warm late September day but she doubted that the sunshine ever permeated the basement flat in Stockwell. The room felt damp, almost as though it had cried oceans of tears for the hundreds of tiny souls whose lives had been stolen before they had begun. She sat for a few minutes watching the passers-by from the knees down as they passed the anonymous building, going about their business blissfully unaware of what was taking place yards from their feet. Slowly, she stood and moved across to a single bed pushed up against the wall furthest from the window and any prying eyes.

As instructed by Sadie a few minutes earlier, she drew the faded olive-green curtain separating the bed from the rest of the room and began to undress. She slipped out of her loose-fitting dress and carefully laid it over the back of the chair along with her panties, all the time thinking, this is wrong; I should run from this place and go home to Nottingham. Mum would be shocked and disappointed in me but she would stand by me, I know she would. If you really believe that, why are you here? asked the other half of her brain. It was a tussle she had been having with herself for the past three days.

Last night, she had been perilously close to telling Gina what she was about to do. They had gone home after the show for their usual Thursday 'girlie night', but she had been so pre-occupied that Gina sensed something was not right.

'Are you okay? Is this still because Peter stood you up on Sunday? Forget about him, Alice, you deserve better. He really is a lying two-faced shit.'

Alice hadn't actually lied about who did the standing up when Gina crept into her room in the early hours of Monday morning after her shift at the Ostrich, eager to hear how her friend's date had gone. Through her tears, Alice had said, there was no date. 'He stood you up?' an outraged Gina had assumed. Alice hadn't corrected her, she had simply replied, 'I don't want to talk about it,' and she didn't.

'No, that's all in the past. I should have listened to you in the first place and not been so flattered by a pop star showing me some attention. I've got really bad toothache. I think it may be an abscess. I'm going to see someone to get it fixed tomorrow.'

This backed up the story Richard had concocted for her being off work for a couple of days. 'I'll tell Larry you had an infected abscess and are on antibiotics,' he had said, as he handed over a manila envelope containing £500, after the show on Monday evening.

'Ouch. I know how painful that is. I had one under an impacted wisdom tooth when I was about your age. I hope you get it sorted.'

She hated lying to Gina, but at least it meant her friend

would be unlikely to try and mediate for her and Peter in the future, in fact, she had vowed she would never speak to him again, calling him an arrogant cock.

Alice had managed to avoid speaking to Peter too, not that she had seen much of him since she had failed to turn up for their lunch date. Perhaps he has finally given up on me, she thought miserably, and who could blame him? And if he knew what I'd done and what I'm about to do, he would never want to speak to me again anyway. She was filled with self-loathing and revulsion at her own behaviour which had led her to this sordid place.

She placed her handbag, containing the large sanitary towel she had been advised to bring, on the seat of the chair with her clothes, and then climbed on to the bed. Silent tears slid from her eyes, drenching her neatly plaited hair, as she mourned the life she was about to take.

She heard the door open and heavy footsteps approaching.

It's not too late, it's not too late, her heart said, but her head was making the decisions. No one need ever know about the mess she had got herself into. How could I possibly love a baby conceived under those circumstances? she thought. It would be a constant reminder of the worst mistake of my life.

Sadie pulled back the curtain. Considering what she did for a living, she seemed a kind and caring person, not what Alice was expecting at all. Sadie hadn't asked many questions. She didn't want to know if the pregnancy was as a result of a missed contraceptive pill or burst condom, or just a careless mistake after a wild night out. She didn't ask why Alice had chosen not to carry the baby to full term and then give it up for adoption to a desperate childless couple who could offer it a decent life. None of that was Sadie's business. All she needed to know was how far along the pregnancy was and that Alice had the cash to pay for the termination.

'It's not too late to change your mind, love,' she said. 'It's not the right thing for everybody. Do you want me to give you a moment?'

Alice shook her head, not trusting herself to speak, tears still streaming unchecked across her cheeks.

'Well, let's get started then. Sit up for me and drink this,' she said, passing over a bone china cup and saucer. Alice recognised the pattern; her grandma had had a tea set just like it.

What would Granny think if she could see me now? she thought. Her grandma had always gone along to watch her perform in dancing shows and competitions, even doing her hair if it required something more than the classic ballet bun. Edna had wanted to go on the stage herself but her father wouldn't allow it. She had been disappointed when the smell of the greasepaint had skipped generation with her daughter, Sheila, showing no interest in theatre at all. When Alice signed her first professional contract for a summer season in Cleethorpes, she had been overjoyed, even going to stay at the holiday camp not once but twice during the sixteen-week run. Please don't judge me, Granny, Alice silently pleaded, as she took the cup and sipped the liquid. It was a shock. She had thought Sadie was offering a cup of tea to calm her nerves before starting the process but realised from the taste that this was not the case. The liquid was pepperminty but also had a hint of the turpentine that her dad used to clean paint brushes when he had been painting woodwork. She grimaced, immediately feeling her gag reflex kick in.

'I don't think I can drink this.'

'You'll have to, dearie, if you want me to help you. Just hold your nose and swallow it all down in one go. The quicker you drink it the less you will notice the taste, like medicine when you were a child.'

Alice rested the saucer on her thighs and used her free hand to pinch her nostrils together as Sadie had recommended. She took a deep breath and drained the contents of the cup.

'Good girl. Now lie back and pop this pillow under your bottom, then feet apart and drop your thighs open. We're just going to try and speed up the process for you,' she said, holding an implement in her hand that looked like a knitting needle.

A few minutes later and Sadie's work was done. Alice had felt a sharp pain deep in her insides but it had only lasted a few seconds.

'You can get dressed now. Did you bring a sanitary towel with you?'

Alice nodded.

'Well, put that in your pants just in case things start to happen really quickly. When you start to feel stomach cramps, a bit like period pains but stronger, I recommend either sitting on the toilet or in a bath of quite hot water until it's all over. And then total rest for a couple of days to allow things to heal properly. If you are still bleeding after a few days, you'll have to go to a hospital to get checked out.'

Alice's eyes were filled with fear.

'A hospital? Can't I just come back here?'

'You could, but I won't be here. I never use the same place twice. I rent the space for a morning, or a whole day if I have a few appointments, then I move on. All I do is provide the service to start a miscarriage. After that you're on your own.'

It was the second time Alice had heard the phrase, 'after that you're on your own', in the space of a few days. She dragged her leaden feet up the stairs from the basement, back into the bright sunshine, before climbing into the back of the waiting black Mercedes, acutely aware that she had never felt more alone in her entire life than she did right at that moment.

CHAPTER 43

It had been a good night at the Ostrich Club. Not only had Gina earned a few tips in the early part of her shift from a crowd of businessmen visiting London from Hong Kong, towards closing time, one of her favourite regulars came in and sat down in a private booth. She strolled across the pocket handkerchief-sized dance floor, making sure her hips sashayed in a provocative manner.

'Vince,' she said, 'you're out late tonight. Shall I call the waiter over to get some drinks? Scotch? Brandy? Or do you fancy sharing a bottle of Moët?'

'I'll have a brandy and whatever you fancy.'

Gina signalled to the waiter, who took their order, then she slid into the booth next to Vince.

'What time do you get off, Gina?'

She scanned the room. There were only two other punters in the club and they were both occupied.

'I can probably slip away in half an hour. Why? What did you have in mind?'

'I've just helped the commercial estate agency I work for negotiate a multi-million-pound deal with an American bank who want to open offices here in London.

My percentage of the commission is huge and I'm high on adrenalin. I feel like celebrating with one of my favourite girls,' he said, reaching for her thigh under the table.

Unlike most of the men who frequented the Ostrich, Vince was young, probably early thirties, Gina guessed, and he was handsome with flaxen blonde hair, pale skin and blue eyes suggesting a Nordic heritage. He was a straight sex man; he didn't need to tie Gina's hands and feet to the bedstead, or have her dress up as a schoolgirl to get his kicks. He was away from his home in Leeds and he fancied some female company, plain and simple. He was one of the few clients who Gina permitted to kiss her on the mouth and, when he did, she could almost allow herself to believe that she was in a proper relationship with him. On more than one occasion, in the afterglow of sex, she imagined what it would be like to wake up each morning with him cuddled in to her. She didn't love him, Gina didn't do love, but it would be nice to have him as her protector. She knew nothing of his home life. Maybe he had a wife and children, maybe he didn't. What she didn't know couldn't hurt her.

'Where are you staying?' she asked, sipping her Babycham.

'Claridge's again, but I thought maybe we could go back to yours, like we usually do.'

She hadn't seen Vince since before Edward had threatened her about having men back to the flat in Barnes.

'I'm sorry, but I have my baby sister staying with me,' she lied. 'We could find a hotel room in Victoria for an hour or two if you don't want to risk being seen with me.'

'Don't be silly. The room is paid for and I couldn't

care less what the snooty concierge thinks. I just like the location of your flat, right on the river. We could be quiet so as not to wake her?'

'No. I wouldn't want to risk it. She's a sweet kid and she looks up to me.'

'I didn't know you had a sister. You've never mentioned her before.'

'It's not the sort of thing that comes up in conversation when you're doing what we do together. And anyway, I know nothing about your family so I guess we're quits.'

'What do you want to know about me?' he teased. 'I'm an only child, parents both living, and I come from Leeds. That's about it really. No big mystery.'

'Do you live at home with your parents?'

'Is that a roundabout way of asking if I'm married?'

'Maybe.'

'No, I'm not. I was engaged for five years but she ran off with the builder who was refitting our kitchen because I'm always down in London for business.'

'And she didn't trust you, which is fairly justified really.'

'It wasn't that she didn't trust me, she just didn't like being on her own all week.'

'Couldn't you have both moved down to London?'

'She's Yorkshire through and through. I don't think the bright lights of London would have suited her. Anyway, she seems happy enough with her builder, in fact they're getting married in December. She always wanted a Christmas wedding.'

'And you don't mind?'

'Not at all, although he could have finished the kitchen before he whisked her from under my nose. It's a right mess.'

'You're funny,' Gina said.

'Ha ha or strange?'

'A bit of both.'

'Best way to be. Come on, drink up. Let's get out of here. Are you okay to walk in those shoes or shall I get us a cab?'

'Is it warm out?'

'Yes. I love an Indian summer.'

'Let's walk then.'

They linked arms and strolled up Regent Street just like any other couple on their way home after a night out.

'So, how about you? I presume you're not married now, but have you ever been?'

'How do you know my husband's not my pimp?'

'I don't. Is he?'

'Of course not. And, I'll have you know, I don't have a pimp. I have a few select clients that I see occasionally and vet personally.'

'I'm honoured to be one of the select few.'

'Are you taking the micky?'

'Actually, no. I like being with you.'

'Clearly not that much. I haven't seen you in what, three, four months? You're not cheating on me, are you?'

'I can't afford you, Gina. I'm ploughing all my money into buying a restaurant in Richmond. I'm a trained chef. I only moved into the real estate game to earn some serious money and then, by chance, the perfect restaurant in the perfect location came on the market. The guy that owns it is retiring so we struck a deal. He stays as head chef until I've earned enough money to buy him out, then I take over.'

The similarity in their situations didn't escape Gina.

They were both working hard at jobs they didn't want to be doing to earn enough money for a fresh start.

'I can see now why the kitchen situation is not ideal,' Gina said, smiling. 'Nowhere to practise your culinary skills at the weekends.'

'I could come to yours and make a fried breakfast for everyone tomorrow morning?'

'The answer is still no. And, if you're so strapped for cash, how come you're staying here rather than somewhere less extravagant? You're sure this sob story isn't just to get you a discount, cos – let me tell you now – I don't do discounts.'

He nodded his head at the doorman who was holding the wooden glazed door open for them to enter the hotel, and guided her towards the lift.

'The company pays for my room and all meals, but not any extras I may have,' he said, winking.

'I'm an extra, am I? Isn't that what they call people who wander around in the background of films? There isn't a camera set up in your room is there?'

'Now there's an idea, except you wouldn't be in the background, you'd definitely be the leading lady.'

'If I didn't know better, I'd say you were flirting with me.'

'And you'd be right,' he said, pushing open the door to his room and barely waiting until it was closed before reaching behind Gina's back to unzip her dress. 'I've missed you,' he said, his mouth closing over hers.

When Gina checked the clock on the bedside table it was 5.45. Vince was sleeping, looking for all the world like a giant cherub from a Botticelli painting. She slid noiselessly from the bed and quietly got dressed before letting herself out of his room and heading down the stairs and out on to Brook Street to hail herself a cab. She hadn't wanted to disturb him by having a shower or even using the toilet, as she wanted to avoid answering the question he had put to her just before he fell asleep an hour ago.

'Do you love me, Gina, even just a little bit?'

And therein lies the problem, she thought, as she gave her address to the taxi driver and relaxed back in the leather seat. I am starting to feel something for him. Not the all-consuming, butterflies in the tummy feeling, but a warm contented glow. I can't let it happen. Nothing good will come of it, I'll just end up hurt when he decides he needs someone by his side in his posh restaurant who doesn't have history as a high-class call girl. Thank God, I've nearly got enough money to buy my little house, then I can do my disappearing act and no one will be able to find me. Even better if the show transfers to Broadway. I can go away for six months or a year and come back to Mortlake with a clean slate.

She paid the driver, and keyed in the code for the outer door to the flats. She had been in a hurry to leave Claridge's without disturbing Vince and, as a result of not having used the loo, was now virtually hopping from foot to foot as she waited for the lift to arrive. She inserted the key in her front door and was surprised to see that Alice hadn't left the little lamp on for her. Poor thing, Gina thought, grateful for the strength of her pelvic-floor muscles which were preventing her from peeing herself, the anaesthetic from the dentist earlier must have knocked her out.

She reached for the door handle of the bathroom and pressed it down, but the door didn't open.

'Alice, are you in there?'

She waited for a moment, listening for the sound of the loo flushing. Nothing.

'Alice! I need to pee, I'm busting. Open the door.'

CHAPTER 44

Gina paced up and down the stuffy relatives' room, periodically glancing at her watch. She guessed she could stay until one o' clock at the latest before she would need to dash home for a quick bath before heading into the theatre in time for the matinee performance. It was past eleven, and there was still no word about Alice's condition.

After calling out to Alice several times from outside the bathroom door and getting no response, Gina had begun to panic. She must be in there, she reasoned, the door is bolted from the inside. Maybe she was feeling dizzy from the after-effects of the dentist's anaesthetic and has fallen and banged her head or, worse still, what if she had decided to take a bath? She could be lying unconscious, partially submerged in the bath and gradually slipping down in the water. She had called out again and was sure she heard a low moaning sound. I need this door open now, Gina thought, grabbing her key and running down the two flights of stairs to Alf's office on the ground floor.

'Alf! Alf!' she shouted, banging on his door.

She heard a shuffling sound and, moments later, a bleary-eyed Alf had opened the door wearing only shorts and a string vest, his rumpled single bed in the background. Under different circumstances, Gina would have found his appearance quite repulsive but she was too anxious about Alice to care.

'Whoa, Gina, where's the fire?'

'Alf, I need you to break down my bathroom door. Alice is in there, and I think she must have fallen and hurt herself. Please help me,' she urged, taking hold of his arm and dragging him towards the stairs.

'That's a job for the fire brigade. I can't be responsible for damaging Edward's private property.'

'There's no time. What if she fell in the bath? What if she's drowning as we stand here arguing? Please Alf, you've got to help me.'

Reluctantly, Alf had followed Gina up the two flights of stairs arriving at the top breathless and sweating. Gina ran ahead and was calling Alice's name repeatedly. She turned as he trundled into the flat and shook her head at him, worry etched on her face.

'Move out of the way,' he said, trying the door handle for himself while exerting a small amount of pressure by leaning his shoulder against it. It didn't give at all. He took a couple of steps back and then lunged himself at the locked door with all his considerable weight. A splintering sound indicated that the wooden door frame, which housed the bolt on the inside, had given way. He pushed the door but something was preventing it from swinging open more than a few inches. 'I think we should call the police, I don't want to be held responsible for what we're going to find on the other side of that door.'

Ignoring him, Gina pushed past, squeezing through the space that had opened up.

'Oh my God,' she said, taking in the sight of her friend

lying in a pool of blood and vomit, 'forget the police, call an ambulance.'

The ambulance arrived within fifteen minutes during which time Gina had carefully moved Alice into the recovery position, lying her on one side to prevent her from choking on her own puke. It was something she had needed to do on many occasions for her own mother after bouts of drinking or drug-taking. She had kept talking to Alice throughout, trying to help her friend regain consciousness.

'What happened, Alice? Tell me what happened,' she repeated over and over.

At one point Alice murmured something unintelligible about Richard, but Gina couldn't work out what she was trying to say.

'Do you know what happened here, miss?' the ambulance man asked, when he arrived. 'Has she taken some medication or any other kind of drugs?'

'I don't know. I came home from work and she was locked in the bathroom. I know she went to the dentist today to have treatment for an abscess on her tooth. Maybe she was allergic to the drugs they gave her, but that wouldn't explain the blood. I suppose she could have started her period,' she continued, almost thinking out loud, 'and came to the bathroom to sort herself out. Perhaps that's when the drugs made her pass out. I don't know. What do you think?'

'It's a possibility, but there's an awful lot of blood. We'll know more when we get her to the hospital. Do you want to ride in the ambulance with her?'

Gina nodded, her face pale from shock, bravely fighting back unaccustomed tears.

'She will be all right, won't she?'
'Don't you worry, we'll look after her.'

Alice had been rushed off on a gurney the moment the ambulance drew up outside Accident and Emergency, leaving Gina to fill in the admission forms.

All the ambulance man had said was, we need to get her to theatre straightaway, she's lost a lot of blood.

That was over four hours ago and, despite her crushing fatigue, Gina had remained awake pacing the small space, unwilling to leave even for a cup of coffee in case the nurses came to give her an update.

'Miss Abbott?' said a nurse in a starched blue uniform, her hair neatly concealed beneath her white cap.

'Yes?' She had maintained the lie she had told Vince earlier that morning in order to get information about Alice.

'The good news is your sister is out of theatre and in a recovery ward. Would you like to be with her when she wakes up?'

'Yes please.'

'Follow me.'

Gina followed the staff nurse along the corridor, her shoes squeaking slightly on the linoleum floor, and through a swing door into the small recovery room.

'She's very weak and she's lost a lot of blood but she should make a full recovery. It's probably best not to mention the baby, we don't want to go upsetting her.'

Baby? What baby? During one of their Thursday night chats, Alice had confided to Gina that she was a virgin. There couldn't be a baby unless it was an immaculate conception. The nurse must have got it wrong, she thought, sitting on the brown upright chair at the side of Alice's bed and reaching for her hand, which was almost as white as the crisp hospital sheets. Attached to her other arm was a monitor whose rhythmic 'bip…bip…bip…' was checking her heartbeat and a drip that was pumping blood into her. The admissions nurse had asked her what blood group Alice was but she had been unable to tell her. It didn't arouse suspicions on the part of the hospital staff as it wasn't the type of thing you would necessarily know about your sister. I don't even know what my own blood group is, Gina thought, carefully watching for any signs of Alice regaining consciousness. What have you been keeping from me? she wondered, gently stroking her hand, and, more importantly why?

'I thought we were friends, Alice,' she whispered, acutely aware of using the words Alice had frequently spoken to her in an accusatory manner.

Alice's eyelids flickered. 'Friends,' she murmured.

'Alice, can you hear me? It's Gina.'

The long eyelashes parted and Alice attempted to focus. 'Where am I?' she croaked.

'You're in the hospital. You're going to be okay. What happened? I came home and you'd locked yourself in the bathroom.'

'The drugs made me sick, and then the pain started. I thought I was going to die. I wanted to die.'

'Don't talk like that. Why would you say something like that?'

'I did a bad thing, Gina. I should never have done it. It was my mistake, I should have been brave enough to see it through,' she said, a note of hysteria creeping into her voice.

'Shh, shh, stay calm,' Gina said, mindful of the nurse's warning. 'Listen, Alice, I had to tell them I was your sister, or I wouldn't have been permitted to stay with you.'

'You told my sister? You shouldn't have done that. Richard said I wasn't to tell a soul. He's going to be so angry with me.'

'No, you've misunderstood. The hospital think I am your sister. I haven't called your home yet. It was too early and then I forgot to bring your number with me, but if you tell me it, I can call them now.'

'No,' Alice said, her voice rising in alarm, 'no one must ever know what I've done. I promised Richard.'

There it was again, Gina thought. Why does Alice keep mentioning Richard? What has he got to do with any of this?

'Is the pain better now?' she asked gently. 'Did the dentist have to take the tooth out?'

'What tooth?' Alice asked, her eyelids beginning to droop, the exertion of speaking beginning to take its toll.

'You went to the dentist, remember? It was the anaesthesia that made you so sick.'

'Sadie made me sick. I drank the poison before she killed my baby. I wish I could go back to yesterday and do things differently but I can't. I'm not the same person I was yesterday and I never will be again,' Alice said, slipping back into semi-consciousness.

The staff nurse was crossing the small space towards her.

'I think we need to let her rest for a while now. We'll be moving her on to the ward in the next hour and visiting is from two this afternoon.'

'I–I have to leave for work at one,' Gina said, the enormity of what Alice had just said beginning to sink in. 'Would it be possible to have ten minutes with her before I go? I'm working this evening too so I won't be able to visit again until tomorrow.'

'I'll see what I can do. Go and wait in the relatives' room and I'll call you when she's settled in.'

'Thank you. She knows about the baby, by the way. I didn't tell her,' she added quickly, noting the look of disapproval on the nurse's face.

'Well, she probably realised from the amount of blood there was before she passed out. It's lucky she was found when she was; she was haemorrhaging so badly that if she had gone undiscovered for another hour or so, she may well have bled out.'

Gina was shaking as she made her way back down the corridor to the relatives' room. If I hadn't left Vince at Claridge's when I did, she thought, Alice would have died, but if we had gone to mine after the Ostrich maybe we could have saved her baby. Alice, pregnant; it didn't seem possible. Whenever they had spoken about boyfriends and sex, Alice had been adamant that she wanted to be a virgin when she got married. Had she been lying? Had she already slept with Peter? A thought occurred to her. Maybe she had told him about the baby and that was why he stood her up last Sunday. What an utter scumbag, she thought. I don't know if I can be in close proximity to him without punching him in the face. How could he be so callous? The only thing that puzzled her was Alice repeatedly mentioning Richard. What had he got to do with any of it and why was he so anxious to keep everything secret? And who the hell was Sadie?

CHAPTER 45

'Have a sip of water,' Gina urged, raising the glass to Alice's lips in her semi-seated position. 'Are you feeling a bit better now?'

Alice nodded, studiously avoiding eye contact.

'I've got to go in a minute if I'm going to get to the theatre on time but I wanted to make sure you were settled on the ward. Are you sure you don't want me to call your parents?'

'They mustn't know about this, nobody can. Please promise me you'll keep this secret for me.'

'Of course, I will, if that's what you want. Look, Alice, there's no easy way to say this. Have you been lying to me about how far things went with you and Peter? It's nothing to be ashamed of. You fell head over heels in love with him and you thought he felt the same way. I just can't believe he would dump you when he found out you were having his baby. I could kill him.'

Alice closed her eyes, a tear trickling down her cheek.

'You've got it wrong, Gina. It wasn't Peter's baby.' Alice took a deep breath. 'It-it happened one night when I got very drunk. I didn't even know I'd had sex, let alone fallen pregnant.'

'But you must have known. If you were a virgin you would have been sore after the first time,' she said, remembering her own ghastly introduction to sex. 'There might even have been some blood.'

Alice fiddled with her fingers. 'There was a little blood but I thought it was my period. Honestly, Gina, I had no clue that I'd lost my virginity.'

'I don't mean this to sound bad, and trust me I'm not judging you, given what you know about my private life, but do you know who the father was? What I mean is, were you sober enough to remember who you went home with?'

'I know the father and he knew about the pregnancy, but I can't tell you. He only agreed to help me after I'd given my word that I wouldn't tell anybody anything.'

With dazzling clarity, it all began to fall into place. There had long been rumours about Richard and his tiny manhood, which would explain why Alice had been unaware of having sex with him. What puzzled Gina was why her friend would ever have put herself in a situation, even when drunk, where they would have been alone together.

'When you say, he "helped" you, do you mean what I think you mean?'

'He gave me money and put me in touch with Sadie. I shouldn't have done it, I know that now. My mum and dad would have stood by me. I feel so wicked.'

'Listen to me, Alice, this is really important. There is a massive difference between a miscarriage and an induced miscarriage. I don't know if the hospital has their suspicions but, if they do, they may well contact the police. Everyone knows that backstreet abortions still go on but they are illegal and you could get into a lot of trouble. You must not mention anything about Sadie and what she did. Do you understand?'

'Yes.'

'You'll have to decide on a story and stick to it if you get asked. It might be an idea to say you were drinking gin and it gave you a headache so you took some aspirin, then you felt ill. They've had to pump so much blood into you, I doubt if they would be able to find any trace of whatever this Sadie person gave you, and they were concentrating so hard on stopping you bleeding that they probably didn't run any tests on your blood apart from to ascertain what blood group you are. Don't look so scared, Alice,' she said, reacting to the terrified look on her friend's face, 'they most likely won't question you after what you've been through, but it's better to be prepared.'

'Why are you being so nice to me? I'm disgusting.'

Gina squeezed her friend's hand. 'Don't be silly. You were unlucky to get pregnant the first time you had sex, but it does happen. You're not the first and you won't be the last and, for what it is worth, I think it is better for a baby conceived in those circumstances not to be brought into the world. A child should have two loving parents or it can seriously screw up their life and, believe me, I know that better than most.' Although one loving parent would have been better than none, she thought. 'You are obviously even worse at holding your drink than you thought. You must have been totally out of it if you can't remember any of what happened.'

'I think it was because I hadn't eaten anything. It was the day my grandma was taken to hospital after her suspected heart attack. I don't remember drinking that much though, just a vodka martini and a glass of champagne, but it must have gone straight to my head.'

'Are you sure that's all you had?'

'I think so, but maybe I had more judging by the dreadful hangover I had the following morning. I felt like I'd been trampled by a herd of stampeding cattle.'

Gina checked her watch. It was five past one.

'Look, I've got to go, but I'll come and see you tomorrow afternoon, okay?'

'Okay.'

'And remember. Have a story and stick to it, no matter what.'

'Thanks, Gina. I don't know what I would do without you.'

It wasn't the first time Alice had expressed the sentiment, and Gina wondered, yet again, if Alice was really ready for the tough world of show business, as she hurried outside on to Fulham Palace Road to hail herself a cab.

'Riverside Mansions, Barnes, please,' she said, 'and will you be able to wait for fifteen minutes before taking me into the West End.'

'So long as you're happy to pay for it, miss.'

Happy didn't come in to it. She had to have a quick wash after her exploits with Vince the previous evening but not until she had cleaned her bathroom floor. Thank goodness it's tiled, she thought, using an old towel to clear up the majority of the mess which could be used as evidence. The bath had been running, along with the taxi meter outside, while she quickly mopped the floor, before dunking herself in the tub for the quickest bath she had ever had.

With her skin barely dry, she threw on some fresh bell-bottom jeans and a floral top, grabbed her jacket and headed out to the waiting cab. It was only then that Gina remembered what Alice had said about only having a couple of drinks on the night she had conceived. Could she really have got that drunk on such a tiny quantity of alcohol, empty stomach or not? she wondered. Some of the other girls at the Ostrich Club had occasionally complained about being slipped a Micky Finn when they had gone back to hotel rooms with their clients. Was it possible that Richard had not only forced himself on her friend while she was in no condition to defend herself but had actually caused her condition by drugging her drink?

The more she thought about it, the more she realised it was highly probable. He was known for having a penchant for young blondes, but they wouldn't give him a second glance unless their judgement had been impaired. I'm going to ask around my contacts in other shows, she thought, and if I find out any other dancers have had a similar experience at Richard's hands, he'll bloody pay for what he's done.

CHAPTER 46

'These have lasted really well,' Alice said, leaning over to smell the roses and carnations in the vase of flowers on the table. 'It was a lovely surprise when you brought them into the hospital. I've never had flowers bought for me before. It was such a thoughtful thing to do.'

From the kitchen, Gina replied, 'No problem,' grateful that her back was to Alice as she waited for the toast to pop up. It was not something she would necessarily have thought of doing but when she had arrived home from the Ostrich Club at three thirty in the morning just over a week ago, she had almost fallen over a huge basket of flowers that Alf had put in her living room with a note.

These came for you this morning. I had them in my office for safe keeping, but then I missed you earlier. An admirer?

Gina had screwed up Alf's note, irritated that he was prying into her private life, and had gone to bed, too tired to think who they may have been from. It was the following morning that she had spotted an envelope nestled in among the aromatic blooms. She tore open the envelope:

Dear Gina,

I woke up this morning and you had gone. What a shame as I was hoping you would answer my question. I haven't got a lot to offer at the moment but one day I will and I'd like to share it with you. Will you meet me tonight at Claridge's instead of going to the Ostrich? If you don't show up I'll take it as a sign that you would rather our 'relationship' continue on a professional rather than personal basis, but please give it some thought, Gina. I think I'm falling in love with you.

Vince xx

She had sat staring at the note, running her fingers over the writing, allowing herself to dream of spending the rest of her life with Vince. The note had talked about meeting up the previous evening but surely, he would understand if she explained that she hadn't received the flowers until it was too late. Damn Alf, damn Alice, damn everything, she had railed, ripping the note into tiny confetti-like pieces. If it was meant to be, I would have got them on time. This must be the universe giving me a sign that this is not the right path for me.

It had seemed a shame to waste the beautiful flowers so she had taken them to the hospital to try and cheer up her friend.

'Here we go,' Gina said, handing the thickly buttered

toast to Alice who was now relaxing on the sofa, soaking up a puddle of sunshine that was streaming through the windows.

'Thank you.'

'Are you sure you feel up to coming back to work today?'

'I'm sure. I think it's a bit like falling off a bike. If I don't go back soon, I wouldn't ever be able to face Richard again, or Peter for that matter.'

'He's been asking after you. Peter, I mean. He said something about you needing to read something in tonight's paper. I don't know what he's on about but if you're coming into work you can ask him yourself.'

'Hmmm, maybe. You did tell everyone that I was off because of my tooth, didn't you?'

'I didn't need to. Larry had already spread the word, obviously under guidance from Richard. Talking of whom, what are we going to do about him? He can't just be allowed to get away with what he did to you. He should be locked up and the key thrown away.'

'There's nothing we can do. I can't come forward and accuse him of date rape without the risk of implicating myself in an illegal abortion, and anyway, as you know only too well, I don't want the stigma of being damaged goods following me around. I hate what happened and I hate that I felt so desperate and alone that I was persuaded by that vile bastard to do what I did. I can't undo any of that, but I can try and put it behind me.'

'I wish you had spoken to me before you went to Richard. If I'd known he raped you, I would have marched you straight down to the police station.'

'But I would still have had people pointing and staring

and I might not have been believed. Rape is very difficult to prove. Richard had me believing that I had instigated the sexual behaviour so he would probably have been able to convince others of it too. They would all have asked the same question. Why would I go to a man's hotel room unless I expected something of this nature to happen?'

'Why did you?'

'Because I'm stupid and gullible and naïve. I truly thought he was just being kind because my parents had been unable to come and see me in the show.'

'Richard and kind in the same sentence. I don't think so.'

'I know that now. Richard only cares about himself. It's been a harsh lesson to learn, but I've done a lot of thinking and growing up in the past week or so. There must be a bit of him that was hoping I would simply walk away from the show. Well, I'm not going to give him that satisfaction,' Alice said, lifting her chin in the same defiant manner that Gina had witnessed on the day of the first audition.

'I'm glad you're feeling stronger now because there is something I think you need to know about that night at the Dorchester.'

'What could you possibly know about that night? You weren't there.'

'No I wasn't, but what I've discovered may change your mind about letting Richard get away with what he did. The whole "two drinks and you were passing out drunk" thing has been bothering me. We've been on a night out together where you drank much more and you weren't passing out. At first I wondered if maybe you had drunk more than that but had blocked the whole episode out of your mind, including the rape, because you felt guilty. But something was niggling at the back of my mind; something a couple of the girls at the Ostrich had told me about. Have you ever heard of Rohypnol?'

Alice shook her head.

'It's a fairly new drug and it has quickly earned the nickname "the date rape" drug. Disreputable men can slip it into a girl's drink and, depending on how much they use, can render that girl totally relaxed so that she will permit them to do exactly as they please while still being responsive to a degree. A larger amount and the victim is almost comatose. I believe that's what happened to you. I don't think Richard meant to knock you out completely but, because of your lack of food that day, the drug had a stronger effect than he intended.'

'Are you suggesting that was his plan all along, to lure me into a private room purely for the intention of having sex with me?' Alice said, shock evident in her voice.

'That's exactly what I'm saying, and it's why I think we need to do something about it. I don't know for sure how many other girls he has abused in this way but I've asked around and it would seem you are not the only one. It could have killed you, Alice, as could the abortion, and it may well kill someone in the future if we don't stop him. You don't want that on your conscience, do you?'

Alice was trying to get to grips with the information she had just received. She had been racked with guilt since the discovery that she was pregnant, believing herself to be totally responsible but, if it was true that she had been Richard's unwitting victim, it changed things. She still felt stupid for putting herself in the position in the first place but it had taken the edge off the guilt.

'Please don't hate me for saying this, and of course I don't want anyone else to fall prey to him, but I don't see what we can do to stop him. Nothing has changed regarding going to the police, in fact, if I tried to report the rape now I would be even less likely to be believed with no physical evidence. I don't see what we could do.'

'There will be something, I just need to think about it. I can't bear the idea of that arrogant prick thinking he has got away with it.'

Alice's defiant mood from earlier in the day was beginning to waver as she and Gina pushed open the stage door.

'Look who's here, Fred,' Gina said.

'Alice, we've missed you. Are you all better now?'

'Yes thanks, Fred. I'm just hoping I can remember all the routines. It's a good job I live with Gina, she's been taking me through the steps for the past couple of days. The downstairs neighbours must have thought we were having a party.'

'That sounds like a good idea.'

'What?'

'We should have a party to celebrate you being back with us. Let's hope it's for good this time.'

'It is, but I don't want any fuss. I just want to settle into the last three months of my contract with no dramas,' she said, following Gina up the stone stairs to the dressing rooms.

'Surprise!' Gina said, throwing open the door to the dancers' dressing room to reveal colourful balloons tied to the back of her chair and a huge bouquet of flowers, wrapped in cellophane propped up against the mirror in her place next to Gina's.

All the girls clamoured around her in welcome and even Hannah was magnanimous when she said, 'We all chipped in for the flowers. You've been missed; the show is better with you in it.'

'Thanks, Hannah, I'm touched.'

'There's been a rumour circulating that you nearly bled to death. Was it a quack dentist you went to? You'd better give us his name so we can all avoid him.'

All the girls nodded in agreement.

'It wasn't that bad really, you know how these things get exaggerated,' Alice said, looking appealingly at Gina for her to change the subject.

'Alice, it's good to see you back.'

Twelve pairs of eyes turned towards the door. Alice's heart skipped a beat.

'Could you spare a minute?'

'J–just a minute then. I don't want to be late for curtain up on my first night back.'

Alice closed the door behind her.

'You're looking well.'

'Thank you, so are you,' she said, her heart pounding in her chest and a blush rising up her neck.

'I'm not going to ask why you stood me up at the Barley Mow. You must have had your reasons and I think in part it was to do with Tammy. When you get a minute, read the bottom of page 27,' he said, thrusting a copy of the *Evening News* at her. 'It might not make any difference to the way you feel about me, but I think it's important for you to know the truth.'

Alice took the newspaper without saying a word. She didn't know what to say. She wanted to apologise for not turning up for their date but what excuse could she give? It was too soon to even think about her feelings for Peter, in fact, too soon to contemplate any kind of relationship with a man.

'I'll let you get ready. Don't be a stranger, Alice.'

CHAPTER 47

The warmth and brightness of the footlights and the knowledge that on the other side of them were hundreds of people, nestled in plush red velvet seats and totally enraptured by the love story that was unfolding on the stage before them, gave Alice a sensation of coming home. This is what it's all about, she thought, as she performed the intricate steps with ease; this is why I came to London. I'm being given a second chance, and I won't screw it up this time. I'll get through the remaining term of my contract and look out for other auditions that will take me away from the shadow Richard has cast over my life. With each spin or kick or lunge, the pain that clutched at her heart relaxed its grip, each droplet of sweat purged her soul. By the end of the first half, it felt as though she had never been away from *Theatreland*.

The curtain came down, and the girls broke from the frieze of their final positions giggling and chatting on their way back to the dressing room for the interval break.

As Alice approached the wings, Richard stepped out in front of her. 'Alice, I'd like a moment after the show, please.'

Frantically, she cast her eyes around for Gina who had been on the other side of the stage at the end of the first half, but she had gone on ahead.

'Erm…' she faltered.

'It's not a request. We need to talk about the amount of time you've had off in contravention of your contract.'

Had she heard him correctly? Was he seriously going to try and penalise her for being off as a direct consequence of his perversion?

'Yes, Richard,' she mumbled, rushing past him.

She ran up the stairs, almost blinded with panic, and, instead of going to the dancers' dressing room, she headed for the toilets and locked herself in a cubicle. Sitting on the closed toilet seat, she hugged her knees tightly to her chest, rocking backwards and forwards. I can't do it, she thought, I can't face him alone. What am I going to do? She heard the outer door open.

'Alice, are you in here?'

It was Gina. She unlocked the door to her cubicle.

'What's wrong? You look like you've seen a ghost.'

'Richard wants to see me after the show to talk about the amount of sick leave I've had.'

'You're joking! He's got a bloody nerve. Well, you're not going anywhere near that creep on your own. I'll come with you, and he can like it or lump it.'

'Would you? Would you really do that for me? But what about the Ostrich Club? Won't you get in trouble with Franco if you're late?'

'I can handle him much better than you can handle Richard. Now come on, we need to get changed for the second half opening.'

The pure joy of being back on stage, doing what she loved, had evaporated by the time Alice tapped on Richard's office door at the end of the performance.

'Come in.'

She pushed open the door and entered with Gina close behind her. A flicker of annoyance crossed Richard's face.

'I don't remember asking to see you, Gina. Haven't you got somewhere you need to be? You're usually out of here like a greyhound out of the traps in Walthamstow.'

'I'm just keeping an eye on Alice,' she replied, standing her ground, 'making sure she's fully recovered from her ordeal.'

The two locked eyes momentarily before Richard dropped his back down to the papers on his desk.

'I wouldn't normally discuss contractual matters in front of a third party, other than an agent of course, but seeing as you both have the same terms and conditions I will make an exception on this one occasion,' he added pointedly. 'You are permitted a week of compassionate leave and two weeks of sick leave within your six-month contract. To give you another week or so to recover after the death of your grandmother, the extra days were entered as sick leave. Obviously, I had no idea that you were then going to have this problem with your tooth,' he said, scrutinising Gina's face as he spoke. 'I could dock your wages, or even dismiss you under the terms of your contract, but I am not a heartless man. I realise this has been an incredibly difficult time for you, so I have decided to allow you those extra days on full pay.'

Alice had been concentrating on her feet throughout his speech.

'Thank you,' she said quietly, without raising her gaze.

'However, there will be no further absences before the end of your contract, or it will result in serious consequences, potentially dismissal. I hope I've made myself clear?'

'Yes, Richard.'

'And Alice, next time I ask to see you in my office, I will expect it to be just you.'

'Unless, of course, Alice has appointed me as her agent,' Gina said pleasantly. 'I've been thinking of my next move once my dancing days are over. Maybe I'll become an agent and Alice can be my first artiste.'

A nerve next to Richard's mouth twitched.

'Be careful, Gina. I know you are only looking out for your friend, but you wouldn't want to get on the wrong side of me.'

'Is that a threat, Richard?'

'Let's say a warning. It would serve you well to remember that no one is indispensable. Now, if you'll excuse me, I have work to do.'

Once safely outside of the door, Gina put her arm around Alice.

'Are you okay? At least he didn't fire you.'

'But now he's got it in for you as well as me.'

'He doesn't scare me with his bully-boy tactics. Franco makes him look like a boy scout. Speaking of who, I need to dash. Let's get out of here. If we grab a cab, you can drop me at Swallow Street on your way back to Barnes.'

CHAPTER 48

'We should go out for lunch tomorrow to celebrate your first week back in the show,' Gina said, carefully reapplying one of her spider-like false eyelashes with a pair of tweezers before pressing on the inner and outer corners of her eyelid to help the glue adhere.

'I'd love that,' Alice replied, loading her brush with powder and dusting it liberally over her face, some spilling on to the peach plastic make-up cape that she was wearing to protect her costume. 'Maybe we could find a pub with live music.'

'Good idea. I think there's one near where you used to live in West Kensington, isn't there?'

'Yes, of course, on the North End Road. They have loads of bands on in the evenings, doing showcases and stuff, but I'm not sure about Sunday lunch.'

'Peter would probably know. Are you two speaking again now?'

Alice thought about the four-line paragraph she had read in the *Evening News* on her taxi journey home after dropping Gina at the Ostrich on Monday night.

I wish to retract the statement I made to this newspaper suggesting that Peter Flint and I were in a relationship. We are not dating, nor ever have, and I apologise to all concerned for any misunderstanding caused.

She had felt a flutter of excitement that Peter would go to such lengths as to have the newspaper print a retraction to prove to her that he and Tammy had never been an item.

'Yes, we're speaking, but nothing more just yet. I asked him to give me a bit of space to come to terms with everything, and he just said to take as long as I need. He is so nice, not your average pop star, no matter what you think,' she said, catching Gina's sceptical look in the reflection of her make-up mirror framed with light bulbs.

'Let me ask him about the live music at the pub, or he might get the wrong idea and think you're asking him out.'

'Shut up,' Alice said, elbowing her friend.

'Oi, watch it, you nearly had my eye out with my tweezers.'

'Sorry. Is it too far to walk there from Barnes? I still haven't properly got my bearings.'

'Probably, and it wouldn't be much fun in this flipping rain. We'd get drenched.'

'They were just saying on the radio while you were in the loo that it's the tail end of Hurricane Bertha. Trust me to choose today to wear my gold sandals into work. It was sunny when we left home this morning. They'll get ruined if it doesn't let up.'

'It is October, hardly sandals season. Haven't you got

any boots?'

'Yes, but I didn't think it was cold enough to wear them. It's funny to think that a weather event on the other side of the world can affect us here. It's blowing a gale too. Do you think we'll get the eye of the hurricane?'

'Is that where it goes all still and quiet before the storm starts up again?'

'Yep.'

'Maybe I'll ask Peter about that too cos I sure as hell don't know. School wasn't my thing.'

'As in, you weren't very clever, or you didn't go?'

'A bit of both, really,' Gina said, good-naturedly.

'I wasn't very smart at school either. Mary's the brains in our family.'

'Have you spoken to them since, well, you know?'

'I rang this morning before you got up. It's so cool having a phone in my room. I can have a conversation without the pips interrupting every few minutes and without nosy neighbours listening in.'

'How do you know I wasn't holding a glass up against our dividing wall?'

'Because I could hear you snoring!'

'You are such a fibber. I don't snore.'

'No comment.'

'I'm not staying here to be insulted' Gina said, scraping her chair backwards on the dressing room floor. 'I'll go and ask Peter about the pub, and you'd better hurry up, it's five minutes to curtain up, and you haven't done your lippy yet. All the others are already down there.'

'Coming,' Alice said, whipping her make-up cape off with one hand and applying her lipstick with the other. She stood back and examined her reflection in the mirror. It's hard to believe that this time two weeks ago, I was lying in a hospital bed, lucky to be alive, she thought, something she hadn't shared with her family when she had rung them earlier in the day. Alice wasn't a fan of keeping secrets, but some things were better left unsaid. With Gina's help, she had started to come to terms with terminating her unwanted pregnancy on the surface, but the scars were deep, and Alice doubted that they would ever completely heal.

CHAPTER 49

'Your mum doesn't mean to be unkind,' Richard said, twiddling the grey telephone cord and swinging around in his chair to gaze out of the window behind his desk at people huddling together in doorways, sheltering from the torrential downpour. 'She's had a lot on her plate lately, and she's just trying to protect you.'

'But Daddy, nearly all the other girls in my French set are going, and even my teacher thinks it would be a good opportunity for me to practise speaking the language. He said that if I'm going to study it for A level, I need to improve my vocabulary and conversation and that exchange visits are the best way of doing it. Please Daddy, will you talk to her?'

'We'll discuss it over Sunday lunch when we're all sat down together. She is just terrified of something happening to you while you're away. I don't think she could cope with any more tragedy after losing your nana. We're all she's got now, princess. She's just trying to keep you safe.'

'But I will be safe,' Miriam insisted. 'The school vets all the exchange homes and it would be such fun to have a

French girl come and stay in our house in return. It's not like we haven't got plenty of room and it would be like having a sister for a little while. You know how lonely I get on my own all the time.'

Richard could imagine his daughter's pretty features forming into a sulky pout. 'Miriam, you know that's not true. You're always having friends round for sleepovers,' he said, allowing his mind to wander, picturing Stephanie, one of his daughter's more curvaceous friends. Only last month she had come into the kitchen of his home when he had been making himself a cup of coffee, wearing nothing but a pair of baby-doll pyjamas. She had leant across him, supposedly reaching for a glass from the cupboard, and in the process brushed her pert young breast against his arm. 'I've always dreamed of being in a West End show,' she had told him. 'I go to dancing and singing lessons, and my teacher says I'm very good. Maybe I could audition for you privately,' she had added provocatively. He had needed to stay facing the work surface until she had left the room to hide his erection.

'Daddy, are you listening?' his daughter demanded, just as Richard's attention was drawn to a noise outside his office door.

'What? Oh yes,' he said, swinging round to face the door as a flash of pink appeared from under it. 'What the hell? Listen, sweetie, I've got to go, the second half is about to start, and someone is at the door. We'll see if we can talk Mum around tomorrow, I promise. Bye darling,' he said, returning the phone to its cradle and crossing his office to pick up what he could now see was a sheet of pink paper. Somewhere, in the back of his mind, he remembered seeing that same pink note paper, but he couldn't quite place it. He wrenched open the door and looked up and down the corridor, but no one was there. Closing it again, he unfolded the square of paper. On it, in letters that had painstakingly been cut out of a newspaper, was a message that sent shivers down his spine:

YOU DISGUSTING PERVERT. DID YOU REALLY BELIEVE YOU COULD GET AWAY WITH IT? YOU ARE GOING TO HAVE TO PAY FOR YOUR DEPRAVITY AND MY SILENCE. I WANT £10,000 IN USED BANK NOTES – YOU HAVE UNTIL MONDAY TO GET THE MONEY

Richard swallowed hard, trying to control his fury. He turned the paper over for further instructions, but the back of the sheet was blank. His hands shook with anger as he reread the words that swum across the page. He couldn't believe his eyes. What the hell does that little bitch think she's playing at? he thought, screwing the note up into a tight ball and throwing it into his bin. She can't seriously think she can blackmail me and get away with it. Moments later, he retrieved the note and smoothed it out with the palm of his hand. Not smart, Richard, he thought, what if the cleaner were to find it? There's no smoke without fire, and there had been occasional rumours previously linking him with naïve, young dancers.

What had changed since Monday? he wondered. Alice had seemingly been too afraid to come to his office unaccompanied so why did she now feel bold enough to blackmail him? Unless this has all been an act, he thought. Maybe she's not the little innocent she has been portraying. God knows, she showed how good an actress she is when she stood in for Tammy in the show. All I had was her word that she was a virgin before the night at the Dorchester. There was no proof at all that I was the father of her unborn child.

The more he thought about it, the more enraged Richard became. You bloody fool, you've been played by a twenty-year-old, he thought, slamming his fist down hard on the table. Well, she's not going to get away with it. She won't get another penny out of me. Holding the note by its corner over his heavy glass ashtray, he flicked open his cigarette lighter and watched as the flame took hold, swallowing up the threatening words. He let go of the sheet and tiny pieces of ash floated on to the rich mahogany of his desk like a scattering of dandruff on the shoulders of a dark suit.

The knock at the door startled him.

'One minute,' he said, hastily removing the ashtray with the smouldering remnants of the note and placing it on the floor at the side of his chair. 'Come in. Ah, Peter, what can I do for you?'

'I was just wondering if you'd heard any more about transferring to Broadway and if you'd given any further thought to my suggestion of Alice being my Melanie.'

Under the desk, Richard's hands formed fists, his perfectly manicured nails digging into the pudgy white flesh of his palms. I wonder if he would be quite so keen on his darling Alice if he knew what a manipulative little bitch she is, he thought. The whole 'falling in love with Peter' thing was probably an act to further her career.

'While I appreciate you are trying to help the girl, and you do of course have your own reasons for that, you need to accept that I am the one making the decisions around here. I'm not saying she wasn't good in the previews, but headlining on Broadway is quite a different matter. To be honest, I'm not sure she could handle it.'

'Really? You seemed keen last time I mentioned it.'

'Yes, well, your suggestion caught me by surprise. Now I've had time to think about it, I'm not sure Miss Abbott can be trusted with something so big.' In fact, he thought, she can't be trusted at all. 'This is her first West End show,' and her last, if I have anything to do with it, he added to himself. 'She needs to prove herself here first before we suggest to the big money men in New York that they should take a chance on a complete unknown.'

'I'm sorry to hear you feel that way, Richard. I'm not sure I would be interested in going if you don't at least give Alice a chance to impress the Americans.'

'Who the hell do think you are? You're a jumped-up former pop star to whom I've given a massive break when no one else would give you the time of day, and you stand there threatening that you won't go to New York unless your little tart goes with you too. Well, I've got news for you. You're not the only guy who can play this role, and if you're not interested in going to Broadway, there'll be a queue around the block of male singers who are. I suggest you concentrate on the job you're being paid to do here, which, according to my watch, means you should be on stage for curtain up in two minutes.'

Peter turned on his heel and marched out of the room. Bollocks! Richard feared that he had gone too far this time. The deal with the Americans was on the proviso that

Peter Flint would be the star in the Broadway production. If that stupid bitch has jeopardised the possibility of the show transferring, I'll bloody kill her, he thought.

CHAPTER 50

'Night, Fred,' Alice said, 'have a nice weekend.'

'Last one out again, Alice? I don't know what you find to do up there.'

'I'm not that slow really,' she said, pushing down on the bar to open the stage door, 'it's just that all the others have got dates and parties and stuff to rush off to.'

'Well, I suppose it's better if you take it easy for a couple of weeks after what you've been through. Plenty of time for all that socialising when you're fully recovered. At least the rain has stopped now. See you Monday.'

'Bright and early for understudy rehearsal,' she said, as the heavy door swung closed behind her, extinguishing the triangle of yellow light that had spilled on to the wet pavement. A hand landed on her shoulder. Assuming it was a fan wanting an autograph, she turned, smiling, an apology ready on her lips. Her smile froze.

'I hope I didn't startle you, Alice? You seemed uncomfortable at the prospect of being alone with me in my office on Monday when all I wanted was a chat about your career. I thought maybe you would feel more relaxed with lots of people around us. Have you ever been to the

White Elephant on the River?' Richard said, his tone light and conversational.

'N-no. But I can't come. I'm on my way to meet some of the girls in the pub.'

'Really? That's not what you told Fred a few moments ago, is it? You must be lying to one of us, and I have a strong suspicion it may be me,' he said, enjoying the look of discomfort on her face. 'That bag looks heavy. Here, let me take it, and we can walk and talk.'

'I'm sorry, I don't know why I said that. It's just that I was planning on going straight home. My first week back seems to have taken it out of me,' Alice said, forced to fall into step alongside him now that he had her bag with her purse in it slung over his shoulder.

'You don't need to lie to me, Alice. I'm your friend, remember? The one that helped you when you got yourself in trouble. Our little secret, eh? I'm assuming you kept your promise not to tell anyone?'

'Of course,' she lied. 'It's something I'm ashamed of. I want to put the whole episode behind me so what would I gain by gossiping about it?'

'That's what I thought, but I wondered if maybe you had confided in your friend, Gina? You two seem to be joined at the hip most of the time, particularly since you moved in with her.'

'It's only temporary. Gina has to move out of her flat soon, but she's letting me stay there until I can find something else.'

'So, you haven't mentioned anything to her about Sadie and... the rest of it.'

'No, I already told you.'

'Good. I just wanted to be sure that you have kept your

part of the bargain before we start talking about New York.'

A black Mercedes pulled into the kerb at the side of them.

'Ahh, here's Max with the car. He can drive us down to Pimlico and, when you've had enough, he can take you home,' he said, opening the door for Alice to get it in.

She hesitated. Sensing her reluctance, Richard got into the car with her bag giving her no option other than to climb in after him.

'You'll like The White Elephant on the River. It's usually full of television and theatre people, movie stars and even royalty, particularly on a Saturday night. You look very pretty tonight; perhaps you'll even attract the attention of someone rich and famous.'

'I'm not looking for a boyfriend.'

'No, I suppose not while Peter is still showing an interest in you. It won't last, though, Alice. He has a bad-boy reputation for a reason. All these young pop stars have one thing on their minds. Bed as many girls as they can in their short-lived careers before they disappear into the obscurity of being a used-car salesman. You'd be better off trying to hook someone with better long-term prospects, even if they aren't as young and handsome.'

'I'm not sure what you're getting at, Richard. Are you suggesting that I only like Peter because he's famous?'

'Isn't that part of the attraction?'

'Maybe I was a bit star-struck at first, but he's nothing like the image the newspapers have painted of him. He even had the *Evening News* print a retraction from Tammy about the two of them being in a relationship because he thought it had upset me.'

Did he now? thought Richard, I must have missed that. He's obviously even more smitten with this girl than I realised, which doesn't bode well for us taking the show to New York without her.

'You know, Richard, I appreciate you offering to take me to this nightspot, but I won't be very good company tonight. I'm shattered, and I'd much rather go home, if it's all the same to you.'

'I'm not going to force you to do anything against your will, Alice, but I did want to have a word with you in private about *Theatreland* transferring to Broadway. The discussions are quite advanced now, and I'm going to have to start giving the New York co-producer an idea of personnel and costs. It's not the sort of thing I want to discuss in front of my staff,' he said, catching Max's eye in the rear-view mirror. 'How about we take a little stroll along the Embankment and I'll get my driver to pick us up in half an hour at Albert Bridge? We can leave your bag in the car so that neither of us has to carry it. How does that sound?'

Richard noticed Alice glance first at the illuminated pathway next to the Thames, with its scattering of couples walking hand in hand, and then at her wristwatch.

'Is New York something you might be interested in?'

'Yes, of course, who wouldn't be?'

'That's settled then. Max, pull over would you and go and get yourself a coffee. Pick us up on the Battersea Park side of Albert Bridge in thirty minutes.'

'Yes, Mr Sherwood.'

The evening was cool rather than cold, with a blanket of clouds that threatened more rain to come preventing the temperature from falling out of double figures. Alice pulled her denim jacket closed and folded her arms across her body as the Mercedes filtered back into the traffic.

'Are you cold? Would you like my jacket?'

'No. I'll be fine once we start walking.'

'Do you know this part of London?'

'Not really. I was living in West Kensington when we were rehearsing, and then Larry suggested I move in with Gina, in Barnes, after my grandma died. I like Larry.'

She sounds nervous, Richard thought, but maybe she's still putting on an act.

'I like Larry too, although we nearly came to blows over you. He was adamant he wanted you in his chorus line, and foolishly I gave in to him. If I'm honest, Alice, I've regretted it ever since.'

'Oh.'

'Yes. You've been nothing but a thorn in my side. There is no denying you have an incredible talent as a dancer and singer, but I'm now wondering if your acting ability outshines them both.'

'I don't follow.'

'Well, before we start talking about Broadway, I think we need to discuss the letter.'

'Letter?'

'Yes. Don't sound so surprised. The letter you pushed under my office door earlier this evening.'

'I'm sorry, but I don't know what you're talking about.'

'There you go again. You have to stop lying to me, Alice, or we'll never be able to trust each other.'

'Honestly, I have no idea what you're talking about.'

'Magnificent, isn't it?' Richard had stopped and was gazing across the murky water of the River Thames at the outline of Battersea power station. 'It's funny how something that was once considered so ugly is now thought of as a thing of beauty. They're considering giving it Grade II listed status. It works in reverse too.'

'I'm sorry, but you're confusing me. Do you mean the power station works in reverse? I don't understand how they generate power, so it means nothing to me.'

'You're very good. Come on, let's cross Chelsea Bridge for a closer look at the old dinosaur. They've already closed part of it down, and there are rumours that it won't be long before it ceases producing electricity altogether. But that's not what I'm referring too. You're very pretty, Alice, but you have an ugly side.'

'If you're talking about me getting rid of the baby, I've regretted it every day since and I think I will for the rest of my life. I should have put more faith in my parents. They would have stood by me; I know that now.'

'So, is that what prompted the letter? Your guilty feelings?'

'I don't know what letter you're talking about.'

'Alice, Alice, you're disappointing me. We both know which letter I'm talking about. When I saw the pink paper, it stirred a memory, but I couldn't quite pinpoint it at first. Then I remembered. It was the night you played Melanie in the first preview, and I bought you those beautiful flowers. You remember those don't you, Alice? You were a little upset I think that they weren't from Peter. But that's all water under the bridge now. Did you see what I did there, Alice?' He laughed a humourless laugh. 'We're crossing the bridge, and there's water under it.'

'Was that a spot of rain?' Alice's voice was high-pitched, her nervousness evident. 'Maybe we should just flag a cab to take us to Albert Bridge to meet up with your driver. If it rains like it did earlier, we'll get soaked.'

'Very possibly, but Max won't be there yet. My wallet is in my coat, and I'm assuming your purse is in your bag, and they are both in the back of the Mercedes, so we have no money to pay. Let's shelter under the bridge and hope it eases off,' he said, taking a firm grasp of her arm and guiding her towards some stone steps leading to the riverbank.

'I don't know. It looks dark down there.'

Richard could hear the fear in her voice. Good, he thought, she needs to be afraid of me, or she'll try it again.

'The path in front of the park is well lit. Once we've passed under the bridge, it will be fine,' he said, keeping light pressure on the small of her back to propel her forward.

The drops of rain were falling faster as they reached the bottom of the steps and ducked under the arch of the bridge.

'Just in time,' Richard said, as the heavens opened and the rain bounced up from the path and the surface of the water that swirled and sucked against the riverbank a couple of feet away from where they were sheltering. 'Now, where were we in our little chat? Ahh yes. The pink paper. I remember seeing the same paper sticking out of the corner of your bag when you came through to the foyer to meet the press. That's how I know it was you. You're not as smart as you think. You went to the trouble of cutting the letters and words out of the newspaper, but you glued them on to a distinctive paper like that. Amateurish mistake.'

Alice had her back against the brickwork of the arch with Richard's hands resting lightly on her shoulders.

He watched as her forehead furrowed. The bitch is still pretending she doesn't know what I'm talking about, he thought.

'You knew I couldn't go to the police. I can't risk them opening an investigation into your rape allegation, even though it would be your word against mine. Mud sticks and I'm damned if I'm going to let a little tart like you, who can't hold her drink, ruin the biggest chance of success I've ever had. I burnt your note. There's no evidence to suggest a motive if anything were to happen to you. I'm not going to give you any more money, Alice, not ten thousand pounds, not ten pounds, nothing. I need to know that you understand that and that you won't try to pull a stunt like this again.'

With a sudden twist of her body, Alice attempted to duck out of Richard's grasp, but he grabbed her arm and spun her round to face him, her back to the river.

'Not so fast. Do you promise me you will never attempt to blackmail me again?'

'I wasn't drunk,' she shrieked, the sound of her voice drowned out against the howl of the wind and the distant rumble of the cars on the bridge overhead. 'You drugged me before you raped me. I hope you rot in hell!'

In that split second, he knew it was too dangerous to let Alice Abbott live. He would never be free of the fear that she may reveal what he had done to her that night at the Dorchester. He took a step forward, forcing her to take a step back. Her foot connected with the slimy mud of the riverbank and she began to fall backwards into the swirling water. He could have saved her in that last instant, when he saw the desperation in her eyes, but instead he gave her a little push to help her on her way.

CHAPTER 51

Alice was falling, arms flailing, but could do nothing to prevent herself from tumbling into the churning water of the Thames. Richard's light grip on her shoulders had been replaced by firm pressure forcing her backwards, her feet losing traction on the slimy mud of the riverbank. Everything felt like it was in slow motion. She seemed momentarily suspended in the air, an observer, as Richard's static figure moved away from her, a look of pure hatred on his face. She opened her mouth to scream, but no sound came. As her body made contact with the surface, displacing the water with a huge splash, the mental shock of him purposely pushing her was replaced by physical shock as the temperature of the water registered against her skin. Water rushed back in to envelop her, filling her open mouth, closing above her as though she were taking her final curtain call.

Down and down she plunged, images of her family filling her mind, her brain unable to communicate to her limbs that they needed to move if she were to try and save herself. As the momentum slowed, Alice knew she had to get back to the surface to take a breath if she was to have any chance of survival. With an almighty effort, she drew her legs in towards her body, pulled her hands above her head into a diving position then kicked her feet and dragged her arms down, forcing her body upwards.

Moments later, Alice broke the surface, coughing and spluttering, gasping for air. As she took huge gulps, trying to fill her lungs, she could feel the tug of an undercurrent on her feet. If I'm going to make it, she thought, I need to be able to swim as unencumbered as possible. Reaching towards her feet, she unfastened the buckles of her sandals and kicked them off, then turned her attention to trying to remove her denim jacket. She grasped the cuff and began to pull it down over her hand, treading water to stay afloat in the choppy waves whipped up by the wind. Writhing and twisting her body, she eventually pulled her arm free and turned in the water to make it easier to drag the other sleeve off. She was now facing the bridge and, through the lashing rain, Alice thought she could see people peering over the edge and pointing in her direction. She wriggled free of the sodden fabric and with a huge effort raised it up in the air to attract attention. It slapped down against the surface, but before she could raise it again, it was tugged out of her grasp by the current and disappeared.

'Help!' she screamed. 'Somebody help me!'

The same swirling eddy that had seconds before claimed the jacket was now coiling around Alice, sucking at her feet. She took a huge breath, feeling the air expanding her ribcage and let herself be pulled under knowing it was useless to fight against it. My only chance is to relax and conserve energy until I reach the bottom of the vortex and then to swim under water for as long as I can hold my breath, she thought, as she spiralled down.

CHAPTER 52

'Come on, sleepy head,' Gina said, pushing the door of Alice's bedroom open, 'I'm the one that was out working until the wee small hours. By the way, you forgot to leave the lamp on for me. I collided with the corner of the sofa. It's a good job I was wearing my boots and not your strappy sandals, or I could have done myself a mischief,' she added, drawing the curtains to allow the daylight in.

She stopped abruptly. Alice wasn't in her bed, and it didn't look like it had been slept in. A smile spread across Gina's face. When she had approached Peter the previous evening to ask him if he knew if the pub on the North End Road had live music on a Sunday lunchtime, he had predictably asked why. 'Would you mind if I join you two, just for a drink,' he had asked, 'it's driving me crazy not being able to see Alice outside of work.' Gina hadn't mentioned it to Alice; she had wanted it to be a surprise. I guess he was more desperate to see her than he let on, Gina thought. He must have waited for her at the theatre after I left and one thing led to another.

Although she still had her doubts about the sincerity

of his feelings towards Alice, there was no doubt that he had done everything he could to dispel the rumours about being in a relationship with Tammy. Maybe it's what Alice needs after what Richard put her through, Gina mused, to feel that someone loves her, even if it doesn't lead to the fairy-tale ending that she's hoping for.

Gina hummed happily to herself as she watched her eggs roll around in the boiling water like barrels of ale in a turbulent sea after a shipwreck. The toast popped up, and she spread it thinly with butter before cutting it into soldiers and lining them up on the side of her plate as though they were on parade. The timer signalled that the eggs were ready and she took great delight in bashing the top of the first one with the back of her spoon before easing the top off to reveal the solid white and runny golden yolk. Just how I like them, she thought, carrying her plate over to the table near the window; perfect eggs on a perfect day. The wind and drenching rain from the previous evening had cleared to reveal blue skies with fluffy white clouds scudding across, and the sun sparkled on the river like diamonds. Maybe I will walk to the pub to meet Alice and Peter as it's such a lovely day. She glanced at the clock on the mantelpiece. It was quarter past eleven. I'll have to get my skates on though if I'm going to have a bath and still be on time.

Half an hour later, dressed in her bell-bottom jeans with inserts of floral fabric and a sloppy ribbed sweater, Gina bounded down the front steps of Riverside Mansions after bidding a cheery 'Good Morning' to Alf. She had had an unusually early finish for a Saturday night. The Ostrich had been virtually empty, which Franco put down to the torrential rain, so they had all been allowed to leave at 2 a.m. Not much good for my bank balance, she thought, but hopefully that won't matter after tomorrow if all goes to plan.

She was only ten minutes late arriving at The Nashville. The place was heaving, with people spilling out on to the pavement much to the annoyance of passers-by. She pushed her way into the crowded interior and moved towards the bar which was queuing three deep, her eyes constantly scanning for Alice's distinctive long blonde hair. The band hadn't begun playing, but the noise was already deafening with people shouting to each other, so it was a wonder she heard her name being called. Her eyes followed the direction it seemed to come from, and there was Peter at the end of the bar, waving to her.

'Excuse me, excuse me,' she said, pushing her way through the mass of people to get to Peter. 'Jeez, it's packed in here. Has Alice gone to the loo? That's brave of her; she's not a big fan of crowds in enclosed spaces. You spoiled my surprise, but I guess you just couldn't wait until today to see her.' Seeing Peter's puzzled look, she continued, 'I take it she did stay at yours last night?'

'No. I haven't seen Alice since the curtain fell last night. I rushed out of the theatre to avoid her as I didn't want to give the game away about today. You two were supposed to be coming here together.'

Time seemed to stand still, the deafening din fading into the background in Gina's head to be replaced by the thunderous beating of her heart. Something was wrong, she just knew it. Why didn't Alice come home last night and where the hell was she now?

'We need to get out of here, Peter,' she shouted, pulling at his arm.

The two of them elbowed their way through the throng, oblivious to the angry looks and comments from fellow customers whose arms they jostled, causing them to spill their drinks on the already stained carpet. Once outside, Gina dragged Peter away from the pub and the main road and down a side street.

'What's going on, Gina? Where's Alice?'

'I don't know. She wasn't in her room when I went to wake her this morning, and her bed looked like it hadn't been slept in.'

'So, you think she may not have been home?'

Gina nodded. Her mind was racing. Where could Alice have stayed? She knew so few people in London and none that she was particularly friendly with apart from herself and Peter. A thought occurred to her. Surely Richard wouldn't have been so stupid as to try anything on with her again? She gasped. 'The note.'

'What note? What are you talking about? Tell me, Gina,' Peter said, taking hold of her shoulders and shaking her slightly.

If Richard thought the blackmail note was from Alice, he could have waited for her after the show to confront her about it. But he's weak, Gina thought. He might be a bully, but he wouldn't dare do anything to hurt her, more for fear of being found out.

She recovered from her slip of the tongue. 'There was a note on the hall table,' she lied. 'I noticed it this morning as I was leaving but I was already running late, and I just assumed it was from Alf. I'm sorry I worried you. It's just me being paranoid. She probably decided to stay over with her ballet dancer friend. It's around here somewhere, but annoyingly I don't know the address. Maybe they stayed up late talking, and she's overslept. Yes, that's more than likely what has happened,' she said, trying to convince herself and Peter that it was a possibility.

'So, should we go back to the pub and wait for her?'

'I guess, for a while. Sorry, Peter, I didn't mean to be so dramatic it's just that, after all she's been through since she arrived in London, I look out for her like I would a kid sister.'

'I know what you mean. She's a real innocent. I think that's one of the reasons I'm so attracted to her. It's hard to believe in this day and age that anyone can have got to twenty totally unscathed by the world around them.'

Little did Peter know what a baptism of fire Alice had endured in London, Gina thought.

'You're right, we should go back to the pub, she may even have shown up by now,' Gina said.

'And if she is there, we can give her a telling off for being so late.'

Please be there, Gina thought, scurrying along to keep up with Peter's long stride, unable to shake off an impending sense of doom.

By 2 pm, when Alice was still a no show, Gina made her excuses and left. Rather than walking, she jumped in a taxi that had just dropped off a fare to get home more quickly in case Alice was there.

'Alf,' she said, anxiously, 'is Alice home?'

'I haven't seen her since yesterday lunchtime. She must have got in after I locked up at midnight last night. Is everything all right, Gina?'

'Yes, of course. I guess she forgot to tell me she was

staying over with friends.'

Gina let herself into the flat and went straight to the bathroom. Alice's toothbrush was still in the pink plastic mug by the washbasin. Wherever she is, Gina thought, she wasn't planning on staying out and anyway, she would have told me. Could there be another emergency at home? she wondered, going into Alice's room and retrieving her address book from the top drawer of her bedside table. Perching on the edge of Alice's bed, she stared at the Nottingham phone number, trying to decide whether or not to ring. It would be pointless to needlessly upset the family if Alice was simply with friends but, if she was missing, every minute she delayed would reduce the chance of her being found unharmed. Barnes was a nice area, but there were perverts everywhere. What if someone had followed her from Hammersmith tube station on her way home last night?

In the end, Gina decided to give herself a deadline of the next morning before getting anyone else involved. She made herself a sandwich as neither she nor Peter had felt like eating at the pub, and settled down on the sofa to watch an old movie.

I must have been more tired than I realised, she thought, when she woke up a couple of hours later to find that the credits of the film were rolling. She stretched and got up to go and turn the television off. The early evening news bulletin was just starting. Gina stared in horror at the screen. Behind the newsreader's head was a picture of a muddy riverbank and in the centre of it was a gold sandal.

'Good evening,' the newsreader said. 'Police have spent the day searching the banks of the River Thames near where eyewitness reports say they saw a person, believed to be a woman, in the water at around ten thirty last night. At approximately three o' clock this afternoon, a gold shoe was discovered about half a mile downstream from Chelsea Bridge, where the police had been concentrating their search. It is not known at this stage if the two are connected but police are appealing for any further eyewitnesses to come forward. If anyone recognises this shoe and can connect it to a missing female, please contact them on the telephone number currently on screen. Investigations will continue at first light tomorrow.'

Gina staggered backwards across the room and collapsed on to the sofa. 'No, no, oh my God, no.'

Moments later her phone started ringing.

'Hello?'

'Are you watching the news?' It was Alf, calling from downstairs.

'Yes.'

'It's Alice's shoe. She was wearing them yesterday when she left here. I remember because I didn't think it was very suitable footwear with the rain on its way.'

'That's what I thought. What should we do, Alf?'

'We'll have to ring the police, especially as you say she didn't come home last night. Poor love, I hope she's all right. Such a nice kid, too. You don't think she threw herself in the river deliberately do you?'

Until that moment, it hadn't crossed Gina's mind that Alice may have taken her own life, but maybe everything had just caught up with her, and she couldn't take any more. There had been an underlying sadness in her demeanour since the abortion, no matter how hard she tried to hide it. Nobody else knows what she's been through, Gina thought, it was my responsibility to keep a close eye on her. How will I ever live with myself if she's dead?

'Are you still there, Gina? Are you okay? I'll ring the police, and then I'll come up and make you a cup of sweet tea, it's supposed to be good for shock.

CHAPTER 53

Less than two miles from where her friends had waited for her in the pub, Alice's motionless body lay partially screened by the bushes that overhung the riverbank. After the supreme effort of battling against and being carried along by the notoriously strong and unpredictable currents of the Thames, which had claimed the lives of many less experienced swimmers than Alice, she had managed to haul herself out of the water before collapsing in a heap and falling into an exhausted sleep. At one point during daylight hours on Sunday, she had woken briefly, shivering convulsively, her teeth chattering. She couldn't determine whether this was because she was the coldest she had ever been in her life or if it was pure fear.

An image of Richard's face, distorted with hate and fury, just before he had released her into the raging torrent of the river, swelled by the torrential rain of the previous few hours, would be etched on her mind for eternity. She had realised, shortly before he pushed her to what he must certainly have believed would be her watery grave, that the ransom note on the pink paper must have been delivered by the only other person who knew anything about the rape at the Dorchester. Gina had been determined that he should pay in some way for the atrocities he had committed, but she could have had no way of knowing what Richard was capable of to protect himself.

When Alice had believed she was going to die, she had screamed at him that she knew he had drugged her before the rape. At least she would go to her grave with the satisfaction that he knew that she knew what a vile and loathsome creature he truly was. The problem was, she hadn't drowned in the Thames, and now that Richard was aware that she knew the whole truth and had attempted to kill her once, she was pretty sure he would stop at nothing until she was no longer a threat to him. What am I going to do? she wondered, curling herself into a near foetal position and hugging her arms around her knees in a desperate attempt to get warm. I can't go to the police because I don't have any proof that he tried to kill me, and there's no evidence of any motive. I can't go to Gina's. If he realises that I genuinely knew nothing about the ransom note, he might be watching the flat intending to frighten her off. I don't know where Peter lives, and I can't go home because I have no money. She drifted back to sleep, feeling entirely helpless and alone.

It was dusk when she next roused, still freezing cold but with the beginning of an idea in her head. When she and Gina had talked about walking to the pub on the North End Road from their flat in Barnes, Alice had checked out a route in her A–Z. If I follow the riverbank until I reach Hammersmith Bridge, she thought, I'm pretty sure I would be able to find my way to Linda's flat in West Kensington. She was hoping Linda would be able to lend her some money and some clothes to get home. If I can just get home, she thought, Mum and Dad will look after me.

Having wriggled out of her denim jacket and removed her shoes to give herself the best chance of survival in the water, she was now barefoot and bedraggled as she began her torturous journey by the side of the river under the cover of darkness. Progress was slow and painful, but she pushed on casting her eyes around her as she walked, desperately searching for recognisable landmarks. Nothing seemed familiar. I could be anywhere, she thought. I might be walking away from the sanctuary of Linda's bedsit if the current carried me further upstream than Barnes. After what seemed liked hours, Alice could see a bridge looming out of the darkness up ahead. There's nothing else for it, I'll have to go up onto the road to find out which bridge it is and try to get my bearings.

Once she had left the comparative protection of the riverbank, she was more exposed to the scrutiny of passing traffic, not that there were many cars around in the early hours of a Monday morning. As she headed for the bridge she became aware of a car's headlights illuminating her steps. Her heart started thumping in her chest. Trying to squash the feelings of unease she kept her gaze fixed steadfastly ahead. The toot of the horn made her jump almost out of her skin. Alice turned to see a black cab with his yellow light on and his nearside window down and relief flooded through her.

'You look like you could do with a ride, love.'

'No, I'm all right thanks.'

'What happened to your shoes?'

'I… I lost them. And my handbag. I haven't got any

money to pay for a taxi.'

'Where are you headed?'

'West Kensington.'

'Go on, get in. I'll drop you home on my way back to central London.'

Alice hesitated.

'It's too far to walk, love, particularly in bare feet.'

'Really? Where are we?'

'Putney Bridge. You'd be better off sticking to soft drinks in the future.'

'I'm not drunk.'

'Maybe not now. The fresh air must have sobered you up. Hop in, before I change my mind.'

It was just beginning to get light as the taxi pulled up outside the house in Avondale Road.

'You get yourself to bed, love,' the taxi driver said, 'and sleep it off. And don't forget to report your bag missing to the police. You never know, some Good Samaritan might have handed it in.'

'Thank you so much. I'll never forget your kindness,' Alice replied.

She waited until the cab had turned onto the main road at the end of the street before sinking to the ground to retrieve the spare key from under the rock painted with pink nail varnish. She scrabbled around in the half-light, her fingernails filling with dark, damp earth frantically feeling for the serrated metal edge of the front door key. Nothing. It wasn't there. Determination gave way to despair, and she began to whimper. It had never crossed her mind that she wouldn't be able to gain access to Linda's flat.

Above her head, a sash window slid open.

'Who's there?' demanded a voice that Alice recognised.

'Ruby? It's me, Alice, please may I come in?'

Moments later the front door opened and Ruby in her faded dressing gown and fluffy slippers, a single roller in the front of her hair, approached.

'My God, Alice. What on earth has happened to you?'

She bent down and put her arm around Alice's waist, pulling her to her feet, then supported her on the short walk to her front room where she collapsed on to a startled Mr Tibbles.

'I'll get you a cup of tea, and then you'd better tell me what's gone on.'

CHAPTER 54

Gina slept fitfully. Every time she began to drift off, it felt as though water was closing in around her, filling her nose and mouth, and she woke moments later gasping for breath and covered in sweat. She could only imagine what it must have felt like for Alice as she desperately gasped for air, all the time her lungs filling with filthy water until she lost her battle for life.

The police had finally left the apartment shortly before midnight. Their questioning was rigorous and at times felt more like an interrogation, and they sifted through Alice's belongings looking for anything that might give them a clue as to why she had ended up in the river. The first thing they had done was confirm her shoe size against that of the gold sandal that had been washed up. They were the same, but Gina knew they would be.

She had given the police as little information as she dared, avoiding mention of the illegal abortion. She had to tell them about the 999 call that Alf had made after the two of them had found Alice unconscious in the bathroom, but she didn't elaborate on the reason behind it. It would be easy enough for them to check hospital records, she reasoned, and then the miscarriage would come to light, but Gina wasn't planning on being around by the time they discovered it. She had already decided that she would deliver the second blackmail note that evening with instructions for where Richard was to leave the money the next day. Once the ten thousand pounds was in her possession, she would simply disappear; it was too dangerous to stick around.

She wasn't afraid of Richard, he was all mouth and no trousers, but if any of the photographs the police had taken of Alice's room appeared on the television news or in the papers, there was a chance that Edward's wife might recognise the flat in Barnes, which could lead to awkward questions. He would be furious, and there was no telling what he might do, particularly as he had threatened her once before. It was definitely time to move on. With Richard's money, she would easily have enough to make up the shortfall on the Mortlake house with some left over to escape abroad until all the fuss over Alice had died down.

Gina brushed a stray tear from her eye as she reached one of her bags down from the top of her wardrobe. All my life I've stopped myself getting close to people for fear of losing them, and when I do allow someone in, this happens. It must be me. I poison everything. Poor Alice. If I hadn't befriended her, she would probably still be alive now. She pulled open one of her drawers and carefully selected a few items of underwear, then repeated the process with tops and trousers. No point in arousing suspicion by leaving with my suitcases, she thought, much better to take smaller bags filled with my stuff over the next three days and leave them under lock and key at Victoria station, ready to catch the early train to the continent on Thursday morning. The police have no reason to suspect me of any wrong-doing but I am part of an ongoing investigation, and I can't risk them preventing me from leaving the country. As for my contract with Richard, that's just tough, she thought, shrugging her shoulders, although she did feel a pang of guilt as she closed the zip on the top of her bag, acutely aware that Larry would take the rap for her not fulfilling it.

If Gina was scared of Edward, it paled into insignificance against her fears of Franco. Already on a final warning with him, she had to call the Ostrich Club the previous evening, feigning sickness, as she had been in no fit state to go to work after the visit from the police. The cloakroom attendant took her message, and she could imagine the prominent vein in Franco's forehead pulsing as the news was delivered. He will have been livid, she thought, especially as he needed to make up money from a soft Saturday night. I reckon I've got a week, tops, of being off ill before he sends the heavies round to put the frighteners on me but, by that time, I'll be a long way from here.

The phone rang, making her jump.

'Hello?'

There was a sniffing sound on the other end of the phone, as though someone was crying, before a voice said, 'Is that Gina?'

'Alice. Alice is that you? I thought you were dead. Alice where are you? The police were here and everything.'

'It's not Alice. It's Mary, Alice's sister.'

The flicker of hope was instantly extinguished. 'Mary,

I'm so sorry, you even sound like her.'

'The police have been here too, and to Mum and Dad's. What happened, Gina?'

'I have no idea. She was in good spirits when I left her at the theatre after the show on Saturday night, looking forward to Sunday lunch at a pub near where she used to live. When I went into her room to wake her on Sunday morning, her room was empty, and her bed hadn't been slept in.'

'Did you report her missing?'

'No,' Gina said, wishing for the hundredth time since she had seen the picture of Alice's shoe on the television news that she had. Maybe, just maybe, if I had reported her missing sooner there might have been a faint chance of finding her alive. 'At first, I thought she might have stayed over at Peter's, but when I arrived at the pub he was there alone.'

'Were they seeing each other?'

'Not exactly, but they've always had a thing for each other, and I thought perhaps it had moved on the next level.'

'Did you tell the police about them?'

'There was nothing to tell. Peter hadn't seen her since the theatre on Saturday night either.'

'That's what he told you, but maybe he was lying. What if they went for a walk by the river and then argued about something? She could have been upset and decided, in the heat of the moment, to end it all. No... no, I don't believe that. Alice wouldn't do that to us. Maybe he pushed her?'

'Mary,' Gina said gently, 'you're clutching at straws here. I know you're upset, but I'm sure the police will get to the bottom of things. There is still a chance that they will find her alive and well,' she said, trying to sound more positive than she felt.

'That's what they said. Until they find her… her body,' there was a pause, during which Gina could hear the rustle of tissues, 'they'll keep searching, but I don't know if I believe them. Gina, I don't think she's dead. We're so close, almost like twins, I think I would know if she'd gone…' her voice petered out.

Tears flowed freely down Gina's face. The hope and desperation in Mary's voice was heart-breaking, almost as though if she believed hard enough that Alice was alive, it would make it come true. Gina was lost for words. What do you say to a nineteen-year-old whose world had just fallen apart?

'Gina, can I ask you something?'

'Anything.'

'Can I come and stay with you for a couple of days? I want to be close to where she went missing. I want to see it for myself. Please, Gina.'

She looked at the bag she had just packed sitting by the front door.

'I'm not sure that's a good idea, Mary. I think it would be too upsetting for you.'

'But I need to touch her things, to breathe in her smell, to feel she's still alive. Please. I'm begging you,' she said, breaking into sobs on the other end of the phone.

How can I refuse? she thought.

'All right, Mary. But just for a couple of nights. When did you want to come?'

'Today. Right now. The sooner I can feel close to her the better. She's not dead, Gina. I know it. She's a really strong swimmer. I told the police that as well but I think they are just humouring me. You believe me, don't you?'

'I want to, truly I do. Call me back when you know what train you're going to be on and I'll come and meet you at the station, okay?'

'Thank you. Alice told me you were the best friend she's ever had and she's right. We'll find her; I know we will.'

Gina returned the receiver to the cradle and walked across to the big windows with their panoramic view of the river. It looked grey and cold, a carbon copy of the sky, with little waves whipped up by the wind. Could Mary be right? she wondered. Could Alice be out there somewhere?

CHAPTER 55

'Please, Ruby, let me stay here for twenty-four hours until I can work out what to do for the best. I didn't know Linda was away on tour again or I wouldn't have come.'

Alice was sipping her third cup of hot sweet tea since arriving at the house in Avondale Road two hours earlier. She was snuggled into Ruby's winter dressing gown, several sizes too large for her, with a towel wrapped around her head, having had a bath in the communal bathroom she had hated so much when she was living there. The heat of the water had finally warmed her through, and the aroma of shampoo and bubble bath had replaced the stench of polluted mud that had dried on her skin. Her clothes, which Ruby had washed for her, were drying on the radiator.

Ruby was shaking her head. 'I don't know, Alice. Your disappearance has been on television and is front-page news. There is a huge police search for you on the banks of the river. I could get in a lot of trouble for hiding you here.'

Alice hadn't told Ruby the whole story of how she had

ended up in the river, but she had revealed that someone had tried to kill her.

'I feel terrible asking you to do this, but I have nowhere else to go. No one need know that you have seen the television report and are aware that the police are searching for me. I'm scared, Ruby. This man has tried to kill me once, but without proof the police wouldn't be able to arrest him. He may try again, and with more success next time.'

'But what about your family and friends? They must be beside themselves with worry.'

'I know, and I feel dreadful for what I'm putting them through, believe me. I just need a bit of time to plan how I'm going to present things to the police so that no one else need ever be frightened of this monster again, but I can't think straight at the moment.'

'You look exhausted. I can't pretend I'm happy about this, Alice. At the very least you should probably go to hospital for a check-up after what you've swallowed in that river. Goodness knows what's in there if the fish can't survive it, and look at your legs and feet; they're cut to ribbons. They could easily get infected, and it would be my fault.'

'I promise it will only be for a few hours,' Alice pleaded.

'Well, against my better judgement, I'll let you get some sleep now that you're all cleaned up and we'll talk about it again when you wake up. Maybe you'll see things differently then.'

'I don't know how to thank you, Ruby.'

'Forget it. I know it's hard to believe, but I was young once and got myself into all sorts of scrapes, although I can't recall anyone actually trying to kill me. They've threatened a few times, mind. Whatever you've got yourself mixed up in, you need to get out of it before it's too late. You're far too young to throw your life away.'

'I think I'm going to go home to Nottingham when this is over. All I ever dreamed of as a child was seeing my name up in lights outside a West End theatre but I'm not so sure the price is worth paying. I wish I'd never come to London.'

'Don't blame London for the people you've fallen foul of, Alice, and never let them make you lose sight of your dream. Now go and get some rest in my room while I pop out and get us something nice for dinner. It'll make a pleasant change to have company; Mr Tibbles and I don't have many guests.'

Alice smiled gratefully as she padded across to Ruby's bedroom, closed the door behind her and crawled under the eiderdown. Within minutes she was asleep.

CHAPTER 56

Peter was pacing up and down the corridor outside Fred's office when Gina arrived at the theatre at six o' clock on Monday evening.

'Where the hell have you been? I've been going frantic. Everyone else was called here for four if they weren't already here for understudy rehearsals. I came to watch Alice at two, but she was a no-show, and then the police turned up. They think the girl who fell in the Thames on Saturday night is Alice,' he said, running his hands through his hair.

'I know. They came to my flat last night after I saw the news report with her shoe and called them. They were there for hours questioning me. I had to tell them we were all supposed to be having a drink together yesterday lunch but I couldn't give them your address or phone number because I didn't have it.'

'I can't believe this. Not my Alice.'

'Try to stay calm, Peter. At least the police are still searching for her, which suggests they haven't given up hope of finding her alive. They took away some of her clothes to get the sniffer dogs involved in the search.'

'They've interviewed everyone, trying to find out who was the last person to see her. It looks like it was probably Fred when she left for the night. Richard's making an announcement on stage at half past six, but I think tonight's performance is still going ahead. I don't know if I can do it, Gina. I think Mike's going to have to go on for me.'

'You can do it, Peter. Alice would want you to. Listen, I'm running a bit late, so I'll have to go and get ready, but we'll talk later. Try not to worry; I haven't given up hope,' she said giving him a quick hug before racing up the stairs.

Gina's belief that Alice may still be alive had been resurrected by Mary, who she had met off the train from Sheffield at 3.30, an hour later than scheduled. That resulted in her being short of time to take Mary back to Barnes and settle her in before leaving for the theatre. They had given Alf an almighty shock.

'Oh my God, Alice! Where have you been? We've had the police here and everything.'

'This is Mary, Alf, Alice's sister. You remember she came down to stay for a few days around Alice's birthday.'

'Of course,' Alf said, 'it's just that you are the spitting image of her, particularly when you're not side by side. If there's anything I can do to help just let me know.'

'Thanks,' Mary replied. She hadn't spoken much in the taxi on the way from the station. It was almost as though she were in a trance.

She had stood by the windows in the flat gazing out on the Thames while Gina bustled around getting ready for work.

'I don't want you going out of the flat, Mary,' Gina said

as she was about to leave. 'I feel responsible for you. If you're going to stay here you have to stick to my rules, okay?'

Mary nodded. 'I feel calmer being here and seeing the river. She didn't drown. I don't know where she is or why she hasn't let us know she's okay but I feel even more certain, being here, that she's alive.'

'Keep thinking like that; there can't be any harm in sending positive energy her way. Now, remember, Alf's on the end of the phone if you need anything, anything at all, and I should be back about half-past ten.'

On her way out of the building, Gina stopped for a quiet word with Alf.

'She wanted to be here with Alice's things,' she explained. 'I didn't have the heart to say no. I don't like leaving her on her own, but I have to get to the theatre. I won't be going on to my other job tonight, so I should be back around 10.30. Will you ring upstairs a couple of times during the evening to make sure she's okay?'

'Of course. Poor kid, and what must those parents be going through?'

The dressing room was very subdued with the girls talking in whispers, if at all. Diane walked over and sat next to Gina, in Alice's place, while she was putting the finishing touch to her make-up.

'Are you okay?'

'Not really, but I guess the show must go on.'

'Well, we're about to find out. Do you want me to wait for you?'

'It's all right. I'll be down in a couple of minutes. It's

not quite half past.'
    'Okay, see you down there.'

Richard stood at the front of the stage, his back to the empty auditorium, waiting for the final stragglers to arrive. Tammy, followed shortly by Gina, completed the company and Richard raised his hands for silence.

'Well, as you all know by now after your interviews with the police, it's believed that the female who was seen struggling in the Thames on Saturday night was none other than our Alice. As it stands, there is no body for the police to formally identify, but the discovery of her shoe would suggest that it was her. Please, if any of you remember anything at all about the last time you saw her, no matter how insignificant it may seem, let the police know. I realise this is very distressing for all of you, but if there's one saying in show business, it's "the show must go on", and I believe that is what Alice would have wanted. Tonight's performance will go ahead as scheduled. Fortunately, you have performed the show without Alice in the chorus line on several occasions, so this shouldn't be too much of a problem. If anyone has an issue with this, please come and see me in my office. Let's do this for Alice. Thank you, company. Larry,' he said to his choreographer who had been standing off to one side, 'a word, please.'

'The girls will be fine, Richard, although Peter looks shocked. Do you think Mike should stand in for him tonight?'

'Of course not. It's a shock for all of us, but we have to get on with it. Anyway, that's not what I wanted to talk to you about. I think it's time that you contacted one of the dancers from your reserve list. What?' Richard said, responding to Larry's look of incredulity.

'That's a bit off, isn't it? We don't even know for sure that the person in the Thames was Alice. For all any of us know, she could have forgotten that it was understudy rehearsal day and she's up in the dressing room right now getting ready.'

'I think we both know that that's not the case, Larry.'

At least, I definitely do, Richard thought. He had spent a very nervous Sunday waiting for a knock at the door from the police, particularly after the news broke in the early evening. He had been so on edge that he had raised his voice to his beloved Miriam when she was whining on about being allowed to take part in the French exchange visit, causing her to run to her room in floods of tears. The knock at the door that he had been expecting had finally come at nine o' clock the following morning. Anita walked into the dining room as he was finishing his breakfast, looking ashen-faced and followed by two policemen.

'These gentlemen want to talk to you about Alice Abbott. They think she may be the girl who fell in the river.'

Richard had since given himself a pat on the back for

his acting skills; his look of horror would have convinced anyone that he knew nothing about it. He had answered all their questions unflinchingly, happy in the knowledge that his driver, Max, would back up his story and say he had driven him straight home from the theatre after a couple of drinks in the packed Four Keys. He was pretty sure no one would be able to say for certain whether he had or hadn't been there on Saturday night, particularly as he was such a regular customer. Max had also volunteered to dispose of Alice's bag once Richard had told him that she had been trying to blackmail him, such was his loyalty to the man who had saved him from a long prison sentence.

'We'll need you to give us details of all your cast members, sir, so that we can eliminate them from our enquiries.'

It had been Richard's idea to call everyone into the theatre early to make things easier for the police to take statements, for which they were very appreciative.

'It just doesn't feel right to move so quickly on this, Richard,' Larry was saying. 'Surely another few days won't make any difference, particularly as the girls are all familiar with the staging without Alice.'

'Are you questioning my judgement, Larry? I do hope not because when this show transfers to Broadway I need to be certain that we are all singing off the same song sheet.'

'If you insist, Richard,' Larry said, biting his lip, 'but, for the record, I think it's a bit premature and insensitive to the rest of the girls, particularly Gina.'

'I wouldn't worry about Gina; when her current six-month contract is finished, I won't be renewing it. It's about time she retired, isn't it?'

Richard marched off the stage feeling satisfied that he had put his choreographer firmly in his place. I run this show, he thought, pushing open his office door. The flash of bright pink against the dark stone floor brought him to an abrupt halt.

His heart started pounding. How can this be? She couldn't have survived the swollen river; I watched her being pulled under by the current. He closed the door and leant back on it, breathing deeply, trying to compose himself before he picked the square of paper up as though it were a red-hot poker. With trembling hands, he unfolded it, and a small safety deposit box key clattered to the floor.

I HOPE YOU HAVE MY MONEY. TAKE IT TO VICTORIA STATION TOMORROW AT MIDDAY AND PUT IT IN THE SAFETY DEPOSIT BOX WHOSE KEY I HAVE SUPPLIED. DON'T EVEN THINK ABOUT GOING TO THE POLICE. I KNOW ABOUT THE ROHYPNOL, YOU SAD PERVERT

Once again, the words were made up from letters cut out of a newspaper. It had to be from the same person. He sank on to his swivel chair, oblivious to the hustle and bustle of Londoners heading home from work that could be seen through the window behind him. He rested his head in his hands, rereading the final sentence over and over again. There could be only one possible explanation, he thought. Alice must have lied about not telling anyone. Gina knows, and it's she who is trying to blackmail me. I've killed the wrong bloody girl.

CHAPTER 58

Edward barged through the doors to the Ostrich Club shortly before midnight.

'Where is she?' he demanded of the barman. 'Where's Gina?'

'I'm sorry, sir, I'm afraid Gina isn't in this evening.'

'Why not? I want to talk to her.'

'That's not for me to say. Maybe one of the other girls could be your companion for this evening?' he said, surreptitiously pressing the green button beneath the bar that alerted his manager to potential issues.

Moments later, the office door opened and Franco strode across to where Edward was leaning heavily on the bar.

'Is everything all right here, Claudio?'

'I want to see Gina,' Edward repeated.

Franco's face registered recognition. This was the same man who had asked to see Gina a few weeks back. He had been drunk then, and it looked like he was heading that way again. It was another very quiet evening in the Ostrich Club, and Franco had to decide whether this guy would be more trouble than he was worth if he persuaded him to settle for one of the other girls.

'I'm afraid Gina is indisposed. She rang in sick yesterday evening, but I'm sure Jenny will be happy to look after you,' he said, beckoning the curvy brunette to join them at the bar. 'What can we get you to drink?'

'Brandy, and whatever she is drinking,' Edward said, allowing the brunette to lead him to a private booth.

'Keep an eye on him,' Franco said to his barman. 'If he starts causing trouble, buzz me and I'll have the boys throw him out.'

Edward watched the manager return to his office. Good, he thought, it's all going well so far. He hadn't touched a drop of drink, but it was imperative for Franco to believe he was already intoxicated if his plan was to succeed.

Edward had wanted Gina out of his Barnes apartment weeks ago but had foolishly allowed her to stay on along with her friend, who was obviously another hooker, he thought, clasping his brandy glass so tight that it was in danger of breaking. Her stupid friend had clearly got herself killed but he couldn't care less about that. He had a more pressing problem. His wife had recognised the photograph of their riverside flat in the paper and had confronted him about it. 'I thought you said it was rented to a little old lady and her poodle,' she had said. 'Why would you lie to me? What are you trying to hide?' An enormous row had ensued with accusations of infidelity being voiced for the first time. In the end, Edward had confessed that he had been renting the flat to a much younger female but admitted to nothing more. His wife had given him a withering look. 'I'm not a fool,' she had said. 'I want that girl gone by tomorrow or you can pack your bags and go and live with her. It's up to you, but I will make sure that none of our social circle will make you welcome.'

Edward was backed into a corner. He had to get Gina out in a hurry but he knew she would resist. She'd already threatened to expose their relationship to his wife, and he wasn't prepared to let that happen. He was afraid of being implicated in anything that might befall Gina, but he was pretty sure that Franco and his heavies had no such fears. He knew that she wouldn't be at the Ostrich Club that night following his conversation with Alf earlier in the evening; it had meant a slight change of plan on his part but, he thought, in some ways it might work better. Provided Alf did as he asked, which Edward was pretty sure he would for the fifty pounds he had promised him, the front door to Riverside Mansions would be unlocked when Franco's henchman arrived to deal with Gina.

Edward downed his brandy flamboyantly, and shouted across the club to the barman, making sure he slurred his words, demanding a double. Once he had Claudio's attention, he started groping Jenny in an inappropriate manner. Within seconds, a burly-looking man was at his side and the door to Franco's office flew open.

'I think maybe you've had enough this evening. I don't allow my girls to be manhandled like that. Are you prepared to leave quietly, or should I have Alberto escort you?'

This is it, Edward thought, I need to get this right. He slammed the key he had been concealing in his hand down on the table. 'It's all right, I'm going,' he slurred. 'You can give Gina the key to her flat back; I never want to see that whore again. I should have believed the doorman at her apartment building when he said he thought she was entertaining a client tonight. That little bitch was supposed to meet me here. It looks like she's been lying to both of us,' he said, hauling himself out of the booth and staggering towards the exit.

'Leave him,' Franco said, putting a restraining hand on Alberto's arm. 'I have a more pressing job for you. I don't like being lied to,' he said, picking the key up off the table and handing it to Alberto. 'I think you need to pay Gina a little visit.'

CHAPTER 59

Mary woke with a start. She couldn't be sure, but she thought she had heard a muffled scream. She listened. Everything seemed quiet. I must be imagining it, she thought, or maybe it was a nightmare, which is not surprising. The whole of the past eighteen hours had been a nightmare since the university principal had called her into his office and delivered the awful news that Alice was missing, presumed drowned. She turned on to her side and closed her eyes to try and get back to sleep. Moments later, her eyes shot open. There it was again, and this time Mary knew she wasn't dreaming. She slipped out of bed and moved silently towards the door. Opening it a crack, she peered out into the darkness of the living room. From what she could see, it all seemed exactly as she and Gina had left it when they had gone to bed. Suddenly, there was a clanking sound and a dim light illuminated the room. Mary's hand flew up to her mouth to stop her gasping. The noise was the lift, but the only reason she could hear it so clearly and see its light disappearing was because the front door of the flat was wide open.

Terrified, Mary closed her bedroom door as quietly as she could and tiptoed back across the room to her bed. She lifted the telephone receiver and dialled 0 as Gina had told her to do if she needed to speak to Alf. The sound of the phone ringing at the other end seemed very loud to her, so she pressed it up against her ear even tighter and put her head under her pillow. It rang six or seven times before it was finally picked up.

'This had better be good,' said a grumpy-sounding Alf, clearly roused from his sleep.

'Alf, it's me, Mary,' she whispered.

'I can't hear you. You'll have to speak up.'

'Can you hear me, Alf, it's Mary. I think someone has broken into our flat. Our front door is wide open, and I heard noises. I daren't speak any louder in case they hear me.'

'I'll come up, Mary. Maybe the door wasn't shut properly to start with, and the wind blew it open.'

'No,' Mary said, urgently, 'I think you should call the police. I'm afraid something has happened to Gina, and they might come for me next. Please, Alf.'

'Stay in your room,' he instructed, 'maybe hide under the bed. I'll call the police. Don't move, Mary, do you hear? Don't leave your room.'

Mary replaced the receiver holding the pillow over it to try and minimise any noise. Clearly, Alf isn't familiar with the bed in this room, she thought, as she lifted the valance to discover storage drawers. She looked around the room, her eyes searching for somewhere to hide, her heart thundering in her chest. The curtains were not full-length, and she couldn't risk the noise the wardrobe door would make if she opened it. Besides, what if they guessed she was in there? She would be trapped. In the end, she stood against the wall behind the door, poised for flight. If anyone opened it, she would have the benefit of surprise and the extra couple of seconds it would buy her could be the difference between life and death.

The minutes stretched out interminably. It all seemed to have gone quiet, but then she heard what sounded like the heel of a shoe against the parquet living-room floor. Mary took very shallow breaths, fearful that the intruder was on the other side of her door waiting to pounce. Salty tears trickled silently down her cheeks. She had come to London to find her missing sister, refusing to believe that she was dead. But what if something had happened to her in this very room and whoever was responsible was now lying in wait for her?

From near silence, there was a sudden cacophony of sound, shouts of 'Police!' and the sound of footsteps.

Mary wrenched open the door preparing to run, but the scene that greeted her rooted her to the spot. The other bedroom door was wide open allowing her to see the back of a heavy-set man sat astride Gina's still body. She was lying half off the bed, her long red hair pooling on the cream carpet like fresh blood, and there were livid purple marks around her neck. The man had his hands in the air in a show of submission.

'This is not what it looks like. The front door was open when I got here. I didn't do anything, I swear. She was already like this when I found her. I was trying to revive her.'

On either side of him, the uniformed police officers with their truncheons raised in the air exchanged looks. 'Don't move,' one of them said.

Mary heard a voice scream, 'Gina!' and, as the man on the bed turned to face her, she realised it was her own.

'What are you doing here? You're supposed to be dead. Richard told me he watched you drown,' Max said, his face a study of fear and confusion.

CHAPTER 60

A light dusting of frost on the grass separating the graves sparkled like diamonds in the bright November sunshine. Alice shivered, and it wasn't only from the cold.

'Are you okay?' Peter said, releasing her hand which he had been holding and pulling her towards his body to share his warmth. Ever since the morning she had walked into the police station in Fulham, bravely prepared to make her accusations against Richard, Peter had barely left her side, insisting she should stay in the spare room of his Knightsbridge mews house, even moving into a hotel for a couple of nights when her parents came down to stay.

'It's just so awful for her,' Alice said, her eyes on the diminutive solitary figure at the graveside, huddled into her hooded coat against the winter chill. 'I know they didn't have the closest of relationships, but for it to end so tragically, without them having the chance to forgive each other, is unimaginably sad. It makes me even more grateful for the relationship I have with my mum,' she added, resting her head against Peter's shoulder.

Alice had confessed everything to her mother and they had shed tears together for the baby whose life had never existed. There were no recriminations and no blame. Sheila Abbott had only once asked her daughter why she hadn't gone to them for help? 'I didn't want you to be ashamed of me,' Alice had said.

'We all make mistakes, Alice. Life is about learning from them and trying not to repeat them,' her mother had responded. 'Your dad and I will always be there for you and Mary, whatever the circumstances. I hope you know that now.'

'It's amazing how little we knew about her, really,' Alice said. 'Even Larry.'

'He's a good sort,' Peter said, looking across to where Larry was standing wrapped up against the cold in a full-length fur coat and matching hat. 'I'm really pleased for him that Anita has decided to re-open the show in London and is pushing ahead with the negotiations for Broadway. To be honest, I didn't think she had it in her. I thought she would crumble when Richard was arrested, and accused of attempted murder, after Max started singing like a canary to try and save his own skin. And then there are the multiple rape charges that have surfaced since you went to the police. What a pair; I hope they both end up behind bars for a very long time.'

'Me too. And you're right, Anita's been amazing, particularly with Tammy falling off the wagon again. It would have been the final straw, for most people. They would have chalked it off as a jinxed show and counted their losses, but it seems to have made her even more determined that the show must go on. It's Miriam I feel most sorry for. She worshipped her dad.'

'It's going to be tough for her when the case goes to court and his picture is splashed all over the front pages of the newspapers again but, hopefully, people won't judge her by the sins of her father. You never know, in the long run, it may turn out to be the making of her. Richard spoilt her rotten. I think her life from now on will be very different, she may even grow up to be a nice person if she accepts guidance from her mum.'

The sort of guidance that wasn't available to Gina, Alice thought, and yet, despite some bad life choices, she became a kind and caring person. She shivered again.

'We need to get you inside. Your body has been through a hell of a lot in the last couple of months, we don't want you catching pneumonia before the grand re-opening tomorrow. How does it feel seeing your name up in lights alongside mine as the co-star of *Theatreland*?'

'Honestly? I feel a bit guilty that I only have this opportunity because something bad happened to Tammy.'

'Well, don't. I told you Tammy would never be able to stay dry for the six-month run. She needs prolonged professional help, which I hope the Melrose will give her this time. Maybe Lynette's judgement as to whether she could handle the pressure of a West End show was clouded by the fact that they were emotionally involved. At least that's all out in the open now, so it's one less thing for Tammy to worry about.'

'I was quite shocked to learn that Tammy prefers women to men. Each to their own, I suppose.'

'Well, I'm just glad you don't,' Peter said, kissing her forehead, the icy tip of her nose and finally her lips. 'It looks like Larry is ready to leave. We can share a car with him and she can come on when she's ready. It was kind of

Giuseppe to offer his café for the wake.'

'He's always adored Gina. He probably thought it was the least he could do.'

As Alice, Peter and Larry made their way towards one of the two cars waiting on the drive of the cemetery, a man, who had been hidden from view behind a large oak tree, approached the lone figure at the graveside.

'Gina?' he said.

She spun round, the wind catching her hood and releasing her long auburn hair.

'Vince! What are you doing here?'

'I read your story in the paper. Losing your mum is tough and I couldn't bear to think of you facing it alone. I care about you, Gina.'

Gina's bottom lipped trembled and more tears rolled down her already streaked cheeks.

'I know she wasn't the best mum in the world but she was my mum. When Max had his hands around my neck, trying to squeeze the life out of me, it was her face I saw. I promised myself that as soon as I got out of hospital I was going to track her down and bring her to live with me in Mortlake. But I was too late. The coroner said that she took the overdose that killed her that same night. It's almost as though she sacrificed her life for mine. Now she's gone, I'll never have the chance to tell her that I loved her.'

'Come here,' Vince said, wrapping his arms around her protectively. 'I have no intention of making that same mistake. I love you, Gina, and I want to spend the rest of my life with you.'

'You can't mean that, Vince. I don't deserve a happy ending. It's impossible.'

'Only if you believe it is,' he said, cupping her face in his hands and brushing her lips gently with his.

ACKNOWLEDGEMENTS

Writing Alice in Theatreland was a different experience from the Liberty Sands trilogy – the complete story had to be told in one book and I hope I have done it justice. I was heartened by the email I received from Justine Taylor, my copy editor, after she had read through the manuscript. She said, 'It's hugely enjoyable, with great characterisation and evocation of London's theatre world in the mid 1970's. Thanks for the vote of confidence, Justine, although I think it must have helped that I lived through that period, and thanks also for your attention to the small details which I believe have made for a better book. See you in a few months for the next one.

Another member of the team is Yvonne Betancourt, my formatter. Once again a great job from you and I appreciate your 'can do' attitude. When presented with a tight deadline you assured me, 'I'll come through,' and you did.

All the covers of my books have been well received but I wanted this one to be a little more menacing. It's a good job I have Angela Oltmann to rein me in as my original ideas were far too complicated. Thanks Angela, I love this cover.

To everyone at Ripped thank you for your support and belief.

My family are the most important people in my life and each of you have helped me in your own way, but special mention must go to my daughter, Sophie, who proof reads for me to make sure there are as few mistakes as humanly possible, something we are both passionate about. I have to share a What's App message from her which brought a smile to my face on a particularly taxing day:

'No, Alice!!! Richard is a slime ball… don't fall for it!! A hotel suite?! Open your eyes woman!!!

Little did Sophie know what was to come.

And lastly, thank you for buying this book and giving me the opportunity to share my characters and their story. I hope you have enjoyed reading it as much as I enjoyed writing it. This is not the final curtain; there will be a new book from me in the autumn.

Other Books by this Author

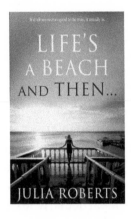

Life's a Beach and Then…
The Liberty Sands Trilogy Book 1

Holly Wilson has landed a dream job but there is one proviso… she must keep it secret, and that means telling lies. Holly hates telling lies. Her latest assignment has brought her to the paradise island of Mauritius where she meets a British couple, Robert and Rosemary, who share a tragic secret of their own. The moment they introduce Holly to handsome writer, Philippe, she begins to fall in love, something she hasn't allowed herself to do for twenty years. But Philippe has not been completely honest and when Holly stumbles across the truth, she feels totally betrayed.

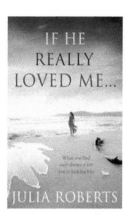

If He Really Loved Me...
The Liberty Sands Trilogy Book 2

History is about to repeat itself in Holly Wilson's life... or is it? Single mum, Holly and her son Harry have an enviable relationship but when Harry discovers she is pregnant again and, for reasons unknown to all but herself, intends to raise the baby alone, he begins to question her decision not to tell him about his own father, who abandoned them before his birth. Upon discovering his father's name, Harry secretly embarks on his search for the truth and uncovers a tragic story. Still reeling from what he has learned, an extraordinary twist of fate brings Harry and Philippe, the father of Holly's unborn child, face to face. Should Harry tell him?

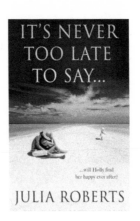

It's Never Too Late To Say….
The Liberty Sands Trilogy Book 3

Holly Wilson seems finally to have it all; a beautiful baby daughter, a son about to embark on an exciting career, a glamorous new job in television, and an adoring boyfriend in bestselling novelist, Philippe. But something isn't quite right… In another part of the country, Carol is reliving memories – dreadful memories – of sins committed against her and those she has inflicted on others. Her carer, Helen, hopes a vision from the past might help mend Carol's broken soul. What links Holly to Carol and Helen? And who is Nick, the handsome stranger who has just walked into her life?

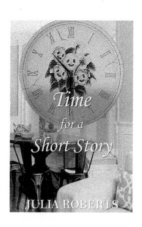

Time for a Short Story
(Kindle version only)

Eloise is still coming to terms with the death of her mother two years previously when she takes a job as a waitress in a tearoom while she is home from university to spend the summer in Guernsey. There she meets regular customer, Josephine, whose hobby is writing short stories. English student, Eloise, offers to read some of the stories and is surprised by how good they are. She organises a special ninetieth birthday treat for

Josephine but when the elderly lady doesn't show up for her usual Wednesday morning elevenses, Eloise gets a feeling that something is terribly wrong. Where is Josephine? And will she ever find out about Eloise's extraordinary act of kindness?

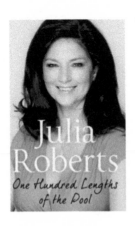

One Hundred Lengths of the Pool
Preface publishing

One Hundred Lengths of the Pool is a memoir exploring Julia's extraordinary life, including surviving the killer disease polio and against all odds becoming a professional dancer. That was the start of a long and varied career in the entertainment industry. In a unique book, each of the hundred lengths is associated with a special moment or memory from her life. However, there is an extra length of the pool that she didn't expect to swim and it has changed her life completely, testing her belief in her favourite saying, 'That which does not kill us, makes us stronger...'

Lightning Source UK Ltd.
Milton Keynes UK
UKHW042011061118
331892UK00001B/8/P